MURDER: TAKE THREE

by
April Kelly & Marsha Lyons

Flight
Risk
Books

MURDER: TAKE THREE
is a work of fiction. No resemblance between the
characters in this novel and any person, living or
dead, is implied or intended.

Copyright © 2012 by
April Kelly and Marsha Lyons

Published April 2013

ISBN: 978-0615555065

Library of Congress: TXu 1-823-345

For additional information about this or any
other Flight Risk Books fiction, or to contact one
of our authors, please visit
http://www.flightriskbooks.com

MURDER IN ONE TAKE
FIRST PLACE - MYSTERY/SUSPENSE
Kindle Book Promos' 2014 International Contest

MURDER IN ONE TAKE
"This perfectly crafted Hollywood murder peels back the curtain on not one, but two worlds, giving the reader a glimpse into the glamour of show business and the slow grind of down-and-dirty police work, blending the two domains in clever metatextual ways. Plenty of snappy banter and clenched-jaw exposition...all the intrigue of Hollywood's big-budget blockbusters."
— *Kirkus Reviews*

MURDER: TAKE TWO
"Kelly and Lyons return to their distinctive brand of mystery starring the LA-based duo (Maureen O'Brien and Blake Ervansky) who combine traditional investigation with the Hollywood perspective. Darker than its predecessor, this installment doesn't sacrifice the humor or turns of phrase that were the hallmarks of the first. Tight and sharp-witted."
— *Kirkus Reviews*

MURDER: TAKE THREE
2014 SHAMUS AWARD FINALIST
Best Indie PI Novel

SHELF UNBOUND'S 2014 TOP 100
Included all three Ervansky/O'Brien detective novels

Also by Marsha Lyons and April Kelly

Murder In One Take
Murder: Take Two

Also by April Kelly

Winged
Valentine's Day

For Carl

PROLOGUE

Maureen O'Brien waits until the canister empties itself through the thin tube running under the closed door. Pulling away the towel which has prevented a backdraft of the odorless gas that, by now, has induced sleep in the occupant of the room, Maureen hears more clearly the driving melodic throb of The Silver Bullet Band resuscitating those Hollywood nights of thirty years ago.

Every evening he sits in the dark for an hour listening to vintage rock and roll—Springsteen, The Police, Robert Plant, Creedence—his winding-down time. This, however, is the last night Leon Querda, AKA Lionheart, will ever hear Bob Seegar rasp on about diamonds and frills.

She slides her hands into the heavy leather gloves that will prevent the garrote from cutting into her own fingers when it snaps over Lionheart's head and slices through his fleshy neck like a wire cheese-cutter tackling a tough, but ultimately giving, pecorino. Maureen moves quickly: the gas is dissipating and she can't afford a wake-up during the procedure.

A blue halo from the sound system's many LEDs frames his chin-on-chest profile as Maureen moves behind the chair. Grabbing a handful of hair, she tilts his head back to expose his throat. But when the head lolls unnaturally to one side, she realizes someone has beaten her to the kill.

Lionheart had gone into the study only a half hour earlier, and a chill goes through Maureen. In five days of surveilling the house to familiarize herself with the target's habits and schedule, she has seen no one else lurking around. The person responsible for this might still be out there, watching her, and that person had the balls and the skills to snuff out a high-ranking CIA asset like Lionheart right under her nose. Suddenly afraid, she snatches up her equipment and gets out of the house, blending into the night as she slips away.

A tall, slender figure, dressed head-to-toe in black, observes with state-of-the-art night vision binoculars while Maureen makes her escape. Bob Seegar runs against the wind, his words falling on dead ears.

Cobalt—or "Co," as it is nicknamed by its neighboring elements on the periodic table—has for millennia been used as a coloring agent in ceramics and glass, from ancient Persian beads to a goblet unearthed in Pompeii's lava-locked ruins, and in the exquisite blue porcelain of both the T'ang and Ming dynasties of China. Only after it was isolated by the Swedish chemist George Brandt, somewhere around 1735, did cobalt's less artistic attributes become recognized in the fields of medicine, magnetics and metallurgy.

The earth's crust is .001 percent cobalt, the bulk of which is concentrated in deposits located in Africa and Russia. But in 1927, a wealthy and gullible New York businessman was shown a cache of cobalt in an isolated section of West Virginia, after which he bought up the seventeen hundred acres surrounding the deposit, established an extraction operation, and brought in miners to winkle out the valuable ore.

The cache was limited, the ore petered out in less than eighteen months, and the financial blow was devastating even *before* the stock market crash of 1929 sent the businessman jumping out the window of his 32nd-floor office in Manhattan.

His widow was grateful to unload the worthless

land and equipment for a half cent on the dollar to one of her husband's associates, a speculator who had already visited the property and confirmed that, although the cobalt was long gone, huge deposits of coal nestled only a dozen yards below the surface of the rolling green hills.

Today, Cobalt, West Virginia, is an active coal mining town with eleven thousand residents, and is still run by the great-grandson of that speculator who so personified American capitalism: if you work hard and are willing to screw over your friend's widow and three small children, God will reward you.

In addition to the mining operation, Cobalt boasts three grocery stores, a two-screen "multi-plex" movie theater, a community swimming pool, a dilapidated roller rink and fourteen churches, among them the non-denominational "Little Blue Chapel" built by the original cobalt miners more than eighty years ago. The Little Blue Chapel is not blue, although it *is* little. The white-painted clapboard structure gets its name from the foot-wide border around the always unlocked double doors of the entrance, a glossy blue frame comprised of thousands of tiny tile squares.

Few Angelenos ever visit Cobalt, it having a notable dearth of personal trainers, sushi bars and Brazilian wax technicians, but Blake Ervansky, a veteran of ten weeks in the LA private eye biz, will fly there twice in the coming months. The first time will be with his fiancée, Jane, as they travel to their wedding in the Little Blue Chapel. Five weeks later, he will accompany her casket to its final resting place in the small cemetery adjacent to the chapel.

"**Why now? And why with no** warning, no discussion?"

"Jeez, Charlie, isn't it about time? You were ten

years younger than I am when you moved out of *your* parents' house."

"Oh, come on. That's different."

Maureen paused in her packing, turned to her father and gave him one of her deliciously evil grins. "Why? Because you were a big tough boy and I'm only a helpless girl?"

Though he knew he wouldn't win this one, Charlie O'Brien stood tall with his hands on his hips as his only child walked right up to him and placed the tip of her index finger on his chest. "Shall I pop the lock on my gun cubby," she asked innocently, "and show you how capable I am of protecting myself?"

He fought the urge to dart his eyes toward the full-length mirror on the wall, a scrolly-edged tribute to female vanity that could trace its lineage to a high-end furniture store on Beverly Boulevard, a Victorian obsession with all things Italian Renaissance, and back to the forge of a 15th-Century craftsman who specialized in ornate glass frames for those mirrors so coveted by Venetian courtesans. Charlie knew the contents of the man-sized safe built into the wall behind that perfect tribute to gentility and depravity had already cost him a housekeeper.

Graciela had been wearing ear buds and listening to post-Menudo Ricky Martin, swaying her ample rear in a middle-aged cleaning lady's version of his narrow-hipped speed grind, while wiping down the shower in Maureen's bathroom. Maureen, thinking Graciela was elsewhere in the house, entered her bedroom and opened the mirrored door of her gun safe to take out her service revolver.

It was never made completely clear how much Graciela saw once she had La Vida Loca'd out of the bathroom. Did she note the make and model of each of the three rifles and eight handguns? Not likely. Did she have time to admire the foam backwall with custom niches for each weapon? No way. Was she impressed by the ingenious quick-release clips that hugged each piece to its vertical nest? Get serious.

Her sharp gasp triggered an automatic response, and Maureen spun around with the first handgun she could grab, an Israeli-built Desert Eagle that looked as though it had been designed to illustrate and define the word overkill. Graciela fainted dead away with a moaned "Christos!" on her lips.

Even Charlie's offer to double her salary couldn't persuade Graciela to continue working in a house where a thing of so much beauty—the mirror she had Windexed to brilliance a hundred times—could hide such evil. If the daughter kept guns in her bedroom, what might the father have in those battered old file cabinets that filled his office? Scripts, he *said*, but now Graciela couldn't help but imagine drugs, body parts, pornography or weapons of mass destruction.

As the tale spread throughout the Hispanic community, no self-respecting Latino male would let his wife go to work in the house whose reputation blackened further with each embellished retelling of the original incident. Which is how Charlie had come to hire the amiable Mrs. Taylor, a second-generation Swiss immigrant unlikely to pick up the static on LA's housekeepers' hotline.

Charlie's hand closed around the slender finger poking his sternum. "I know what you have and I know what you are capable of. But I'm a father with a valid license to worry about my kid no matter *how* old she is."

Her moving was a touchy topic. Charlie's current inamorata was the owner of a successful diner in Nevada, and she had been peripherally involved in

Maureen's most recent investigation, one involving a murderous magician and a man-eating tiger. She had skillfully convinced her father she was moving out because of her twinges of jealousy about his every-other-weekend trips to Nevada, and Denice's alternate weekend stays at their house.

That was preferable to his knowing the truth, that Maureen feared she was the target of an assassin who might or might *not* be CIA. If she were to be killed, she didn't want Charlie—or, for that matter, her potential step-mother—to become collateral damage.

The pink diamond sparkled under bright white spots in a Rodeo Drive jewelry store, lights specifically selected and aimed to provide dazzling evidence of the quality of bling showcased by the exclusive shop. A pair of what looked like padded chopsticks lifted the stone from a black velvet-lined tray, carefully placing it on the closed fingers of the pretty blonde whose trembling hand rested palm down on the display case.

Gerard Duval had seen a lot of pretty blondes trembling in his store through the years—if Los Angeles has one dependably renewable resource it is pretty blondes—but they were mostly Clairol, the trembling came from coveting the cash value of the bauble they held, and the buyers were often generous "uncles" of advanced years.

This young woman was a kindergarten teacher, and she had been arguing with her beau—some kind of detective—about size and price for a half hour, an argument Mr. Duval had witnessed a hundred times before. Normally, though, it was the check-writing male pushing for the smaller, cheaper engagement ring stone, while the female flogged that whole "two months' salary" business for all it was worth. Here, in a surprising reversal, the detective championed the larger gems, while the teacher refused to consider anything over a half carat. That is, until Mr. Duval had brought out the pink diamond.

The jeweler prided himself on always spotting that precise love-at-first-sight moment, and he knew it had come for the teacher when she saw the faceted, heart-shaped gem. "Perhaps the lady would like to step outside and view the stone under natural light."

Jane looked up in disbelief. This stranger was going to allow her to be alone with the most beautiful thing she had ever seen? Her eyes misted with both gratitude for his trust and the desire to wear the precious pink heart on her finger for the rest of her life.

Mr. Duval smiled and nodded, so, with a hopeful glance at her future husband, she turned and walked like a somnambulant toward the door. A gentleman standing there quickly opened it and Jane stepped out into the afternoon sunlight.

Blake Ervansky turned to the jeweler with a mock-serious look. "You know, she could be halfway to Compton before either one of us realized we'd been shafted."

"Unlikely, sir. My doorman is a former Navy Seal who can still run a six-minute mile. Your fiancée would be body-slammed to the ground before she made it to Wilshire."

Blake lifted his eyebrows in surprise. Reserved Mr. Duval had a sense of humor.

"Now, with the lady outside, might we proceed with a discussion about payment?"

"Yeah, yeah, whatever it costs I'll write a check." Now it was the jeweler's eyebrows that expressed surprise. This was a working man, not a millionaire, and he had no idea Charlie O'Brien had called that morning and instructed Mr. Duval to put everything over $20,000 of the ring's cost on his own account. "What I really need to know is—and please don't be offended—is that diamond tacky?"

"*Tacky?*" Mr. Duval blanched at the insult.

"Hey, I don't know jack about jewelry, but I've never seen a heart-shaped diamond in an engagement ring. Or a pink one. And the last thing I want is some snobby trust-funder looking down on Jane like she has no taste."

Though Mr. Duval respected Blake's protective motive, he was still incensed at the implication he might try to foist off a bit of geological kitsch onto an unsuspecting young couple. He did not want to lose the sale, however, especially since the detective was apparently a friend of Mr. O'Brien, a long-time, big-spending customer.

Jane came back into the shop at that moment, carefully balancing the diamond on the back of her hand, so Mr. Duval was able to respond to Blake's inadvertent insult while simultaneously sealing the deal with the fiancée.

"Before you ask to see any other stones," he said to her, knowing full well she had no intention of looking at anything else, "let me tell you a little about the unique color and cut you have so wisely chosen to consider."

While Jane listened, enthralled, and Blake felt himself shrink from six-foot-four to four-foot-six, Mr. Duval described the legendary Darya-i-Nur, or "Sea of Light" diamond, the 185-carat pink gem that is the most cherished of the Iranian Crown Jewels. Then he mesmerized her with the legend of The French Blue, an exquisite heart-shaped diamond commissioned by Louis XIV. The 67-carat stone was lost for almost forty years after disappearing in 1792, and when it eventually resurfaced it had been cut down into an oval to disguise its origin. Ultimately purchased by and named after Henry Hope, it became one of the most famous and mysterious jewels in history.

Once he was certain he had vetted both cut and color well enough, the jeweler turned to the humbled detective with a smile. "Shall we select a setting?"

A couple miles away in the large back yard of a Beverly Hills mansion, the crew from Guerrera Gardens & Landscaping carefully raised the massive top-piece of the water fountain they had been working on all week. Once it was fitted into the ten-foot-wide Parian marble base, they would have only the vertical water pipe and the decorative finial to install.

Ricky Guerrera nervously directed four men as they lifted the top-piece on two pairs of crossed beams. The supports themselves weighed thirty-five pounds each, and when you calculated in the weight of the big topper, each man had to manage a hundred and forty pounds as the crew jockeyed it over the top of the snow white center bowl. After lowering the top-piece into the corresponding carved slot of the base, they relaxed a little, relieved now of the main weight.

Ricky Guerrera kicked off his sturdy work boots, brushed the bottoms of his feet to make sure no grit stuck to his socks—if he scratched the valuable marble his father would kill him first and fire him second—then stepped into the dry fountain to remove the long bolts holding the four beams in the shape of a large double X.

Ricky was aware that Micah Deifenschlictor, one of the world's leading movie action heroes, watched the fountain assembly from inside the house. Micah wasn't a patient man, and he had only decided to redo his landscaping and install a water feature two weeks ago, so Guerrera Gardens was working around the clock to satisfy the impossible delivery requirements of the star and to justify their enormous fee. Ricky's father, Carlos, normally oversaw all installations for Hollywood A-listers and anyone else willing to pop for the stiff prices on his fountains, waterfalls, Koi ponds and "contemplation pools," but a sciatica flare-up had kept him in bed for the past couple days. A $10,000 bonus was tied into the completion of the fountain by the end of today, and Guerrera senior had made it abundantly clear to his son failure was not an option.

So when Micah came out into the yard and told him to knock off until Monday morning, Ricky was caught between a rock and a hard-ass. "Uh, Mr. Deifenschlictor," he said shakily, "I can get the water pipe in and the finial cemented on in less than an hour, if you'd like to—"

"Come back Monday," Micah interrupted. "I'll open the gate for you at 7:00."

Decades of weight-lifting and "alleged" steroid use had transformed Micah's body into a six-foot-two-inch column of steel-hard muscle. The tattooed warning "Death Before Dishonor" stretched ominously over the bulge of his left biceps, and his neck was a smidge wider than his military crew-cut head. Micah was *not* accustomed to being challenged.

Ricky Guerrera swallowed nervously. If he said more, he might get punched by the star of *Steel Fist*, *Two Steel Fists* and *I, Army*, but if he screwed the pooch on that bonus money, he'd get his butt kicked by Guerrera père. Carlos was shorter than his son, balding and asthmatic, but after browbeating and intimidating Ricky daily for all the boy's twenty-five years, Carlos was definitely the more threatening of the pair.

The kid was about to speak up to make one last pitch for completing the fountain, when Micah smiled and threw his large, veiny arm around Ricky's narrow shoulders. "Tell your old man I'll still pay the bonus. I just want some quiet and privacy to work on a new script for the rest of the weekend."

Ricky spoke to the crew, instructing them in Spanish to load the van for an imminent departure, then checked the time and began making notations on a clipboard. Micah followed the workers out to the Guerrera Gardens van, where he handed each of them a fifty-dollar bill. This more than compensated for their lost hour of overtime, so a muchas gracias chorus followed the star's return to his house. And once the gate closed behind the departing truck, he settled in to work alone for the rest of the weekend.

Elsewhere that Saturday afternoon, Maureen O'Brien continued to pack for her move, and Blake Ervansky wrote a check for an engagement ring, both unaware the next job offered to E&O Investigations would be trying to prove Micah Deifenschlictor had not murdered his agent. That decision—to take on their third major case as private detectives—would bring unimaginable grief into Blake's life, and would alter his relationship with Maureen permanently and irrevocably.

Sunday night, her last there as resident "lady of the house," Maureen lay awake in her childhood home. It was only a matter of time before Charlie would ask Denice to relocate from Nevada and move in with him, and Maureen had made peace with herself about that. Her father deserved all the love and happiness Denice Cantrell apparently brought into his life, especially if he lost his only child.

When Lionheart's assassin came after her—and Maureen had little doubt he would—there was a long shot chance she could get him before he got her. If he was working alone, a former agent Lionheart had screwed over, for instance, that might end it. But if her would-be killer was working through official channels, another would be sent, and then another, until the job was done.

Goal one was protecting her father, and the first step in that process was tomorrow's move. She would breathe easier once the van from Starving Students pulled away from the big Spanish house on Acacia and headed down Nichols Canyon on the way to the three-bedroom, fourth-floor apartment on Doheny Drive. Maureen wondered if her roommates had moved in.

Opting for a larger place with a couple roommates had almost magically reduced Charlie's uneasiness about her moving out. Of course, he didn't yet know who her roomies were, so he was still living in the bubble of ignorance that had his daughter only a twelve-minute drive away in space shared with two girls her own age.

The man in the wetsuit wore latex gloves, not to keep his fingerprints off the surfaces in the house—his DNA would be everywhere in the place anyway—but to keep his victim's blood off his own skin. He knew he would be the prime suspect and he didn't want the cops finding Cody Mason's blood in the U-joint of the shower drain at his own home.

Punching in the code to override the security system, then another to open the wrought-iron gate, the killer slipped inside and turned left. He moved along a hedge of nandina that fronted the eight-foot stone wall, stopping a few yards in to grab a bush and pull it out slightly, breaking one prominent branch almost completely through, and stripping a few leaves before releasing the evergreen to pop back against the wall.

His big hands were clumsy in the gloves, but he finally got the little plastic bag open and shook out one of the only two pieces of evidence the Beverly Hills Police Department would find at or near the murder scene. He unhooked the D-ring on his belt, removed the child's baseball bat it held, then reached up and used it to scuff the dust and debris on top of the wall above the bush he had bent. After carefully securing the bat to his belt again, he unsnapped the leather scabbard on his left hip and took out a finely-honed knife with a ten-inch blade.

While Cody Mason was being slaughtered in his own kitchen, Charlie O'Brien lay awake in a cherry wood four-poster in Madison, Nevada. Denice, known locally as "Dolly," slept soundly, a faint hiss issuing from her parted lips every four or five seconds.

Charlie had flown in last night, not wanting to hang around while his daughter moved out. Maybe knowing in two days he would go back to an empty house for the first time in almost thirty years had pushed him into making tonight's stupid mistake with Denice.

His timing had stunk, unusual for a former comedy writer. When he had proposed—without a ring, without fanfare, without even dropping to one knee—Denice had minutes earlier locked up the diner for the night, after having been on her feet since 4:00 A.M. Even his cloddish choice of words, "I want you to grow old with me," had been wrong. Nice going, Charlie, he thought, what woman could resist the lure of getting old?

Charlie had fallen in love with Denice Cantrell almost on first sight, and had known he wanted to marry her only weeks into the their relationship. But now, because he had blurted out his off-the-cuff proposal the same weekend he was "losing" Maureen, he had come across as needy, as though he thought he could slot Denice into the emptiness left behind by his only child's departure.

"Hey, you," she had said, gently laying her hand on his cheek. "You don't have to be in such a rush to find her replacement." Then she had kissed him lightly before stripping off her uniform and stepping into the shower. She didn't seem angry; she didn't even seem disappointed, but Charlie felt he had let her down. He knew Denice had not lived an easy life, and that made him want to wine and dine her, dance and romance her, dazzle her with gifts and attention. Instead, he had presented his proposal with all the panache of an ox looking for a second ox to help him pull the wagon full of boulders they would haul until some distant day when they both dropped dead in the harness.

Is it a temporary setback, he wondered, or have I jumped the shark with her? Charlie decided the next time he asked her to marry him he would ride in on a white steed, cape swirling, and sweep her off her little Reebok'd feet.

"Name your price; money is no object."

Those two clichés should have been music to Blake's ears. First, because he had spent twenty grand for an engagement ring two days earlier and second, because all good things come in threes. Unfortunately, the words were spoken by someone Blake couldn't stand, defense-attorney-to-the-stars, Gail Hatcher.

Blake had arrived at the office on Sunset earlier than usual Monday morning, intending to get a jump on several small jobs that had come in since he and Maureen finished their last investigation a few weeks earlier. Gail Hatcher could easily have faxed, texted phoned or emailed, but her choice to be standing outside the office at 8:30 A.M. was an indication of the size and seriousness of the case. Blake might have been able to ignore electronic attempts to communicate, but there was no way to pretend the woman herself was not impatiently tapping a red-soled, designer shoe on the hardwood floor outside the door of E&O Investigations.

Once they were inside, Blake directed Hatcher to the fishbowl conference room, then ducked into the kitchenette to make coffee. He tossed one extra scoop into the paper-lined drip basket—one didn't make it through a face-to-face with Hatcher drinking weak-ass joe.

The offer had been served with a side of Gail's usual brusqueness. If Blake would drop everything else and start working full-time to keep her client from being framed for murder, she would write a $100,000 retainer check right now, and give him carte blanche to charge any hourly rate he wanted.

God, it was tempting. Blake had only left the Beverly Hills Police Department in January, and he still missed the dependability of that weekly paycheck. So far, he and Maureen were doing very well, but he knew those lucrative peaks could just as easily be separated by wide valleys in the future. Maureen didn't really need to worry; her father had made a fortune off a successful TV series. Although, with her moving out today, maybe some of the parental largess would taper off.

"Mrs. Hatcher, I don't think I'm putting too fine a point on it when I say our previous encounters have been adversarial. So pardon my skepticism when you choose to pluck *me* from a veritable garden of LA investigators. And I'm not sure I want to get plucked by you again." They both knew he was referring to the several complaints she had filed against him with his superiors, complaints as substantial as fog, designed to obfuscate with fog's fleeting effectiveness.

She trilled a laugh, fanning the air with one hand as if brushing away the last drops of past water under forgotten bridges. "When we were on opposing sides, Detective, of *course* I engaged you with a spirit of healthy competition, but I always thought you were the best and brightest at the BHPD. Which is why I want you on my team now, and why I've come to you first with this very generous offer."

"I'll run it by my partner and get back to you later today."

"Sorry, not good enough. I'm leaving in exactly ten minutes, and if you aren't holding my check and I haven't hired your firm, I'll take the offer directly to my second choice. So you'll have to decide right now if you *really* need to discuss it with that little cupcake you call a partner."

She didn't raise her hands and make air-quotes around the word partner; her intonation did the job quite effectively, but when she saw his glare, she knew she'd have to pull back or risk losing him. "Oh, fine. I'm sure she's very good at *whatever* it is she does for you, but who exactly calls the shots at this place?"

It was one of her standard half-goads, half-dares, and he wanted to kick her out of the office, hear the clickety-click of her rapidly retreating stilettos as he emptied his Glock into the floor behind her. Yes, the fantasy was tempting, but she had guaranteed the retainer was free and clear, that he kept it all even if it took him only a day to prove her client was not a murderer, and that's what tipped the balance for Blake. Maureen wouldn't balk at a unilateral decision that brought in so much cash, would she?

"Okay," he said, picking up a pen and flipping to a clean page in the yellow pad that lived on the conference table, "who died?"

***

MAXIMUS
The Centurions await your orders,
Excellency.

DELMONICUS
Very good, Maximus Clemidius. Tell
them we march against Tiberius
tonight at half past the Ides.

MAXIMUS
Hark! Footsteps! Stand back, my
liege, lest an assassin's dagger find
your entrails.

DELMONICUS
Nay, loyal Max, 'tis only Exaynus, no
doubt bringing news of the supply
wagons.

MAXIMUS
Hmmph. I care not to hear words
delivered by the Emperor's catamite!

DELMONICUS
Stay, Maximus. Judge not the boy for
the beauty Zeus granted him. He is
loyal to our cause and has since last
Christmastide been of an age too great

to interest the lecherous Tiberius.

***

That leaden dialogue comes to you courtesy of the execrable film, *Double-Crossing the Rubicon*, a 1972 tits 'n' togas bomb notable for making *Plan Nine From Outer Space* look like a cinemagraphic paragon by comparison. In fact, the only lasting impact of *Rubicon* was its introduction of eighteen-year-old Micah Deifenschlictor, fresh off the proverbial turnip truck.

When Micah's striking good looks generated hot buzz from the women unlucky enough to have been taken by a date to see the movie during a theater run best measured in hours, several agents bellied up to the trough and tried to sign "the boy with the Greek physique." To a man, they told him he would have to shorten or change his unwieldy last name, which the guy from William Morris said looked "like the chorus of 'Old MacDonald' took a dump in a bowl of German consonants."

The young actor stood firm, unwilling to tamper with his surname and disrespect the memory of his Bavarian father. Only Cody Mason, an independent agent less than a year out of Wharton, supported Micah's choice. "I'll make you famous enough, kid, that they'll all *have* to learn how to spell your name." And that's exactly what he did over the next decade. Micah Deifenschlictor became the top young action hero of the early 80's, and then when every reporter, reviewer and talk show host finally learned how to spell and pronounce Deifenschlictor, Micah had a Roseanne Barr/Arnold/Thomas/Barr brain fart and told his agent he wanted to drop the cumbersome surname, revered father be damned.

Cody, who had spent ten years imprinting his client's challenging moniker on the public, now had to rebrand Micah as being worthy of induction into that pantheon of celebrities known by a single name. Hundreds of column inches in *People Magazine* were freed up to cover other stars when the man with the Greek physique became plain old Micah. And every dyslexic entertainment show reporter breathed a sigh of lerief.

There was less than a four-year age difference between them, so the physically blessed actor and his pipsqueak agent became more like brothers than business associates. The two famously caroused the Hollywood club scene those early years together, with Micah frequently playing wing man for Cody, sifting through a constant flow of willing young women like a blue whale inhaling a cloud of krill. Micah always held back the quality for himself, but Cody was more than satisfied with the quantity directed his way.

In any long-term relationship there will inevitably be rough patches, and the two men—called behind their backs the geek and the Greek—hit them all, sometimes in public, sometimes with loud and harsh words, but never with physicality. Micah's mother had drilled into him that you *never* strike a girl, and you never, *ever* strike someone smaller than you.

Every few years they wallowed through a conflict that had Micah sending out signals he would consider new representation, and Cody engaging in the scalpel-precise character evisceration Hollywood agents do so exquisitely behind the scenes.

The first—and many claimed the worst—of these conflicts occurred when Micah enlisted in the U.S. Marines at twenty-two, right as Cody was getting his client's price and recognizability up enough to ask for single-card credit on the next movie.

"You putz! Tell me you're joking!"

"Fuck you, Cody. It's a done deal. I signed all the papers this morning."

"So what happens to *Kiss Her, Kill Her?* Psycho parts like that don't come along every day. It's a sign I've finally got them taking you seriously. You go off to play soldier and some jerk-off like Harvey Keitel will chew up that role and shit out a Best Supporting Actor nomination!"

"I'm sure my fans will turn on me for serving my country," Micah responded sarcastically.

"You're not even *from* this country!"

Micah had chosen a hidden-away restaurant to drop the bomb on his agent. Dan Tana's was as safe a place as any in LA to air celebrity dirty laundry, but Cody still lowered his voice when he went in for the kill.

"This isn't about serving your country. This is about putting a bigger hetero stamp on your ass, isn't it? Too many of those new pansy mags voting you fan fave, am I right?"

He had hit the mark and he knew it, so Cody Mason leaned back with a look of triumph, Sigmund Freud discovering a cigar is sometimes more than just a cigar. Micah glared back, hoping his acting was good enough to convey a refusal to dignify Cody's accusation with a response, but knowing what his agent said was slam-dunk accurate.

After a couple minor movie roles playing macho men—well, technically, macho *boys*—Micah realized merely acting the part of a gladiator, gang banger or studly deputy didn't make you manly. Especially when you were wearing make-up and your signature tousled locks came from a curling iron and a flitty stylist named Tr'Shawn. Micah knew, even if Cody was too short-sighted to figure it out, that a couple of years in the toughest branch of America's military would codify his masculinity at a level that could not be compromised by wearing make-up, having surfer-boy highlights, or unwittingly gathering a growing fan base of gays.

The Vietnam fiasco was a dead man walking by 1976 and the U.S. hadn't yet chosen its next venue for the disposal of X percent of its young male population, so Pvt. Deifenschlictor spent his time after boot camp at a small Marine base on Oahu, amping his butch quotient while keeping out of the line of fire.

While Micah surfed and served, Cody built his small agency into a boutique dynamo, rejecting offers to be absorbed into one of the behemoths like CAA or ICM. He stayed pissed-off for about as long as it took his biggest client to get through basic training, then spent the rest of Micah's hitch planning on how to capitalize on the actor's selfless service to his adopted country.

The lead in *Steel Fist* was waiting for Micah when he mustered out, along with a just-shy-of-nude photo shoot for the hot-hot-hot *Cosmo Magazine*, which had already featured Burt Reynolds and several other big names, so the geek and the Greek—both considerably matured—resumed their relationship.

Steel Fist killed. It had been filmed for only five million dollars, but grossed seven times that amount in the initial world-wide release, and would later double that figure from video rentals and then DVD sales. Micah's time in the Marines had softened his Bavarian accent and hardened his body. He now had everything needed to become a leading man.

Two Steel Fists came out eighteen months after its prequel, putting Micah firmly on the A-list—if not for talent, for earnings potential—and he and Cody were inundated with scripts for their next project. This brought them to the brink of another one of their legendary squabbles, as Cody's instinct was to change things up, go for a romantic comedy or one of those highly acclaimed Merchant-Ivory films, to make sure Micah didn't wind up typecast as brainless beefcake.

In the meantime, Micah had been approached by one of his old Marine buddies who had written a movie script. This in itself was not unusual, as approximately seventy-two percent of the people within a star's gravitational field will eventually go to him or her with an idea (inevitably revolving around their *own* profession or life experience) or a garbage script. *Three Steel Fists* stretched credulity to a wafer-thin membrane. In it, Micah would play a mercenary with a heart of gold and his predictable fists of steel. His buddy would be a one-armed martial arts expert who supplied comic relief, in addition to that all-important third fist.

Cody had a cow. Dreck like this could undermine everything he had worked for, so he called in a favor and Micah's old Marine pal suddenly got an offer to do rewrites on a script everyone in the business except him (and Micah) knew would never be made into a movie. Cody anonymously underwrote the payments to the former Marine, while persuading Micah it wasn't a violation of the "no man left behind" code to walk away from *Three Steel Fists* and do a rom-com with newcomer Jessica Lang.

The occasional comedy and art-type movie kept him from being known *only* as an action guy, but there was no denying Micah's career hinged almost entirely on charging through fire, explosions and general mayhem wearing low-slung fatigue pants, loincloths or leather greaves, sweat glistening on the ripped planes of his bare chest, and wielding a weapon that could be, interchangeably, an AK-47, a gem-encrusted sword or a glowing rod that fired atomic death rays. His nearest competitor in the action field, Harrison Ford, might be a much better actor, but Micah had it all over Indiana Jones when it came to pecs, lats, deltoids and sweat rivulets.

As the 20th Century counted down to its panicky Y2K close, Micah moved through his mid-forties. The famous rock-hard muscles took more and more work to maintain, so the star searched for a way to keep his professional edge.

The history of anabolic steroids began when the Nobel Prize for Chemistry was awarded to Adolf Friedrich Butenandt, a German biochemist, for his groundbreaking work in the development of synthetic testosterone in 1939. As if there weren't enough of the real thing sloshing around the Fatherland *that* year. Further research by other scientists led to anabolic-androgen steroids, famously used for jump-starting growth in undersized children, and FDA-approved later for the treatment of burn victims.

As with most drugs that come onto the market, an off-label sub-market for AAS sprang up, primarily around body-builders and weight-lifters, but other competitive sports were not immune to its abuse. In fact, it was the slow-motion sport of baseball that finally blew the lid off the dirty little secret of steroids.

The physical changes were gradual, so it took Cody Mason years to realize his client was juicing. He blamed it on the muscleheads at the gym where Micah lifted weights, one of whom was that "writer" from the old Marine unit on Oahu. Although Micah had *not* done *Three Steel Fists*, he maintained a close relation-ship with the guy, even throwing him a small part in every movie he made.

The original body of "the boy with the Greek physique" had been a true gift from Mother Nature.

The hard, muscular frame of the twenty-something man had been forged by the U.S. Marine Corps. But the increasingly cartoonish and improbable body of the aging Micah was a legacy from the steroids.

Cody Mason realized he had to get his most profitable client out of the public eye, out of loincloths and low-slung fatigues, and into business suits that would cover the veiny bulges. Which is why Pinnacle Pictures was formed.

Micah reluctantly swallowed his disappointment, morphing his fear about the encroachment of the next generation of hard-bodied young action stars into a willingness to step aside and make way for them. He embraced his role as movie maker and studio head, a role his agent had sold him as much more powerful than being a piece of meat in front of the cameras, ordered around by a series of ever-younger directors.

Although Cody owned half of Pinnacle Pictures, Micah was in charge of day-to-day operations at the studio located on a hundred isolated acres in Tujunga. (Pronounced with an *h*-sounding letter *j*, as though you were trying to cough up a clot of hair and phlegm.) Its northern boundary ran contiguously with the border of the Angeles National Forest. In its first eight years of operation, Pinnacle had hosted production on dozens of commercials, numerous corporate training movies, a slew of infomercials and seven feature films. Pinnacle was ready for the next big step, funding and producing movies of its own. That's why Micah was developing the script of *The Devil's Platoon*, an action movie he would direct. He and Cody jointly advanced the thirty million up-front dollars out of their own pockets, and were rolling the dice on a strong return two years down the road.

Cody Mason could not have chosen a worse time to get himself gutted like a rainbow trout.

Blake carefully maneuvered his Mercedes around the landscaping van in the driveway of Micah's sprawling home, while elsewhere in Beverly Hills, Det. Libby Johnson secured and searched the scene of a savage homicide. Blake pulled up near the open garage, which housed an Escalade, a Lamborghini and a camo-painted Humvee. Seeing Gail Hatcher's black Jaguar crouched like a tensing Rottweiler reminded Blake to give Maureen a heads-up. "You should let me take point. The lovely Mrs. Hatcher has a real hard-on about you."

"Duly noted. I will be nothing more than eye-candy in a non-speaking role."

He had filled her in on what little he knew after picking her up at the house, where the Starving Students truck was already being loaded. The job of supervising the rest of the move was turned over to Mrs. Taylor, Charlie's housekeeper.

Gail Hatcher opened the front door after Blake's knock, dispensed with the greeting and proceeded straight to: "Let's go. The media are already on the story." She held the door open and aimed her left arm toward the sunken living room. As the two detectives passed by, Maureen sketched a subtle curtsy, missed entirely by her partner, but noted and filed away by Hatcher in the brain fold where she kept her list of who's naughty and nice.

Micah posed in front of a picture window, pre-tending to be watching the Hispanic men working with pitchforks and spades to break up a ten-foot wide strip of ground bordering the back wall, but *actually* bestowing upon the two people who were going to save his ass a good look at that famous inverted triangle. Broad, solid shoulders formed the impressive line across the top, and he held his hands behind his back, the right one loosely gripping the wrist of the left, emphasizing even further the narrowing angle down to the aforementioned ass.

"Micah," Gail said, "I'd like you to meet detectives Blake Ervansky and Maureen O'—" She stopped as though searching through a long list of possible Irish suffixes for the winner. Even Blake could see what she was doing, so he dryly provided the answer.

"O'Brien. Maureen O'Brien."

"Of course. Sorry, it's been a stressful couple of hours," Gail said, doing a perfect take on sincerity. Maureen flashed her a smile that conveyed two crude words as clearly as if she had spoken them aloud.

The introductory snark took the edge off Micah's dramatic turn from the window, and he was annoyed to find all eyes were not on him when he sighed and pivoted to face them.

"It's very nice to meet you, Mr. Deifrins—"

"Micah, please," the star said, moving toward Blake with his hand extended, cutting him off before he mangled the name any further. As the two men shook hands, Maureen observed that although Blake was inches taller, he looked almost delicate compared to the bulked-up celeb.

The sleeves of the logo-emblazened knit shirt stretched tightly over biceps that bulged even in their relaxed state, and his pectorals pressed out against the soft fabric as if they had been oiled and pumped up for a body-building competition. Maureen masked her personal distaste, smiling warmly when Micah released Blake's hand and enveloped her small one in two meaty mitts.

"Miss O'Brien."

"I also go by one name; you can call me Maureen."

Micah leered, delighted by the pert little redhead, assuming his impressive physique was working its erotic magic on her. He wondered what it would be like to bang a copper-topped spinner like—

"Okay, why don't we all have a seat," Hatcher snapped out, her crisp order bringing Micah back to the business at hand. She turned to Blake and Maureen with a scowl that would have been right at home on the stone face of a medieval church gargoyle. "Before we start, let me remind you both that you are my employees, and I am Micah's attorney. Every word said here today is covered by privilege, so you will not share *any*thing that comes out in this room with law enforcement. Not now; not ever."

"We're familiar with the concept of privilege, Mrs. Hatcher, but before we deposit your check and commit ourselves to being bound by it, I'd like to ask your client one question." When she shrugged her assent, Blake turned to Micah, who sat forward expectantly, an earnest expression on his face. "Micah, did you kill Cody Mason?"

The star's eyelids did a quick jolt and his brows tensed as the reminder of why they were here hit home, but big boys don't cry. Micah cleared his throat so he could answer clearly, though softly, "No." Then Blake confirmed to Hatcher that he and Maureen agreed to be bound by privilege, and for the next hour his questions and the star's answers shaped the framework in which the two investigators would be working. And that framework didn't look any too solid.

First, Micah had no alibi. He told Blake he had been home alone from the time the gardeners left around 3:00 on Saturday afternoon until 7:00 this morning when they returned. He described a volatile, forty-year relationship with numerous very public battles. He readily revealed he and Cody had recently taken out life insurance policies on each other with Lloyd's of London, the only company willing to cover each man for the staggering amount of $15 million until *The Devil's Platoon* was released.

"We each had to pay $500,000 up front to secure the policies. And if the movie wasn't ready to go in twelve months, we would have had to pony up another half mil each."

Blake raised his eyebrows. "I know I'm only a working stiff, but that sounds like a hell of a lot of money." He might as well have said a hell of a lot of *motive*, and Hatcher cut her eyes at him, conveying a "down, boy" warning.

Missing the flying subtext in the room, Micah responded. "Oh, we never would have paid the second premium. We only needed the policy in place through post-production." He explained they didn't want any heirs or survivors coming forward and encumbering *The Devil's Platoon* in the event of the death of one of the two principals. "Cody's lawyer wrote the contract so that if one of us died, our ex-wives could only get the insurance money to fight over, with no claim on the movie."

When Blake was told the two men had five ex-wives between them, he thought the deal sounded legitimate, but he knew it would trigger a hard look from the police. He really wished Hatcher's client had even a shred of an alibi. "Okay, is there any way we can prove you never left this house last night?"

Micah concentrated, then looked at Blake and shook his head.

"No security cameras?" Gail asked. "Nothing to record the comings and goings?"

Micah brightened. "Yes! There's a closed-circuit thing Security Pro rigged up at the gate. I never had a reason to look at any of the footage, but I assume it works."

"Show me," Maureen said, standing. They were

the first words she had spoken since the introductions, and Micah figured she could no longer resist the urge to be alone with him.

"Come on," he said. "It's in the utility closet by the master bedroom."

She followed him out of the room as Blake turned to Hatcher. "Do you believe he didn't do it?"

"What I do or don't believe is irrelevant to Micah's defense. And *should* be irrelevant to you and the cup...I mean your partner."

Meanwhile, the cupcake herself was looking at the pod of security equipment in the tiny room, aware of Micah standing close enough behind her that she could feel his warm breath on the crown of her head. And then, the inevitable: his hand flattened against the small of her back, curving as it slid down to lightly squeeze a firmer-than-expected glute.

Although Maureen didn't move, her thoughts merrily danced with possibilities. Even in this tight space she had several options for terminating the unwelcome grope, actions with consequences ranging from ten-on-the-pain-scale hurt to Micah's testicles, to a shattered nose, to a quick death. She chose not to exert immediate physical control over him, sensing long-term emotional control might be more effective in the pursuit of truth in this case.

She slowly turned, letting her breasts graze his gonzo six-pack and causing him to moan softly even before she looked up and aimed the full force of her lovely blue eyes at him. "Micah," Maureen breathed huskily, bringing one hand up and resting it on his bulging pectoral muscle, making sure to rotate the heel of her palm where his nipple strained the knit fabric. "You can't imagine how strong my feelings are right now, but if I let those desires take over, how clear-headed am I going to be in helping my partner prove your innocence?"

At the mention of the partner, Micah instantly understood the cause of her unnatural resistance. "Are you and that Cub Scout getting busy?" Her shy glance down confirmed it, an embarrassed, wordless yes. But Micah couldn't blame her for making do until he came along. "How serious is it?"

Those long black lashes fluttered up once more. "I can honestly say I have *never* felt for him what I'm feeling about you right now." Her smile implied erotic promise, but Micah knew she was right. If he moved in too quickly on this bangin' piece of ass, her nerdy BF might not do everything possible to clear him of the inevitable murder charge. No, Micah decided to let the Cub Scout enjoy a few more weeks of riding this little firecracker. The wait would only prime her more. With a wink at his zillionth easy conquest, he turned all business.

"The SD cards only rewrite every thirty days, so both cameras should show my gate never opened last night."

Twenty minutes later, as Blake backed his car around the gardening company van, then pulled out through the open gate, Maureen was finally able to vent. "Drive through the nearest car wash and leave the windows down. I need a shower."

"The old horndog put the moves on you?" he asked with a grin.

"Hey, I just took one for the team, so you do *not* want to mess with me. Besides, I have in my pocket something that could, if horndoggie isn't lying, give us the proof that will wrap up our part of this case before sundown. Ta-da!" She pulled out an SD card and held it up for him to see.

"Please tell me that's not the original."

"Don't be daft. I didn't even touch the original, so when the police pull it they won't be finding *my* prints on it."

"Did your romantic interlude yield anything else?"

"Yeah. Now that Micah thinks I'm his next booty call, he was more forthcoming about his familiarity with that surveillance system than when we were all together in the living room."

Blake considered that for a moment, realizing it was Hatcher who had suggested there might be video, prompting her client to "remember" the cameras at the gate. He wondered if the two of them were working together on some kind of cover-up. Or, at the very least, a refashioning of the information he and Maureen would have access to.

At the end of the block, Blake turned and pulled around to drive behind Micah's property, only to find access by anything wider than a golf cart would be impossible. He and his partner peered down the pathway (by law there are no alleys in Beverly Hills) between the eight houses, four fronting each of two parallel residential streets. In an effort to utilize every square inch of overpriced land, each owner had pushed himself snugly against the rear of a neighbor he had most likely never met, creating a racy image of spooning real estate.

"I wonder how the garbage gets picked up," Blake said.

"Rickshaw?"

"They wouldn't put the cans out front in such an exclusive neighborhood, would they?"

"Maybe. But they'd have to be designer cans. Gar*bazhe* by Givenchy."

Back at the office of E&O Investigations, they settled in to watch everything that had moved in front of Micah's house from noon yesterday until the file had been pulled and copied this morning.

Side by side images showed the views from two digital cameras, each fixed high-up on the wall on opposite sides of the gate. The street, the first few houses across the street in both directions, and Micah's gate were all clearly visible. As Blake and Maureen ate their sandwiches from the deli next door, they logged all activity.

The comings and goings were what they expected through the afternoon hours and early evening: a SoCal Builders' delivery truck, three busses full of tourists, neighbors driving in or out, but as night approached, the Sunday evening traffic tapered off. Two kids on bicycles raced home for dinner, an SUV pulled up to the curb and parked one house down, a little VW with a Pizza Hut sign mohawking its roof slowly cruised by, the driver obviously scanning house numbers. After 11:00 P.M. the street was deserted, remaining so until the time code read 4:36 A.M., when a dark sedan slowly approached Micah's gate. Blake and Maureen sat up and paid close attention to the car as it rolled into view on one camera and out of view on the other. Halfway through the drive-by a hand shot out of the driver's side window, firing a missile high in the air. The plastic-wrapped LA Times did not clear the gate, however, smacking the top bar and falling on the street side. The sedan was already out of frame when the paper hit the pavement.

Nothing but the occasional power-walker for almost ninety minutes, then a speeding car lurched to a stop in front of a neighboring house, disgorging a young man with a script in his hand, one of an endless number of runners bringing TV actors all over town their words for the week. The kid was back in his car in under a minute, then off to the home of the next sitcom star waiting to see how naturally funny he or she would be later on. After that, all the predictable Monday morning activity began: a school bus picked up children carrying chef-prepared lunches in their designer backpacks; sleepy neighbors pulled out of their driveways, trying not to spill their coffee or drop their cell phones as they began the daily commute; the SUV left the curb and drove away; United Package Express made a delivery next door; and at 7:02 the van from Guerrera Gardens pulled up to the callbox. As the driver pushed the button and waited for the gate to open, he turned around, obviously speaking to someone in the back. The side door slid open right as the gate began rolling aside, and a man stepped out, scooped up the newspaper and hopped back in before the van started forward. When Blake's car pulled up to the gate, they ended their log.

Gail Hatcher picked up on the first ring and Blake gave her the good news. "If your client is telling the truth about his front gate being the sole ingress and egress to the property, and assuming he doesn't have the ability to leap tall buildings in a single bound, the Beverly Hills Police are going to have a very hard time pinning this murder on him."

"That's all well and good, but I still need you to follow up on those phone calls from last night. I want to have that timeline before the cops do."

Micah had told them about three calls around 11:00 the night before. The first call was from Cody to Micah, touching base like he supposedly did every night around that time. Micah had claimed his agent said he heard something downstairs and cut the call short to check. When he didn't hear back, he tried Cody's cell and got voicemail. Micah said he assumed Cody's cat had knocked something off the kitchen counter, that Cody had checked it out, then gone to take a shower and get ready for bed.

"It bothered me, though, when he didn't get back to me, so I waited another few minutes, then called him on his land line. Cody always leaves his cell in the kitchen overnight, but if I yell loud enough when the machine picks up on the land line, he can hear me all the way upstairs."

"And did he pick up?" Blake had asked.

"No, and then I went to bed, a choice that's going to haunt me for the rest of my life."

Micah said he tried both cell and land line shortly before the landscapers arrived that morning. Then he'd called Cody's assistant and left it to her to check on her boss.

Blake no longer had law enforcement's right to pull phone records, so he figured the police were going to get that information before Gail Hatcher. But when he walked back into the conference room, Maureen had a little surprise for him.

Lt. Rhee looked up as Libby Johnson strode into his office. "Where's Jimbo?" he asked.

"Still at the scene. I'm here to put together a list of who we should talk to, then I'll swing back and pick him up so we can start making the rounds." She gave her first impressions of the crime scene, telling the lieutenant it appeared the perp or perps gained access to the property by going over a stone wall.

"How high?"

"High enough that LeBron would have needed a boost to get over it."

"So, he used a ladder or an accomplice. Unless, of course, the killer is Spider-man."

"We ruled out Spidey when we found a button in the grass under where the wall was breached." The initial guess on time of death was between 10:00 and midnight last night, she told him, and the victim's assistant discovered the body shortly after 8:00 this morning.

"You getting anything helpful from her? Or him," he added quickly.

"Her and not really. She was still a basket case when I left, but Jim was talking her down." Libby went through the rest of what she knew so far. The killer got in by breaking a pane of glass in the door to the kitchen, had apparently confronted the owner there, and had used what the coroner could already tell was a *really* big knife.

"What jumps out for you?" the lieutenant asked.

"Three things. First, no defensive wounds." Rhee nodded, understanding the implication that either the perp had moved with fatal speed to catch the victim off guard, or the dead man had known his killer and not anticipated the attack. "Second, nothing appears to be missing, and trust me, you could keep a fence busy for a month unloading the electronics, artwork and jewelry in that place."

Another vote for a personal motive, thought Rhee. "Any suspects?"

"That's number three. There was a threatening message on his phone from last night. The assistant pulled herself together long enough to identify the caller."

"Drum roll?"

"Yeah. That muscle-bound movie star with the last name that looks like a spilled can of alphabet soup."

While Blake spoke with Gail Hatcher, Maureen looked again at that SUV parked on the street near Micah's house. It had suddenly occurred to her that as they rapidly advanced the security footage, looking primarily at Micah's gate, she hadn't noticed anyone exiting the car when it parked last night. And now, after a second look, she knew no one had gotten *in* it this morning before it pulled away.

Blake walked into the conference room while his partner keyed something into her computer. "Hatcher wants us to put together a time line from Micah's phone calls last night," he said. "But this is now an active homicide for BH, so I don't think any of my old buddies there are gonna be willing to share."

"We don't need them. I already pulled the cell tower hits, the land line call times, *and* I'm running the plates on a suspicious vehicle."

"How? We don't have access anymore."

But Maureen had, for the heck of it, entered in the hush-hush code that had been issued to them when they were temporarily furloughed from the BHPD to work on a celebrity murder. The star's influential father had exerted some kind of pressure on the Governor and suddenly, Blake and Maureen were duly licensed private investigators with a secret access code issued by the office of the Police Commissioner. "Well, they *did* cancel our old code when we quit, but apparently the Commissioner's office hasn't noticed we still have our double-oh-seven clearance left over from the Roberts case."

This bureaucratic blunder would give them official fact-finding power until the day some low-level bean counter discovered it. Already it had given them the information Gail Hatcher wanted on the phone calls, along with the name of the owner of the mystery SUV. Maureen watched the screen, waiting to learn who Gregory Wartham was. "Hey, Blake, look at this."

He moved behind her chair to look at the screen. Greg Wartham, owner of the SUV that had sat all night a short distance from Micah's house, had been arrested a couple times for petty stuff: trespassing, worthless checks, violation of a restraining order. But the information that interested Blake and Maureen was that Wartham was a "reporter" for the supermarket tabloid *Star Views*, a foreign-owned rag that specialized in slimy showbiz gossip, both real and fabricated.

"A paparazzo," Blake said. "That makes things interesting."

He wasn't at his apartment in Van Nuys, but the landlord volunteered to Maureen that Greg Wartham usually drank lunch at a place called Casa Vega on Ventura Boulevard. After braving the hard glare from the valet when Blake parked his car at a meter on the street, the two detectives fell even further in the guy's esteem as they walked through the small lot looking for the SUV. One glance inside when they found it told them they had caught a lucky break, so Maureen went into the restaurant, while Blake stayed outside to call Hatcher.

If bats drank margaritas, Casa Vega would be their regular watering hole. Maureen stepped out of a sunny LA afternoon into what felt like the black hole of Calcutta, and had to stand still a few seconds while her eyes adjusted to the almost non-existent light. When she could make out the bar straight ahead, she went to it.

"One Anchor Steam and one Pepsi," she told the bartender who, curiously enough, did *not* have over-sized alien eyes to make up for the lightless working conditions. She put a twenty down while he poured the drinks, then stepped into the main room to find her man. Greg Wartham sat alone in a booth, the remains of a large Mexican combo plate pushed to one side, and a half-empty glass of beer in his right hand. He appeared to be nodding off. Poor baby, Maureen thought. Up all night spying on people and now he needs a nap.

When she returned to the bar the drinks, change and her partner were all waiting. "And?" she asked the still-blinking Blake.

"If he has anything to sell, we can get up to ten grand in cash from a bank a half mile from here."

Greg's head popped up with beer-modulated alertness when the two strangers slid into the round booth from either side.

"Hi, Greg," Maureen said. "Mind if we join you?"

"That's rhetorical, right?" he asked, noting he was now penned in. "Who are you?"

"Names aren't all that important for this," Blake said. "We'd like to make an offer for whatever you got on your little stakeout last night in Beverly Hills."

Greg looked from the brown-haired guy to the sweet young thing, trying to figure out what kind of trap they were luring him into. "I don't know what you're talking about."

Blake leaned closer so he could drop his voice very low and still be heard. "We're *talking* about the audio equipment in your car. It's more sophisticated than what the LAPD uses on their drug busts."

"Are you cops?" Greg asked, a nervous look on his face.

"No," Maureen said, "we're two people who can afford to pay more than *Star Views* will for whatever you overheard at a certain action hero's house last night. Cash, under the table."

"Well, then I guess we're all shit out of luck, because I didn't get anything." He lifted his glass and drained the remaining beer. "That's the problem with anonymous phone tips. Half the time it's only somebody yanking your chain."

"And what was last night's tip?" Maureen asked.

He shrugged. Might as well tell her. After all, he couldn't sell what he didn't have. "Okay, a guy called around 9:00 to say a long-married, Oscar-winning actress would be heading to Micah's for a bit of the old horizontal mambo while her husband is off on location. The photographic proof would have been worth boo-coo bucks, and the audio—" he stopped himself and turned toward Blake. "Are you *sure* you're not cops? 'Cause if you *are* and you lie about it, my attorney says—"

Maureen laid a hand over his. "Dude, we're after dirt, same as you. Only we're after *different* dirt."

He admitted he was hoping to record pillow talk, sexy conversations, even phone calls that would prove the two celebs were having an affair. And if his photo capture made the cover, he'd have gotten a huge payday. "All I got, though, was a lost night of sleep and an actor talking to his agent."

"Land line or cell phone?" Blake asked.

Greg was beginning to suspect maybe he *did* have something worth selling. Not to his scuzzy boss, for sure, but maybe these two were dumb enough to pop for a couple hundred bucks. Suddenly Greg turned coy. "Haven't you heard, Mr. *I'm-not-a-cop*? Tapping phones is illegal. I could go to jail if I did something like that."

"A thousand dollars," Blake shot back.

Holy shit, this guy is serious, Greg realized. But will he come looking for a refund when he hears the worthless crap I recorded? Greg's slight hesitation prompted Blake to up the offer. "Each. Assuming you recorded his cell *and* his land line."

The paparazzo made his decision. "You did say cash, right?"

Greg Wartham did *not* have taps on Micah's phones, as they quickly learned, but only listening devices planted through the house—no doubt put there by a bribed household employee. Now they knew why he had jumped into his car and sped away after he had taken the money and turned over the recordings in the parking lot of that bank. All Maureen and Blake had was the audio of Micah's side of the three calls. By matching the times of the calls against the phone record Maureen had already pulled, they could prove Micah was home during the window of opportunity in which Cody Mason was killed. Or at least the window they expected the medical examiner to certify.

Of course, none of this could be used in court, and even the discovery of their possession of the material could jeopardize any future defense for Micah. A good prosecutor would have the digital CCTV coverage thrown out once a judge heard an employee of the accused had beaten the cops to the evidence, removing the SD card, perhaps even replacing it with an altered version. The paparazzo's recordings were guaranteed to be ruled inadmissable.

None of that mattered, however, as Gail Hatcher only needed the "proof" as an insurance policy. She intended to sit on the discovery Blake and the cupcake had made. If her client panicked after being arrested, she could soothe him with the assurance that he could *not* be touched once the police did due diligence. If the cops failed to find something, she could nudge them in the right direction with a slip of the tongue, instantly retracted, quickly denied. And if anybody connected with the BHPD deliberately tried to hide evidence and frame her client she would ask for a private meeting, then threaten him or her with evidence that—while not meeting the standards of the court—was strong enough to derail a career.

After Blake called Hatcher to give her the news,

he and Maureen decided to call it a day. Now that the attorney could rest easy about her client, she was in no rush to get transcripts of the calls. End of the week was fine, she had magnanimously told Blake.

"I'm not coming in tomorrow," Maureen said, as they locked the office. "I've got to unpack at the new place and pick up Charlie at Burbank Airport late in the day."

"Then let's make it an official E&O Investigations holiday. Jane's ring is supposed to be ready by 11:00, and I want to swing by her school and put it on her finger in front of all the little rug rats."

"Well, aren't you the romantic boyfriend."

"*Fiancé*," he corrected, test-driving the transition title between boyfriend and husband.

When they got to the unmanned underground parking facility, Maureen did a fast visual sweep. This was exactly the kind of spot she would choose if she wanted to ambush someone. Blake noticed her high-alert check of the unoccupied concrete warehouse for cars. "Afraid Micah's lurking around, ready to declare his undying passion?"

"Yeah," she replied, "something like that."

Blake drove her to Charlie's house so she could pick up her car and head over to the apartment. It was 5:30 and they had earned $100,000 for one day's work. If the two detectives could have gotten a peek into the immediate future, though, it's unlikely either of them would say it had been worth it.

"Miss Larsen and Mr. Vasky sittin' in a tree, K-I-S-S-I-N-G." Their cadence was off and half of them only faked their way through the spelling part of the traditional childhood taunt, but all twenty-six kindergartners giggled with delight as the *really*, really tall man got down on one knee and asked their teacher to marry him. And then there were cookies!

Blake had cleared his visit with the principal before walking to Jane's classroom, a bakery bag of Snickerdoodles in one hand and a two-carat diamond ring in the other, so word had spread quickly among the faculty. The glass pane in the door of room nine filled with the faces of female teachers looking in at a scene off the cover of a Harlequin Romance novel.

When the dashing hero got to his feet and took Miss Larsen in his arms to kiss her, squeals broke out among the children, and several faculty hearts beat faster. Then the cookies worked as well as gags to quiet the kids, while everyone came inside to hug Miss Larsen and shake hands with Prince Charming.

While Blake inspired romantic fantasies at an elementary school in the San Fernando Valley, his partner took clothes out of a wardrobe box and hung them in the smaller-than-it-had-looked closet. No doubt about it, most of her stuff would have to go back to her father's house. The problem with Los Angeles weather is it doesn't have the dramatic mood swings of cities like Chicago or Syracuse, so people don't have "seasonal" clothes. You are as likely to require a short-sleeved tee on a February afternoon as you are to need a light jacket on an evening in July, so you can't stash half your wardrobe for six months of every year.

For the time being, Maureen would have to leave most of her clothes in the three tall cardboard boxes that crowded one side of her new room. The bigger issue was where to put the guns. She hadn't brought all of the them, only two handguns and one rifle, but eventually she wanted them all nearby. She checked under the bed, deciding that was probably the best place. She would have a handyman build her a long,

flat wooden box on rollers, but she would order it as a
sweater storage unit, rather than a gun case. For the
time being, she wrapped the rifle in a bath towel and
slid it under the bed. The handguns—one almost
dainty and one dead serious—would be on her every
time she left the apartment until her problem with the
possible assassin was over, one way or another.

Maureen flinched at a thud on the other side of
the wall, but it was only one of her roommates shoving
a night stand into place.

In a taxi headed for McCarren Airport in Las
Vegas, Charlie tried to banish his sadness about
Maureen moving out by working on his campaign to
win the heart of Denice Cantrell. Well, he already
had her heart, along with every square centimeter of
her delightful body. What he wanted now was her
presence every day. But Dolly's Diner had been her
very successful baby for ten years, and she didn't seem
likely to abandon it to move to LA with him. Charlie
couldn't see himself thriving in a small place like
Madison, Nevada, either. He could operate his blog
from anywhere—he'd been doing it from a booth in
Dolly's off and on for three weeks now—but his home,
his daughter, and every friend he had were all in Los
Angeles.

Charlie tackled the problem as though it were a
script and he had to hammer out all the plot points to
bring the story to a satisfactory conclusion.

Det. Libby Johnson waited impatiently for the
search warrant. Micah whatever-the-fuck-his-last-
name-was had given logical-sounding answers for
everything when she and her partner Jim talked to
him at his house yesterday afternoon, but too much
didn't add up. He claimed there had been some calls

between Cody Mason and himself Sunday night—conveniently right around the M.E.'s estimated time of death, she had noted—but the victim's cell phone wasn't anywhere to be found, so Jim was back at the station running down the phone call times to compare with Micah's statement and the conversation he claimed he had inadvertently recorded with his agent. Libby, meanwhile, waited for the world's most obnoxious judge to finish his lunch? Poker game? She didn't know *what* he was doing back there, but if his assistant didn't send out that signed warrant soon, Libby intended to go in chambers and kick some black-robed ass.

When she and Jim confronted Micah about the threatening message on the victim's land line, he had sheepishly claimed that was how the two of them always talked to each other. Last night they had looked through the security video from the star's gate to see if he was lying about leaving his house, but Libby knew he could have easily used a ladder to scale his own back wall to get to the murder scene. Of course, he would have needed a vehicle or a pair of wings to get to and from the victim's house in the tight time frame, but she would figure that one out later.

Right now she wanted to search Micah's closet for a jacket missing a button. And if she didn't find that jacket, she was going to dig up all the flowers that had been planted yesterday morning along the back wall of the property, where she suspected all the bloody evidence was buried.

Libby normally chose hard evidence over gut feeling in homicide investigations, but there was something about that actor that didn't set right with her, beyond his creepy overdeveloped body and the multiple stuffed animal heads that gazed down from his walls.

While Jim had gone through the rote questions in Micah's living room, Libby had strolled over to an enormous glass trophy case with overhead lights illuminating the weapons it housed. Little white cards—like the ones on museum exhibits—gave the name of the movie in which each gun, knife, chain saw or broad sword had appeared.

By the card that read *I, Army* was a long-bladed knife with a casket-shaped handle, what the bayou folks back in Louisiana used to call an Arkansas toothpick. Libby glanced over to make sure Micah wasn't watching her, then tilted her close-cropped head right up to the glass. Unless she was very badly mistaken, that was dried blood along the razor edge of the toothpick.

Independent living is *so* overrated, Maureen decided, as she slowly made her way east on Magnolia Boulevard, checking the rearview mirror periodically for anyone staying behind her too long. She hadn't washed a load of laundry since she was a student at UCLA, and only *then* when she had forgotten to bring something home with her sheets and clothing on her Thursday night returns. Graciela always laundered, ironed, folded or hung everything neatly for Maureen's drive back to campus Monday morning.

The cap had come off a bottle of mouthwash in the move, and the set of bed sheets she had packed was soaked with thirty-two ounces of minty freshness. Maureen had trekked down to the laundry room, only to find all four washers in use. Back upstairs she dumped the soggy bundle on the floor of her room and went to the kitchen for something to drink. When she opened the fridge door and looked at the pristine shelves—empty except for an open box of Arm & Hammer baking soda—it dawned on her that she would have to buy groceries. And not only the staples like milk, cereal, bread, eggs and coffee, but all the supporting players: salt, pepper, catsup, mustard, hot sauce, napkins, toilet paper, dish soap and few dozen other things one housekeeper or another had always ensured were stocked in Charlie's kitchen.

If it weren't for this whole *somebody's-probably-going-to-kill-me* issue, I'd move back home now, she thought. When she dropped Charlie off at the house, Maureen would leave the wet sheets for Mrs. Taylor and pick up another set to put on her bed tonight.

Pulling in next to baggage claim, she saw Charlie waiting at the curb with his laptop and a carry-on, both of which he tossed into the back before climbing in on the shotgun side. On the plane he had come up with a plan guaranteed to persuade Denice to move to LA, so even the sadness over Maureen's moving out couldn't completely dampen his mood. As he shut the door and Maureen pulled away, Charlie wrinkled his nose. "Did somebody throw up peppermint schnapps in here?"

Jane couldn't take her eyes off the beautiful ring. *Her* beautiful ring, she had to keep reminding herself. A part of her felt guilty—she knew it must have cost a lot—but that part shrank as she recalled a childhood longing for pretty things she knew she would never have. And last night, Blake said he and Maureen had made $100,000 for a single day's work. It was an unimaginably large amount, more than double what Jane made in ten months of teaching.

"So, start planning the wedding," Blake had said.

Once the busses had pulled away with their little charges, Jane sat at her desk flipping through the bridal magazines provided by her co-workers after Blake's classroom proposal. Apparently, putting on a wedding was as tactically challenging as mounting an expedition to scale Kilimanjaro, and Jane felt overwhelmed. Flowers, food, cake, bridesmaids' gifts, the all-important dress with a capital D. Hotel space to book. Restaurant, chapel, rehearsal dinner, reception, invitations. Oh, Lordy.

Jane knew tradition dictated the wedding was to be paid for by the bride's father, impossible in this case, as Carl Larsen, a partially disabled coal worker, had barely kept food on the table and a roof over the heads of his wife and five children all these years. Even with Jane sending half her take-home pay back to Cobalt every month, the family barely got by, clear examples of America's working poor. It was hard enough for her parents to accept money from their own daughter; how humiliated would they be to attend a fancy wedding knowing someone else had paid for it because they couldn't afford to?

Not all the bridal magazines were recent, having sat in desk drawers for months, to be pulled out and sighed over periodically, so Jane looked through the twelve-page spread on the Kardashian wedding. She felt herself getting queasy reading the prices of the various elements of the lavish affair, especially in light of how briefly that particular till-death-do-us-part had lasted.

The idea of wasting so much money on what is really only a great big party, bothered Jane, so she closed the magazine, putting it back with the others and deciding to return the entire stack tomorrow.

Libby Johnson directed the crew of detectives and uniformed officers who searched Micah's house. So far, no jacket matching the threads of the torn-off button had turned up, but three guys were digging in the flower bed where Libby hoped they would find a set of bloody clothes and Cody Mason's cell phone. She was certain she already had the murder weapon, having bagged the Arkansas toothpick first thing. And her fingers were crossed about the two hairs the M.E. had found on the victim's body, hairs not belonging to Cody Mason.

The mystery of how Micah, a man pushing sixty, had gotten to the murder scene and back so quickly was about to get less mysterious.

"Yo, Johnson, come look what I found in the garage," Det. Willis said.

Stepping into the huge garage, Libby noted the three parked examples of conspicuous consumption, but those weren't why Willis had called her in. Hung on rubberized pegs high up on the wall were racing bikes, one for an adult and one for a child.

"Take down the bigger one but don't let the tires touch the ground." Once the bike was securely held by two uniforms, Libby reached her gloved hands under the streamlined seat and tested the weight. Titanium frame, she guessed, and easily hoisted over the back wall by a man with Micah's strength.

"Wrap it carefully," she told the officers, letting the weight settle back onto their hands. She felt sure the tire treads contained evidence that would prove the bike had been ridden within the last few days, and she looked forward to questioning Micah about it.

When do I get to see the new place and meet your roomies?"

"Well, nobody's really settled in yet, so probably not for a while." As soon as Charlie opened the front door and flipped on the foyer lights, Maureen headed toward the laundry room with her wet sheets. "Hey, Charlie?" she called over her shoulder. "Would you mind if I grabbed a few things out of the pantry while

I'm here?"

His normal response would have been "help yourself," as Charlie O'Brien was the quintessential mi-casa-es-su-casa guy, but a rapid mental calculation told him this might be the way to convince Maureen to move back home. He knew she was accustomed to privacy and a full complement of household amenities. In his effort to compensate for the early loss of her mother, Charlie had, rightly or wrongly, parented his daughter not only with love, but by purchasing every little thing she ever wanted and ensuring she never had to lift a finger around the house. He knew he was lucky she hadn't turned out like those overprivileged Hollywood brats who keep LA's rehab centers in the black and disgrace themselves in the tabloids every week.

So, she's sharing tight digs with two other girls and privacy is out the window, he thought. She had made a comic story out of the wet sheets and laundry room adventure on the drive from the airport, but her father heard it as the first of many rude awakenings facing Maureen in the wake of her self-emancipation. Charlie didn't like to use the word *spoiled*, with its unsavory implication of rottenness, but he knew his daughter was at the very least *dependent* on his open-handed generosity. And that was peachy keen with him, especially if it brought her back home. The sooner she got fed up with "reality," the better.

Maureen returned from the laundry room with a new set of sheets. "Did you hear what I said?"

"What? No, I was checking my messages."

"I'm wondering if I could maybe take a few things from the pantry." When she didn't get an immediate, magnanimous go-ahead, she continued. "Uh, coffee, salt, mayo, stuff like that."

Perfect, he thought. She doesn't even have the

basics. "I don't know. Mrs. T. didn't bring groceries last Friday because I was leaving, so until she gets here in the morning, I'm kind of low on things."

On salt? Maureen wondered skeptically. But this wasn't her home anymore, and by her own choice, so she would have to quit relying on Charlie for everything. "That's okay. I'll stop by the store on my way back to the apartment."

The last thing Jane wanted that evening was a fight with Blake. Not after the ring; not after the romantic proposal. And that's why she soft-pedaled her reluctance about pricy nuptials.

"But doesn't every girl *dream* of a big, wonderful wedding?" Blake asked.

"No, *dopy* girls dream of big, wonderful weddings. Smart girls dream of big, wonderful *husbands*," she replied, dropping her hand and cupping it where it counted. "And I am going to have that whether my wedding makes *Access Hollywood* or gets performed by a Justice of the Peace."

Blake willingly allowed himself to be distracted, returning her attentions in kind, but no way was he letting her off the hook on the wedding. Jane had claimed it was all too much bother for her to put everything together, but he knew her hesitance went right back to her impoverished childhood and her resultant uneasiness about "wasting" money.

If any woman ever deserved a lavish wedding, with her as the lovely center of attention, it was Lisa Jane Larsen, and Blake intended to make that happen whether she wanted it or not.

Libby Johnson sat across from Micah and his attorney, wondering if the rumors about his steroid use were true, whispers that had floated through

Hollywood for many years. As a former college athlete who had come *this* close to turning pro, Libby had witnessed or heard about AAS abuse on more than a few occasions, and was familiar with the side effects. With his ridiculously overdeveloped body, Micah could be the poster-oaf for juicing. Might Cody Mason have been the victim of 'roid rage?

Det. Johnson knew Gail Hatcher would stop her client from answering pretty much everything she wanted to ask, but decided to try the old catch-more-flies-with-honey gambit. "As you know, you are not under arrest, but I'm talking to everyone who was close to Cody Mason so I can piece together a picture of why this tragedy occurred."

"I understand," Micah replied, his voice conveying subdued concern. "And I want to help."

Libby glanced down at her notes, using that few seconds to put a shy smile on her face, a look as out of place there as a nun at a cockfight. "You know," she said, gazing up through her lashes at the muscled freakshow. "I've been a big fan of your movies for a long time."

"Well, thanks; I'm flattered," he said, wondering what it would be like to bang a bald woman.

"In fact, I'd really love an autograph. I mean, if it wouldn't be too presumptuous of me."

Micah's attorney narrowed her eyes, wondering what was going on. Gail Hatcher had seen Libby Johnson do many things in interview rooms: growl, threaten, browbeat, even throw a chair. She had watched her play cat-and-mouse with suspects, turn their words against them, tell lies about accomplices supposedly spilling their guts in another interview room, but she had never once seen Det. Johnson simper. Good God, thought Gail, she can't be *attracted* to this ambulatory clump of testosterone, can she?

In answer to the detective's question, and on very familiar turf now, Micah reached over and pulled the spiral-bound pad to his side of the table. He gave the obviously mesmerized black woman a wolfish smile as he took the ballpoint from her, making sure to let his fingers graze hers with promise. He clicked open the pen and signed the single name with a flourish.

Libby filed away the fact that Micah was right-handed, the first piece of data she had gleaned so far, then masked her disgust when he stroked her palm with his middle finger on returning the pen. "I guess one of the reasons I always admired your work was that you were not only an actor, but an athlete as well. I played a little B-ball in college myself."

"Hoops, all right. I'm impressed."

Gail Hatcher could not figure out what was going on. Micah might be trying to lay groundwork for a hook-up, but what was Libby doing? Gail decided to keep silent and watch what unfolded.

"Didn't I read that you qualified for the Olympics back in the late 80's?" the detective asked, using a ploy that worked on actors and other narcissists.

"It was actually the mid-70's," Micah corrected, secretly pleased she thought he looked fifteen years younger than he was. "And I *did* make the team. But then a movie role came up and I had to drop out."

"Weight-lifting, wasn't it?"

"Yeah. And it was tough choosing between a Gold Medal and a Golden Globe," he said, trotting out a line Cody had come up with thirty-five years earlier."

Oh, hell, why don't the two of them get a room, wondered Gail.

"I'm dying to know, what did you lift back then?"

"I qualified with 475 pounds," he said, raising both arms and flexing his guns to emphasize the point.

"So, I guess it would be no trouble at all for you to

lift a racing bike over the back wall of your property if you wanted to get to your agent's house in a hurry and an automobile wasn't an option."

Micah's smile died away, but Gail Hatcher nodded appreciatively. Ah, she thought, it had only been a spoonful of sugar to make the medicine go down.

The acronym LOL took on an unpleasant meaning for Libby Johnson over the next few days, as the Lloyd's of London representative bird-dogged her every move. Lloyd's, in the dapper personification of Mr. Garrett Smythe-Whitt, had fifteen million reasons to want Micah Deifenschlictor charged, prosecuted and convicted of the murder. Only then would Lloyd's be off the hook for the life insurance payout.

Aware of the potential public relations nightmare which would follow the charging of a Hollywood icon, Lt. Rhee cautioned Libby to pursue the case with deliberation and delicacy. Nattering in her other ear, however, was Garrett Smythe-Whitt, who was "cheesed-off" about everything from the lack of a tea station in the break room, to what he perceived as Libby's slow-walk in arresting Micah.

Her multiple chats with the prime suspect had yielded nothing more than the desire to hose herself off after each contact with him, so Det. Johnson impatiently awaited results on the knife and the bike. Without the victim's cell phone, the semi-threatening answering machine message from Micah on the land line was too flimsy a thread from which to hang an arrest. The words implied motive, but the time of the call brought opportunity into question. And so, she waited for test results on the knife that could pin down means.

All the while, Mr. Garrett Smythe-Whitt—his initials fueling a dark fantasy in every cop whose path he crossed—challenged her investigative techniques, the crime lab's slowness, even the integrity of a police department he implied might be searching for a scapegoat to avoid bringing charges against a well-known movie actor. And he did all this in a whiny, nasal British accent that made Libby want to jam a crumpet down his throat. Thursday afternoon, when she got word the lab report was in on the Arkansas toothpick, Libby announced she was leaving to visit Micah's dug-up back yard again. To keep the Lloyd's of London bloodhound off her scent, she went out the back door, in again through a rarely used side door, and down to the forensics lab.

Five minutes later Lt. Rhee took her call, then slipped by LOL's GS-W to join her downstairs. They found some privacy in the morgue, where a cheesed-off Libby Johnson told him the results. "The good news is we definitely have a match for the knife used to kill Cody Mason. The bad news is the dried blood on the blade is fake. Special-effects movie blood."

"Any chance he cleaned the blade, then dipped it in the fake stuff to throw us off?"

Libby Johnson shook her head, letting the lieutenant know that was the first question she had asked on reading the results. "Ray said the blade could have been scoured, but the wooden handle would have absorbed at least trace amounts of blood."

"Duplicate knife?"

"Jimbo's already checking. I called him while I was waiting for you to get down here."

Ray Perez, one of the CSIs, pushed the door open and alerted them to the imminent arrival of Smythe-Whitt. In a dramatic stage whisper, he warned, "The British are coming! The British are coming!"

Nearly forty-eight hours after her less-than-

fruitful discussion with Blake about the size and cost of the their wedding, Jane sat at her desk dreading the next go-round with him. The school busses had all pulled out thirty minutes earlier, and most of the faculty was rapidly following suit.

Her fiancé's "surprise" had been waiting when she got to her classroom that morning: a Beverly Hills-based wedding planner with a résumé consisting of lavish nuptial "events" for Broadway stars, senators' daughters, Oscar winners and gazillionaires whose shiny-new trophy wives wanted to give a bejeweled middle finger to the prior Mrs. Moneybags.

While Vanessa Baird paged through expensive possibilities for her consideration, Jane's queasiness returned, despite the wedding planner's attempt to reassure an obviously reluctant bride-to-be with the news that Blake had pre-approved a hefty budget. She presented it to Jane as being able to do "the fun stuff" without having to worry about cost.

Far from providing reassurance, Vanessa's words had exacerbated Jane's anxiety. By the time her little charges were scrambling off the busses and Vanessa Baird was packing up her designer satchel of over-the-toppiness, Jane feared she was about to be the first person older than five to throw up in her classroom.

Ginger ale from the cafeteria had quieted her stomach, and she had gone about the day with her usual enthusiasm, glancing frequently at the beautiful pink heart on her left hand. She glanced at it again now, then at the wall clock, knowing she would have to leave soon and talk to Blake. This time, though, she wouldn't be so timid. She couldn't leave him with the mistaken idea she was only being coy about not wanting to spend a fortune on a big wedding four or five months down the road. If marriage is about give and take, Blake was going to have to give on this.

Jane sighed as she took her purse from a drawer. Would he call the whole thing off? Would he ask for the ring back? She didn't know, but thinking about it triggered her nausea again, and she knew she'd have to stop at a drug store on the way home for something to put her out of her misery.

Maureen gave a relieved sigh when she got to the office Friday. Apartment living was wearing thin after only three days, as were her new roommates, so the cozy suite felt like the next best thing to her father's house. She decided to bring toiletries, bath towels and a blow-dryer Monday, so she could start showering here before Blake arrived each day, instead of at her new place.

The deal with her two roomies was that *they* were supposed to share one of the bathrooms and Maureen was to have sole use of the second one, since she was taking responsibility for the lease and all the utilities. But earlier, while one of them belted out Cher's *"If I Could Turn Back Ti-yimc"* in her own shower, the second one, unable to hold it any longer, sneaked into Maureen's bathroom for a lengthy sit-down.

When Maureen tried the door, she discovered it was locked, and heard a flush. Then, when the door finally opened, she was advised to "light a match" before entering. Maureen's several sucky trips to the grocery store this week had not included the purchase of air freshener or Lysol spray, so she had to wait for the underpowered exhaust fan to render the room only slightly less toxic than present-day Chernobyl.

The office voicemail included a political robo-call, two inquiries from potential clients, an order for a thin crust with sausage and mushrooms—E&O's number was, unfortunately, only one digit off from the West Hollywood Domino's—and a message from Blake saying he wouldn't be in today. Fine by Maureen. The only things she had to do were transcribe the rest of those eavesdropping recordings the tabloid weasel had sold them, email them over to Gail Hatcher, and do phone follow-up with the possible clients. The politician and the pizza guy would have to get along without her.

A few hours later, having gotten Gail's confirmation on the transcripts, and having set up a Tuesday appointment for a man who wanted a couple weeks surveillance on his possibly shady business partner, Maureen was able to relax and enjoy the solitude.

After walking over to Ziggy's and picking up a corned beef on pumpernickel, she sat in the fishbowl conference room with her lunch of sandwich, potato chips and Acqua Panna spread out on paper towels before her on the table. She had propped the glass door open, as the outer office door was locked and she wanted to be able to hear if anyone came knocking. Of course, if Lionheart's assassin paid a visit, he would be undaunted by a locked door. The killer could be anyone, official or no, but was there really any reason to believe he would come after her? She had not witnessed a thing, only coming upon Lionheart's body afterwards, so she wasn't a danger to whoever did it.

Maureen realized she was attempting to make the threat go away—at least in her mind—so she could justify moving back in with Charlie. She didn't have room for all her clothes and guns, she was rapidly learning how ill-suited she was to domestic chores, and she missed her father. Not to mention one of her roommates was a total pig.

She understood most people hearing about a woman almost twenty-eight years old still living at home would conjure up an image of an unemployed slacker taking advantage of parental tolerance, but she and Charlie had never related on a parent/child basis. Maureen genuinely enjoyed his company. After an initial flash of attraction, she was settling in to a comfortable relationship with Blake. She could not picture herself spilling her guts to him any time soon with details of her CIA wet work, but she was learning not to bristle up and snap when he made one of his infrequent pokes at her dark past. The pokes were not mean-spirited, were never made in front of anyone else, and were gradually providing a much-needed release valve for Maureen. Knowing he *knew*, and didn't despise her for it, gave her at least a tiny bit of wiggle room in her own self-loathing.

If Maureen were completely honest with herself, she would acknowledge that Jane and Denice had also improved her life. Jane was younger than Maureen by four years, and still had a naive, small-town lack of sophistication about her, but she was intuitive, kind and funny, a perfect partner for Blake. And she had unselfishly thrown a lifeline to Maureen during a recent blowup between father and daughter over his new companion.

What was it about Denice that both rankled and soothed Maureen? She couldn't figure it out, never having walked the occasionally bumpy terrain of a mother/daughter relationship. She only knew Charlie was mad for the lady, and so Maureen would continue forging whatever bond would be necessary for future accord in the house she desperately hoped she could return to.

She tried to talk herself out of being a target, but kept coming back to the reality that someone had known she was in Lionheart's house when they beat her to the killing punch. Why wouldn't they allow Maureen do the job if they wanted him dead so badly? God knows she had reason enough to murder that evil bastard. Or was someone putting together a black-mail dossier on her? Video of her going into the house and coming out after Lionheart was oh-so-very dead. Maybe taking out the CIA bureaucrat right under her nose was the assassin's way of taunting Maureen, leaving a sword to dangle over her head.

The trash can rang eight times before going to voicemail. A middle-aged man in uniform at the sign-in desk of the Century City high-rise had heard the can ring every fifteen minutes for the past two hours. Assuming someone had accidentally tossed their cell phone away while jettisoning an empty machiatto cup, he had pulled the can around and into the polished, sheltering arms of the large, U-shaped reception desk, intending to take the liner bag home with him when the second-shift guy showed up at 3:00.

He had done this before, sometimes coming up with real treasures. A diamond tennis bracelet whose clasp had failed right as its owner knuckled the can lid to drop in a sheaf of presentation papers after an unsuccessful sales pitch upstairs. A pair of fifth-row tickets to a Hollywood Bowl concert, thrown away by a young man storming out of the building after the receptionist for the penthouse law firm turned down his marriage proposal. Even the Faux-lex watch on the desk man's wrist was a rescue from the lobby's main receptacle.

He would haul the bag home, dump its contents on a tarp in his kitchen, then sort through the mess with gloved hands. There was at least a cell phone in it today, so maybe there would be a small reward for its return. And if not, hey, free cell phone.

The case against Micah Deifenschlictor went into a spiral dive Friday afternoon when results came back on the bicycle. The decomposition of the tread contents indicated it hadn't been ridden for months, confirming Micah's claim he had last taken it down at Christmas, when his little boy visited for a week and they had biked into the Beverly Hills commercial district for breakfast every morning.

Libby Johnson had ordered the digging crew to go down another twelve inches. The house had been tossed twice, and every bit of ground between it and Cody Mason's house had been scoured for trace. No bloody knife, no jacket matching the button and worst of all, no cell phone to break Micah's alibi.

The two hairs on Mason's body didn't match the prime suspect, nor did they cross-ref with anyone in the national database. And Garrett Smythe-Whitt was hemorrhaging Earl Grey and slagging-off Libby Johnson to anyone who would listen. If she failed to make the case against Micah, Lloyd's of London was out fifteen million dollars, and Smythe-Whitt, who had approved the policy, was likely out of a job.

Libby had been certain she had the right guy, so her frustration grew as each puzzle piece reconfigured itself so as not to fit. She had an able-bodied young officer make the climb over Micah's wall, then run to Mason's house and climb over *that* wall. Factoring in Micah's age, 58, and his obsession with weight-lifting instead of any kind of cardio, the task would have been nearly impossible without the bike or some other vehicle. Libby had viewed the gate security recordings and knew Micah never left through the front. She needed that cell phone to rule out the smarmy muscle freak. *Or* to nail his ass to the wall.

Libby's partner hung up as she approached his desk. "Jimbo, any luck?" she asked.

"No, and I think his voicemail must be full, 'cause now it only rings and rings. I've called every fifteen minutes for most of the afternoon."

"Give it to one of the uniforms on the next shift so we can keep calling. If that phone was dumped by the killer, somebody's eventually going to hear it."

"By the way," Jim said, "the propmaster on *I, Army* confirmed there were *two* identical Bowie knives custom-made for the film and both went missing when the movie wrapped."

***

CODY MASON HOMICIDE
Case No. BH12-3-114H
TELEPHONE TRANSCRIPT: Call #1 (Part A)

T/D:	10:48 P.M. - 3/25
LOC:	2 mins 45 secs
ST/T:	10:48:20 P.M.
E/T:	10:51:05 P.M
T/F:	To (310) ████████ (cell)
	From (310) ████████ (cell)

SOURCE: (310) ████████ (accidental recording by MD)

MD: Micah

CM: S'up, asshole?

MD: Fuck you, dwarf.

CM: Yeah, you wish. How's the script?

MD: I got the story roughed out. I'll give it to Harry tomorrow so he can start plugging in the actual words.

CM: Yeah, great. Listen, about this
casting shit—

MD: Don't even start.

CM: Newsflash, I own half the picture and
I get a vote.

MD: Oh, cut the hard-ass. These guys
have had a real rough time since they
left the Corps. Homeless, broke,
PTSD, you name it.

CM: So you write 'em a big fucking check.
What you *don't* do is let a bunch of
amateurs jeopardize our first feature.

MD: And how exactly does casting *actual*
Marines to *play* Marines jeopardize it?

CM: You ever see that lousy airline
commercial a few years back? The one
where some ad flack had the brilliant
idea to use *real* stewardesses? A
bunch of mile-high cocktail waitresses
hamming it up for their big break.
Jesus! It was like watching robots
with lip gloss and hooters. The flack
got shitcanned and the next spot
featured real actresses. (FIVE
SECOND PAUSE) You still there?

MD: Look, most of the guys will only have
one or two lines. Me and Dom carry
all the important dialogue.

CM: (SNORTING NOISE) Dominic! You
want to tell me how a flunky you
threw a four-line bone to on all your
movies is suddenly second lead? Why

not Jake Gyllenhaal, like I suggested?

MD: Wow, look at the clock. It's time for your late-night snack, so why don't you go have a nice big bowl of go-fuck-yourself.

CM: Hey, I'm just saying we both have a lot on the line here. Don't go all touchy-feely and put it at risk.

MD: Way ahead of you. I got a dialogue coach lined up to walk each of them through his lines until he sounds like Sir John frickin' Gielgud. And, trust me, these guys know the combat stuff.

CM: (SIGHING SOUND) Okay, you big homo, I'm gonna go along with you on this.

MD: We're doing a good thing, Cody.

CM: Yeah. Piranha—

(CALL DISCONNECTS)

TELEPHONE TRANSCRIPT: End Call #1 (Part A)

***

Charlie O'Brien isn't expected or invited, but he drives toward his daughter's new place anyway, a huge, ugly potted plant belted into the passenger seat next to him. As housewarming gifts go, it is perfect: the wide-spreading leaves will take up too much space in an apartment he is fairly sure Maureen already finds claustrophobic. In addition to being big and useless, the plant requires watering every other day to keep from wilting, thus adding one more annoying responsibility to the list of them Maureen has no doubt discovered since moving out.

Having observed the passive-aggressive behavior of dozens of actors with whom he has worked, Charlie finally has an opportunity to apply those skills in his efforts to get Maureen to come back home. Overtly, he will continue to support her quest for independence, but off-camera he'll keep tightening the screws until she breaks.

As part of his charm assault, he has brought small gifts for her two roommates. Foregoing chocolates in case either girl is dieting, Charlie has had Gerard Duval make up two pairs of earring jackets. A stud can be inserted through the center of the little circle made up of ten-point diamonds, instantly turning a simple stone into a framed statement piece. Maureen will be constantly reminded by her roommates what a terrific father she has. *While* she's watering her plant, he hopes.

His cover story for the visit is that he wants her to join Denice and him at a black-tie gala a week from tomorrow, the first lavish, star-studded event since the Oscars after-party almost four weeks ago. Part of Charlie's plan to win over his crush, Denice, is to impress her with major-league show business glitz. Let the diner owner from tiny Madison, Nevada, feel like Cinderella at the ball. And, as a clincher, he has asked Mr. Duval to build another piece of jewelry for him, a diamond and pearl necklace guaranteed to take Denice's breath away.

Enjoying happy thoughts of restocking his lonely house with both of the women he loves, Charlie finds a guest spot in the underground lot and eases his Alfa Romeo into it. Getting out, he pats his pockets to make sure he still has the two tiny jewelry boxes, then goes around to unbuckle the second seat belt and hoist the unwieldy plant onto his hip. On the elevator up to the fourth floor, with leaves swarming his head, Charlie notices the potted monstrosity also emits an ungodly stench. Better and better.

He places it on the floor before ringing the bell, the easier to present his gift with a hearty "Ta-da!" when Maureen or one of the other girls opens up. Charlie automatically tilts his head to the angle that has enabled him to look his child directly in the eye ever since she reached her adult height of five-foot-four at age fifteen.

But when the door swings open, Charlie finds himself staring, not into Maureen's electric blue eyes, but at a wet mat of gray chest hair.

Libby Johnson and her partner had driven south to a duplex near Baldwin Hills to pick up Cody Mason's cell phone, and were listening to all his voicemail messages on their drive back to the station. The only important one, the call from Micah, appeared to confirm what he had been telling them from the beginning. "He's not our guy," Jim said, hitting the end button on Mason's phone through the plastic of the evidence bag.

"We don't know that for sure yet."

"Come on. The M.E. says Mason was most likely dead by 11:30 and the call was placed at 11:15."

"No, Micah *says* he's calling at 11:15."

"I know you like him for this, Lib, but the time of the call is right here on the screen, and—"

"Like that couldn't be faked," she interrupted.

"—*and* you can bet it's going to match the time of the cell tower hit. Not to mention we've already heard the supposedly threatening call that came in on the land line a little while later. Face it, he's alibi'd."

She stared straight ahead as she maneuvered the car through the Friday quitting-time traffic crawling north on Sepulveda. Realizing Jimbo was right didn't make it any easier to swallow. And if Micah hadn't killed Cody Mason, who had?

What Libby didn't know was that a new person of interest was about to be handed to her like the ending of a lousy play you can't wait to walk out of.

The dripping old man threw his arms wide in greeting. "Charlie!" Unfortunately, the exuberance of the gesture compromised the tenuous hold of the knot in the bath towel encircling his pot-bellied middle. As the towel hit the floor, Charlie found himself staring at the flaccid, uncircumsized penis of comedy writer Max Keller.

"Jesus, Max, cover that thing up!" Charlie turned aside, the hideous plant providing a more welcome view than an 86-year-old schlong.

Bracing a hand on the doorjamb, Max was able to squat deeply enough to retrieve the towel from the floor. After his nude, arthritic plié, he straightened and wrapped the towel around himself again, securing the knot more tightly this time. "You only look away 'cause you're envious. Come on in."

While Charlie hoisted the plant and entered the apartment, Max continued his monologue. "Yeah, my ex used to say it reminded her of a Sharpei puppy. And when I was just a kid writing for Uncle Miltie, we had this contest where we lined up quarters—"

"Max," Charlie interrupted, "can we for the love of God move the topic off your schvantz?"

"Oh, I get it, deep down you're worried you're gay. No sweat, I already put away the temptation. So, what's with the plant? We recasting *The Day of the*

Triffids?"

"Housewarming gift for Maureen. Is she here?"

"Not home from work yet. Sit, relax."

Charlie sat on the couch, while Max settled in one of the armchairs. "So, you're one of the roommates," Charlie began tentatively.

"Yeah, and between you, me and the bedpost I've gotten more tail in the past week than I have in the last ten years." Max saw Charlie blanch, and hurried to clarify his claim. "Not your kid, Charlie! Maureen's like a granddaughter to me." He leaned forward, dropping his voice to a comedically conspiratorial level. "I'm talking about Ethel Rosen. Don't let the walker fool you; she's insatiable in the sack."

"*Ethel* is the other roommate?" Charlie asked in disbelief.

"I know what you're thinking, too soon after Sol's death. But the woman has crazy needs, if you catch my drip. And between her hormone patch and my boner pills, we're a match made in a Rexall pharmacy. Last night, we—"

"Dad?" Charlie was relieved to see Maureen in the doorway.

"Hey, I'm gonna go put on some pants," Max volunteered. "You two get acquainted." As he left the room, Maureen noticed the potted monster.

"What's with the plant? We recasting *Little Shop of Horrors?*"

Oh God, Charlie thought, what did I do to my kid? She's turned into Max Keller with fresher references. "Max and Ethel? Seriously?"

"Women my age bore me. Besides, they were both living in total dumps." Maureen flopped down on one of the armchairs, giving the plant the evil eye as she caught a whiff of its armpitish aroma.

"They lived in dumps because their only income is

Social Security," Charlie said. "So, of *course*, they can upgrade to a Beverly Hills-adjacent mid-rise."

Looking like a teenager nailed for texting while driving, Maureen sheepishly coughed up the truth. "Yeah, well I may have slightly misrepresented the rent to them."

"You're subsidizing."

"Gosh, I wonder who I learned *that* from."

"Cute. The diff is I made twenty million in salary alone on *The Brothers Gunn*, forget about the two-hour repacks for the third world movie market, so I can afford it. You're just a working girl now, so unless you're planning to kill me for the inheritance, this set-up is terminal."

"Charlie!" Ethel Rosen lurched into the room, popping her walker forward ten inches, then catching up on foot. "Max told me you were here."

Charlie stood and crossed to her, bending to peck her cheek. "I stopped by to see if we could all go to Spago for dinner. My treat."

Maureen's look at him over the snot-green leaves of the plant said: *the apple doesn't fall very far from the tree, now does it?*

Charlie's look at her over Ethel's silver-blonde wig said: *this conversation isn't over.*

An anonymous phone tip directed the BHPD to Frank "Goody" Goodwin, a 41-year-old independent talent agent who had been trying to poach Micah away from Cody Mason for years.

Goody was brought in for questioning on Saturday, and was unable to explain how the victim's cell phone ended up in a lobby trash can eighteen floors below the suite of Goodwin Talent. He played down his interest in Micah, admitting he had given it a whirl and offered a contract should the geek and the

Greek ever split up, but said it was routine business, no biggie. His alibi for the time of the murder fell apart with one phone call.

On Sunday, a search of the area around Goody's condo building turned up a knife behind a dumpster, a duplicate of the one at Micah's house. And this knife had *real* blood along the edge. That was enough for a judge to sign a search warrant, resulting in the discovery of a jacket matching the button and threads found under the hedge at the crime scene. The jacket had been dry-cleaned, and the button had been professionally replaced, but it hung in Goody's closet like the final juicy clue in a TV cop drama.

At 7:30 on Sunday evening, Frank Goodwin was arrested for the murder of Cody Mason, and Micah was off the hook. Libby Johnson couldn't understand how she had been so wrong, deciding never to listen to her gut again. From now on, it was hard evidence or nothing.

***

<u>CODY MASON HOMICIDE</u>
Case No. BH12-3-114H
TELEPHONE TRANSCRIPT: Call #1 (Part B)

T/D:	10:51 P.M. - 3/25
LOC:	Ø mins 18 secs
ST/T:	10:51:05 P.M.
E/T:	10:51:23 P.M.
T/F:	To (310) ███████ (cell)
	From (310) ███████ (cell)

SOURCE: E&O Investigations - illegal
recording purchased from
unnamed tabloid reporter

(**TRANSCRIBER'S NOTE:** This is a partial,
following continuously from Transcript #1, as
(310) ▓▓▓▓▓▓▓ claims he realized at this
point he was accidentally recording call from
(310) ▓▓▓▓▓▓ and hit stop record. Remainder
of call contains only the voice of
(310) ▓▓▓▓▓▓.)

(PAUSE)

MD: Probably your cat knocking something
        over in the kitchen.

(PAUSE)

MD: So, go downstairs and check it out.

(PAUSE)

MD: You're right. It's probably nothing,
        but give me a call back anyway.

(PAUSE)

(CALL DISCONNECTS)

TELEPHONE TRANSCRIPT: End Call #1 (Part B)

***

Maureen was already working on her side of
the double desk when Blake strolled in around 9:30
Monday morning. She looked up from her computer to
find him vogue-posed in the doorway of their office.
  "Notice anything different?" he asked.
  She gave him the once-over, but couldn't discern
any new article of clothing. "Haircut?" she ventured.
  "Nope. You're looking at a married man." As

proof, he offered up his left hand, which now sported a gold band on the ring finger.

"Ah, now I see it. You *do* have that I-just-lost-my-cherry look. What happened to the wedding planner you hired last week?"

"Apparently, she scared the hell out of my fiancée. Somewhere between the $200-a-bottle champagne and a wedding dress with its own mortgage, Jane's eyes rolled back in her head and the only word she could choke out was *elopement*."

Blake recapped the whirlwind weekend for his partner: the Friday flight and drive to Cobalt, West Virginia; the meet-the-family Saturday; Sunday morning's wedding in The Little Blue Chapel; and the flight back last night. Maureen knew he'd been looking forward to a big wedding, so she asked if he was disappointed.

"Strangely, no. Jane's been uneasy from the start about spending a lot of money on what is in essence only a party, and as she pointed out to me Thursday night when she made her case for eloping, I expected *her* to do all the work. So, when it came down to me pitching in on decisions about bridesmaids gifts and centerpieces, I took the easy way out."

"Well, I'm happy for both of you."

He told her she was in the minority on that one. His parents were ticked off at him because they had never met Jane, and his old partner, Artie Lassiter, felt he had been screwed out of throwing the bachelor party. "When the school year is over, we'll fly out to Minnesota to charm and disarm the Ervansky clan, and I figure a case of St. Pauli Girl ought to bring Artie around."

Blake asked Maureen if anything had happened on the homefront while he was gone, so she told him about their client meeting the next day. "Oh, and in case you haven't heard, they arrested some agent last night in the Cody Mason homicide. From what I saw on the news this morning, he's the real deal."

"That clears the way for you to date Mr. Musclepants," Blake said with a grin, ignoring the scowl she shot his way. "Maybe you can bring him to our house this Saturday. We're having a little drinks-and-buffet thing to celebrate the nups. Lt. Rhee's coming, along with a lot of the guys from the old squad."

"Sorry, but Charlie's dragging me to a black-tie gala at the Hilton."

"Can't he bring a date instead?"

"He *has* a date, but he's afraid the cheeseburger queen won't know how to dress or act, so I have to be the hired Tim Gunn for the night."

This was an exaggeration of what Charlie had actually said, as he had no fear Denice Cantrell would embarrass him in any way around the celebrities at the gala. He only wanted to make sure she didn't feel awkward or "less-than" around the kind of women who had Jimmy Choo on speed dial. He had enlisted his daughter in case a subtle adjustment on makeup, hair, wardrobe or accessories was needed.

Maureen had been to dozens of these "glamorous" events, and knew exactly what to expect in the way of cuisine, entertainment, bullshit conversations, and unwelcome advances. It was the last place she expected to run into Lionheart's killer.

***

CODY MASON HOMICIDE
Case No. BH12-3-114H
TELEPHONE TRANSCRIPT: Call #2

T/D: 11:15 P.M. - 3/25
LOC: Ø mins 17 secs
ST/T: 11:14:57
E/T: 11:15:14
T/F: To (310) ▮▮▮▮▮▮▮(cell)
       From (310) ▮▮▮▮▮▮ (cell)

SOURCE: VM on cell (310) ▮▮▮▮▮▮▮.

???:   You have reached the voicemail of—

CM: Cody Mason

???:   —who is unavailable at this time.
      Please leave your message after the
      tone.

(BEEP SOUND)

MD: Hey, douchebag, how long does it take
      to strangle a cat? Call me when you
      get this. It's 11:15 and I'm hitting the
      rack in another half hour.

(CALL DISCONNECTS)

TELEPHONE TRANSCRIPT: End Call #2

***

The first week of April was busy for everyone. Blake and Maureen nailed down the surveillance gig at their Tuesday meeting. It wasn't the kind of money Gail Hatcher had handed them the week before, but it was good, solid income and it would establish them as good, solid investigators, instead of the "celebrity detectives" they had unwittingly become after their first splashy case.

Jane Larsen-Ervansky, relieved now of last week's burden, happily spent her after-school hours planning the party she and Blake would have Saturday night. She was much more comfortable with a budget for beer, wine, munchies and Italian food than she had been with the wedding planner's proposed expenditure of only marginally less than the gross national product of Venezuela.

Libby Johnson built her airtight case against Frank Goodwin that week, though Goody maintained his innocence, claiming the action star had called him Sunday morning to set up a meeting late that night.

"He told me he was finally ready to dump his representation, so I agreed to meet him at a beach parking lot off Pacific Coast Highway between Sunset and Point Dume."

"At 11:00 P.M.?" Libby asked dryly.

"He said he didn't want Cody to know. And he for sure didn't want any paparazzi seeing us together before the deal was done."

Nothing about his story held up. Micah admitted he had toyed with the idea of signing with Goodwin Talent several years earlier during one of his and Cody's classic squabbles, but denied he would ever have seriously considered a move. As to the secret meeting the night of Cody's death, Micah claimed he knew nothing about it. When the BHPD went through Goody's phone records for the day of the murder, they found no incoming calls from any of Micah's cell, home or work numbers.

By Friday, Libby was satisfied she had the right man. Frank Goodwin had murdered Cody Mason with premeditation.

Garrett Smythe-Whitt reported back to Lloyd's of

London each day that week, his emails becoming less founded in truth as he prayed for a miracle that would put Micah Deifenschlictor back in the starring role of this whodunit. His prayer was not answered.

Maureen turned slowly, assessing herself in the door-mounted "full-length" mirror of her new bedroom. Full-length if you're a hobbit, she thought, checking out not the beautiful dress she wore, but whether the ankle holster showed when she moved.

The gown was a Roberto Cavelli: vine-patterned ecru lace over a satin underslip, with a mermaid-tail flare from the knees down. The gun was a Walther TPH: six .25 ACP rounds in a detachable magazine, with enough blowback to require a firm grip for dependable operation. Sofia Vergara had worn an identical dress to The Golden Globe Awards a couple months back, but to the best of Maureen's knowledge, Ms. Vergara had *not* been strapped at the time.

Satisfied the Walther was undetectable under the soft draping, she rotated her right ankle to make sure movement was not restricted by the holster, then red-carpet-walked a couple of times around the room to adjust for the added weight. Her Baby Browning was almost two ounces lighter, but Maureen had put in more firing-range time with the Walther.

Trying to ignore the sounds from the adjacent bedroom that indicated her two roommates were going at it *again*, she did a fast dip-and-snatch, pulling the gun out from under the lace and satin, and aiming it at herself in the mirror. Three more practice pulls, then she picked up her tiny designer bag and left for her father's house.

***

CODY MASON HOMICIDE
Case No. BH12-3-114H
TELEPHONE TRANSCRIPT: Call #3

T/D: 11:33 P.M. - 3/25

LOC: Ø mins 42 secs

ST/T: 11:33:03

E/T: 11:33:45

T/F: To (213) ▮▮▮▮▮▮ (land line)
          From (310) ▮▮▮▮▮▮ (cell)

SOURCE: Answer machine on
         (213) ▮▮▮▮▮

CM: Hi, this is Cody. I'm unable to take your call right now, but if you'll leave your name and digits after the beep, I'll get back to you as soon as I can.

(BEEP SOUND)

MD: Hey, asshole, pick up the phone. (PAUSE) Cody! (PAUSE) MASON!!! (PAUSE) You inconsiderate prick! While you're jacking yourself off in the shower, I'm sitting here thinking somebody broke into your house and stole your fuckin' Picasso. If you don't pick up I'm coming over there to kick your ass! (PAUSE) Fine. Be a dick. I'll talk to you in the morning.

(CALL DISCONNECTS)

TELEPHONE TRANSCRIPT: End Call #3

He checked his perfect, hand-tied bow tie in the polished steel of the refrigerator door. No prefabs for Charlie O'Brien. "Kickin' it old school," he murmured approvingly, as Maureen entered the kitchen.

"Well, ain't you tuxed up beyond all recognition," she growled in the gravelly voice of Charlie's most famous TV creation, private eye Max Gunn. Charlie turned to her.

"Boy, that voice and that dress do *not* match. And you are going to have drunk celebs glomming onto you all evening. You want I should carry a blunderbuss to scare them off?"

"Nah, I'm already packing."

Charlie's eyes darted to her tiny clutch, worried she was telling the truth. Maureen saw his concern, opened the designer bead fest, and showed him the meager contents: miniature hairbrush, lip gloss, a pack of tissues and a roll of breath mints. His look of relief convinced her she was right in holding some things back from him. "Where's Dolly?"

"Still getting ready. And let's start calling her by her real name, okay?"

"Sure. And what do we have here?" she asked, noticing the jewelry case on the granite counter top.

"A little bauble to make my lady shine among the glitterati." He opened the velvet case.

"Whoa! I see you're putting another one of Mr. Duval's children through college."

"I am nothing if not a man of generosity," Charlie replied, deftly slipping in a subtle reminder of the perks awaiting her return to the fold.

Like so many of Gerard Duval's creations, the necklace was understated and exquisite. It was a single strand, twenty inches long, and the pattern was: pearl, pearl, diamond, pearl, pearl, half-inch cylinder of Turkish filigree, then a repeat with the diamonds and pearls reversed. The icy diamonds beautifully counterpointed the warm, creamy pearls, while the filigree gave the piece a Victorian look.

"Charlie?"

He shut the box and put it behind his back as Denice entered the kitchen. Charlie was used to seeing her in a waitress' uniform or in nothing at all, so he was gobsmacked by the vision that glided into view. Even Maureen, who still believed true beauty was the exclusive province of the young, raised her eyebrows in surprise.

The dress was a fitted column of midnight blue with a deep, square neckline and long, tight sleeves that belled at the wrists. The art deco pattern traced on the bodice in silver bugle beads gave the illusion of curve, trompe l'oeil discreetly filling in for the breasts Denice had forfeited to a mastectomy twelve years before. Her face, which was lucky to get a swish of blush and a flick of mascara every morning before she hurried out at dawn to open the diner, was made up with the skill she had mastered as a Las Vegas showgirl, scaled back to look perfectly natural in non *va-va-voom* stage lighting. Her sable brown hair was a touseled mane of shoulder-length waves that gently swayed as she turned her head from father to daughter, then back. "Jeez, don't look so shocked. I told you I could clean up and pass."

As stunning as the willowy brunette was in her gown and makeup, it was the necklace she wore that riveted Charlie and Maureen. An inch-wide ribbon of diamonds hugged her slender neck like a choker, dipping to a vee at the base of her throat. The perfect stones threw fire in fifty directions as she moved her head, flaring even under ordinary kitchen lights. In the center of the sparkling vee nestled an oval-cut blue sapphire that had to weigh three carats.

Charlie felt behind himself till he connected with the knob of one of the drawers in the island, pulling it out and slipping the rectangular jewelry box inside. "My God, you are breathtaking," he said, lifting his hand and doing a finger twirl to indicate he'd like to see the three-sixty.

Denice smiled, then began a slow turn. As soon as her face was away from them, Charlie and Maureen looked at each other, his shoulders and hands lifting in a *what-the-hell?* gesture that smoothly transitioned to a welcoming reach-out as the pivot was completed. "I am the luckiest guy in the world."

"And don't ever forget it, Slick," Denice said, stepping up to lightly touch his bow tie as his hands went to her waist. She pecked his cheek, then turned to Maureen. "So. Do I pass muster?"

"You shine-up re-e-al nice," Maureen drawled in Max Gunn's voice.

"I'll get my bag and then I'm ready to go." She trailed her manicured nails along Charlie's shoulder as she turned to leave.

"Holy crap," Maureen said softly, once Denice cleared the room. "That can't be real, can it?"

Charlie didn't think it was his place to enlighten Maureen about Denice's past, but when she was still in her teens, Denice—then known as Dolly—had run with Frank Sinatra, Sammy Davis, Jr., playboys, princes and rock stars. "Oh, it's real all right."

Maureen gave him her illest evil grin. "Looks like Charlie O'Brien's gonna have to up his game."

"Don't you worry, kiddo," he replied slitting his eyes at her. "This old hunter still remembers how to catch a fox."

Maureen pointed at the drawer in the island where her father had hidden the now-outclassed necklace. "So, can I have it?"

"Like *that's* gonna happen. You had your chance and blew it, remember?"

The tiny restaurant on Laurel Canyon at the base of Lookout Mountain Avenue would do a booming business that Saturday night. Because of its out-of-the-way location, San Fernando Valley people rarely made the two-mile trip down Laurel to eat there, and the folks in Hollywood had too many other choices to bother fighting the traffic north for a mile, so even a high-volume night like a Saturday only pulled in a few dozen of the locals whose homes lined the twisty little roads up in the hills.

Tonight, though, the parking lot would fill with cars belonging to teachers and cops, and two recent police academy grads would earn some after-hours cash shuttling partygoers up the mountain to the home of Blake Ervansky and Jane Larsen. Every couple of trips, the rookies would also carry trays of food: hot hors d'oeuvres the first hour; eggplant parm, lasagne, grilled sausage and garlic rolls the second hour; dessert and cheese platters the third hour.

Lt. Aldin Rhee and his wife, Kathy, unfashionably on time, got into the back seat for one of the earliest shuttle runs, finding Libby Johnson already riding shotgun. As the young officer pulled out of the lot, Rhee inhaled deeply. "What is that wonderful smell?"

"I have a tray of stuffed mushrooms, clams casino and mini quiches on my lap," Libby said.

"*You* cooked?" Lt. Rhee asked, hastily adding, "No offense."

"None taken. No, as I was about to climb aboard, some guy in a chef's get-up ran out of the restaurant and handed me a tray and a hot pad to put under it."

"You could tell everybody you cooked," Mrs. Rhee suggested.

Libby looked over her shoulder at the lieutenant's wife. "Kathy, for a bowl of lies to be swallowed it has to contain at least a teaspoon of truth. Nobody's buying me cooking."

"Are you two going to make the announcement at the party?"

"We thought about it," Rhee said to his wife, "but we don't want to take the focus off Blake and Jane's special night."

Charlie worked the room with Denice, and Maureen was glad she had brought her own car. She had been attending events like this—fundraisers, bar mitzvahs, award show after-parties—since she was a child, and the glam had long ago dulled for her. She would stick around for another half hour, then put in an appearance at Blake and Jane's party, where nobody would be talking about their latest series, movie or life sensei. No, cops talked about important things: the Dodgers, the price of gas, the boobs on the tranny they'd busted for soliciting the night before.

Still, it was gratifying to see her dad so happy. As he talked to the same old people and laughed at the same old jokes, he never moved away from Dolly. Denice. His hand was always at her waist or resting on her shoulder or passing her a glass of champagne. Charlie was obviously smitten by the woman Maureen worried could break his heart if she didn't feel the same. Maureen had thought at first that Dol—Denice was nothing more than a jumped-up waitress angling for a millionaire, but the diamond and sapphire necklace had kind of blown a hole in *that* theory.

Maureen turned and headed toward the seventy-foot-long buffet, intending to check out the caviar before leaving. When she was still a dozen yards from the elongated repast, she swept her eyes down the line of people chatting as they filled their plates. There, salad tongs in hand, was the assassin Maureen had been expecting for three weeks.

The party was in full swing as Artie Lassiter finished his toast to the newlyweds. "...although *why* she settled for him when she could've had me is a mystery we're *all* still scratching our heads about. But, heck, they seem to be hopelessly in love, so raise your glasses for my old partner, Blake, and his *new* partner, Janie."

After the round of cheers died down and everyone went back to the hard work of making a Saturday night count, Blake slipped through the crowd and found Artie. "Hey, thanks for keeping it clean."

"I can be a real fuckin' gentleman when I want to," Artie said.

Blake shook his head. "So, what do you think of the house?"

"Sure looks a lot better than when you bought it. And the hardwood floors are a big improvement over that baby-shit-green shag carpeting."

"Harvest Gold," Blake corrected.

"Spoken like a guy who never changed a Pampers. Call me in a couple years when you've got two kids and a diaper pail full of 'Harvest Gold.' Where's the other woman?"

"She had a thing with her dad tonight, but she said she'd try to get by later."

"I heard you two scored big on that Cody Mason homicide. Was it really a hundred thou for one day's work?"

"You don't expect me to bill and tell, do you?"

"Well, I know a couple PIs who are kicking their own asses for turning down Hatcher's deal." Before Blake could react, Artie's attention was drawn to the attractive woman in her late thirties who smiled at him from across the room. "Hold that thought. With any luck at all I'm gonna walk out of here tonight with that school librarian's phone number."

"You're livin' large, Lassiter," Blake called after him. Artie was gone, but his words stayed with Blake. Why would Gail Hatcher tell him he was her first choice if it wasn't true? Maybe she thought he'd be less inclined to take the job if he knew he was sloppy seconds. Or thirds, if Artie's info was accurate. He tried to get back into the celebratory spirit, but that niggling little cop tic in his brain wouldn't let him.

CIA agent Terry Patton put the ladle back in the salad dressing holder and looked up to see former co-worker, Maureen O'Brien, directly across from her. Terry froze.

"I believe you're looking for me," Maureen said in a low voice.

"Jesus, no." Terry glanced left, then right. "I'm working something. I didn't even know you were going to be here. Are you on the job again?" She set down her plate and cautiously moved toward the end of the table. Maureen shadowed Terry's movements, each doing a visual for weapons, and assessing their handbags. Both assumed there was a knife in the other's bag, and *definitely* a piece at the ankle.

"I'm out permanently. This is my non-pro milieu," Maureen said.

When they cleared the buffet table, they stepped over to an open spot on the floor, neither trusting the other enough to move into a corner, even for privacy.

"You need to tell whoever's in charge I didn't kill Lionheart."

Terry looked at Maureen for a long time before making a whooshing sigh. "I know. I took him out at the Company's request."

Over the next few minutes Maureen learned her last job for Lionheart had been totally off the rez and that she had carried out his unauthorized covert op with no back-up, no protection. The Company had then moved heaven and earth to find out the identity of the rogue operative Lionheart was running.

"They sent me to watch him," Terry said, "and that's when I saw you slurking around. I didn't know what was going on, so held off until I made sure you intended to kill him."

"But why? Why not let me do it?"

Terry shrugged. "I remember you had a problem with the takedowns; thought I'd save you the grief."

"This one would have been a pleasure. That bastard blackmailed me with something he had on my father."

"So everyone got what they wanted. Or deserved," Terry said.

"And I can stop walking around with hardware stuffed every place but up my ying-yang."

"I'm sorry I didn't tell you. I wasn't sure I could trust you enough to know the identity of your pinch-hitter."

"Well, I thank you for the favor. What does the Company know?"

"Only what I reported. That Lionheart is dead and the rogue agent has faded into the mist. The case is closed. You don't have to worry."

Maureen and Terry had not been close when they worked for the CIA, even when they became the last remaining agents on Lionheart's infamous and failed "Operation Angel of Death" team. But Maureen now felt genuine gratitude toward Terry, who grinned and said "Never underestimate the ying-yang as a place to stash a weapon."

Until that moment, Maureen hadn't realized how tightly wound she had been since Lionheart's death. While Terry drifted off into the crowd, returning to her assignment—a foreigner suspected of laundering illegal arms sales cash by bankrolling American-made independent films—Maureen went to find her father and say good-night. All of a sudden she was in the mood to party hard.

Jane was in the kitchen rinsing and stacking empty trays to go back to the restaurant, when Stacy Bonner, the librarian from her school, walked in and offered to help.

"I think I have most of it under control, but you could put those glasses in the dishwasher for me."

Stacy checked the door to make sure they were alone, before saying, "So, the hunky linebacker with the silver sideburns. Is he gay, married or anything else I should know about?"

Jane smiled. Of the three cop/teacher match-ups she had high hopes for tonight, Artie and Stacy were her starred couple. "He's straight, a widower for ten years, and a genuine diamond-in-the-rough."

"Hm-m-m."

Jane felt the "hm-m-m" was too noncommittal, so she threw in: "And his boys are grown and living on their own. You know what, let's leave this stuff." She took Stacy's arm and led her back to the party.

Blake and Libby had rehashed the recent March Madness play-offs until they had bored everyone else around them and been left alone.

"So, how are you coming along on the Cody Mason case?" he asked.

"As of this morning we have a match between the guy in custody and the two hairs found on the vic, so we're taking it to the grand jury."

Blake nodded, took a sip of his Pepsi, then tried to sound as casual as possible when he asked, "What time did the 911 call come in on that?"

Libby turned and gave him a long, hard look, not fooled by his nonchalant expression. "What's your interest in the Mason case? Because if you're working for Frank Goodwin and pumping me for—"

"I am *not* working for Goodwin. Or anybody else connected to the case," he replied, telling the truth, but not the whole truth. "I'm only making small talk."

Libby snorted. "And I'm a five-foot-three white debutante."

The doorbell rang and Blake left to bring in a tray of lasagne for the buffet table. He spent ten minutes with Jane, accepting congratulations from her co-workers and his former workmates, but when he saw Artie break away from the librarian and head for the beer cooler, Blake intercepted him. "Artie."

"Exactly the guy I wanted to see. You got a book I could borrow? We're going out next Friday and I need something to talk about with her."

"Back in my room; help yourself. Listen, did one of those PIs you mentioned happen to say what time Hatcher offered the Mason case to him?"

"Hell, Ervansky, we were shootin' the shit, not taking each other's deposition. And why do you care? You got the payday, not them."

"Can you at least give me names?"

"Beau Prince and Jimmy Barone."

A tray of eggplant parmigiana rang the bell, so Blake left Artie to his brew and book search.

A half hour later, Blake found Keesha, Lt. Rhee's assistant, and her significant other out on the deck overlooking the pool. "Hey, Keesh; hey, Fran."

"Look at you all grown up and married," Fran said, giving him a warm hug.

"Bound to happen, good-looking guy like me. So, Keesha, how big a box of See's candy would you need to give me a harmless piece of police information?"

"There's a half-pound minimum, but it can go as high as two pounds if it requires stealing evidence or falsifying documents," she said, playing along.

"Fair enough. What time did the 911 call come in on the Cody Mason murder?"

She closed her eyes and searched her organic hard drive, taking less than ten seconds to come up with, "The call was logged at 8:15 A.M. on Monday, March 26th. That'll be one pound, mostly dark Bordeaux and Cashew Brittle. No raspberry creams."

Gail Hatcher had been waiting outside the door of E&O Investigations that morning when Blake arrived at 8:30.

An hour later, still in her designer gown, but now without the ankle holster, Maureen proceeded to blow off a month's tension. When she arrived, Blake tried to pull her aside for a confab, but she told him it would have to wait till Monday. She then chugged an Anchor Steam and hauled the first man she saw onto the dance floor.

The crowd applauded as Artie Lassiter recreated John Travolta's slick moves from the steamy twist number in *Pulp Fiction*, and Maureen tossed her hair and channeled Uma Thurman. He was showing off for his librarian, but Maureen was trying to lose herself for a while. The crowd stepped back to give them room, cheering and clapping while the music blasted. Det. Willis tried to cut in on the action, but when the partiers realized his idea of the twist was sticking his butt out and wiggling it, they booed him and shoved Artie back onto the cleared space in the living room.

Artie and Maureen both knew the twist is all

about the knees and the shoulders. As he bent back, his knees swaying from side to side, she leaned forward, shimmying over him to the encouraging shouts from every guy in the room. When Maureen held her nose, raised one arm, and sank down in the classic "swim" move, Artie topped it with a spirited rendition of the jerk, throwing a bad-boy wink at the librarian who clapped along with the crowd.

When the song changed, Artie put on sunglasses and led the crowd in a spirited Harlem Shuffle. Blake watched, making a mental note to slip an extra twenty to one of the valets to take the obviously sloshed Artie home later on. But at the evening's end his ex-partner was nowhere to be found and Blake assumed Libby or Rhee had driven him home.

Despite the fact that Blake and Jane had told everyone "no gifts," gifts had been forthcoming. The teacher side of the guest list had given a full set of Calphalon pots and pans, a surprise the couple had welcomed. Between them, Blake and Jane's ragtag collection of cookware, picked up piecemeal from yard sales, discount stores and his mother's hand-me-down distributions, did not lend itself to gourmet experimentation. The law enforcement contingent, having been subjected to the Monday morning recaps of Blake's weekend home improvement projects for the past three and a half years, chipped in to get a $500 gift certificate for The Home Depot.

Beginning with the kitchen makeover, Blake had slowly transformed the house, mostly by himself, one challenge at a time: master bath, master bedroom, guest bath, hardwood floors. The gutters still needed to be refitted, and the second and third bedrooms were pretty much as they were when he bought the place, so Blake knew he was at least a year away from completion, but the gift card windfall jump-started his interest in pricing out the second bedroom makeover he and Jane had discussed on the flight back from West Virginia. He headed out on Sunday morning for The Home Depot in the west valley, a fact-finding expedition only, he had told Jane. She stayed behind to tackle the party cleanup, although he assured her he'd be home in two hours to move the furniture back where it belonged and bag the garbage for Monday's pickup.

As he waited for the green light at the bottom of Lookout Mountain, Blake glanced across the street to the little restaurant that had supplied the food for his party the night before. It was closed, as was the mini grocery store attached to it, and the parking lot was empty except for one car: a bronze Mercedes 550SL, the fraternal twin of his own silver car. Both had been gifts from a grateful client.

Instead of making the left turn to head up Laurel when the light changed, Blake turned right, then made a sharp left onto the tiny side street that would give him access to the parking lot, a near-impossibility this time of the morning on a weekday. He checked the plate on the SL. Apparently Maureen had been the one to drive Artie home in his own car last night.

Blake passed the lot again an hour and a half later and the Mercedes was gone.

"I think we may have a problem," Blake told Maureen when she breezed in Monday morning.

"Not me. I'm on top of the world."

"And what's got you so chippity-cheerful all of a sudden?"

"I'm moving back into my dad's house."

"Didn't you move out like two weeks ago?"

Maureen plopped down in the chair on her side of

the desk. "Yeah, well apparently I'm not cut out for cooking, cleaning or putting up with roommates."

"You're such a princess."

"And her highness wishes she had more than two middle fingers to flip you off. What's this problem you think we have?"

Blake told her about his earlier calls to two of LA's best-known private investigators: the famous Jimmy Barone and the infamous Beau Prince, each of whom had confirmed an offer from Gail Hatcher to keep the stink off Micah Deifenschlictor. Barone's offer had come to him by phone around 6:30 the morning after the murder, and Beau Prince had awakened to Vampira ringing his doorbell at 7:15.

"I'm not sure what your point is," Maureen said. "Are you P.O.'d about being her third choice?"

"No. But I am curious how Gail Hatcher knew to be hustling up a hired gun that early, when the 911 call didn't come through until 8:15. By 8:30 she was already here trying to stuff a hundred thousand dollar check down my shorts."

"Give me a few seconds to expunge *that* mental picture." Maureen squinched her eyes closed. "Okay, gone. Look, in LA it isn't unheard of for the 'people' of a show business mover and shaker to remove anything personally incriminating *prior* to calling the police. Drugs, special-interest porn, frilly panties with *his* initials."

"Hello? Anybody here?" A knock accompanied the voice, and since Blake's side of the desk was closer to the office door, he got up and stepped into the lobby.

A few moments later Maureen heard the front door close as Blake called out, "Something came for you."

"Fan mail from some flounder?"

"No," he said, walking back into the office and

putting a vase overflowing with red roses on the desk.

Blake pretended to be working on the surveillance schedule for their new client, while Maureen removed a card from the small envelope, read it and smiled. She then moved the flowers to the credenza behind her and dropped the card into the wastebasket the two shared. She turned to Blake. "So, who's up first?"

Blake volunteered to take opening day of their two-week stakeout, and they decided to alternate days after that. They discussed hiring a part-timer to take up the slack on the grunt work if jobs kept coming in, then made cold calls to businesses until it was time for lunch. Maureen lost the coin toss, so she got up to walk over to Ziggy's New York to pick up their order. She hadn't said a thing about the flowers all morning, and it was driving Blake nuts. When she slung her purse onto her shoulder, he nodded toward the roses. "Those are really beautiful."

Maureen glanced back at the roses and smiled. Crossing to the door, she said, "Charlie's happy I'm coming home."

Blake tried to resist, he really did, but a couple minutes after Maureen left, he couldn't help himself. Reaching into the wastebasket, he retrieved the little card and read: *Thank you for Saturday night. You're a peach. Love, Artie.*

As he drove home late Monday several things bothered Blake. What, if anything, had happened between Maureen and Artie on Saturday night? And why did everything about Cody Mason's murder feel *off?*

Maureen hadn't lied; well, not exactly. She'd only made a statement about Charlie's response to her returning home, never actually claiming *he* had sent the flowers. Blake's error, he now realized, was in not asking her a question. Nothing so pointed as *hey, did you by any chance boink my old partner?* Something more subtle. Maybe a bit jokey, like *are those from a secret admirer?* Or head-on: *so, who sent the flowers?* Instead, he had made the brilliant observation that the roses were "pretty." Well, duh, you doofus.

Six years of police work should have taught him that bonehead observations do not solicit answers; questions do. And now the time for a question on this one had passed.

He *had* asked questions on the Mason homicide, or at least searched online for answers. After he and Maureen had eaten their sandwiches from Ziggy's, she had gone back to cold-calling businesses, but Blake had started looking into Gail Hatcher's connection to Micah Deifenschlictor. The only thing he came up with was a domestic violence complaint filed by the second Mrs. D. against Micah fifteen years earlier. Hatcher had debunked the allegations in about three seconds, proving first that the wife had a lover; second that her bruises and split lip had come from said lover, *not* Micah; and third that the whole thing was a ploy to get a bigger divorce settlement. Jimmy Barone had been her investigator on the case.

Okay, so they had a history and maybe Micah would naturally call her first, but how would he have known about Mason's murder so early? Blake didn't buy Maureen's pre-sweep-for-incriminating-evidence theory, because Keesha had mentioned a few of the items found in Mason's house by the police, items your nearest and dearest would want to dispose of to protect your rep. If an advance team had tried to sanitize Cody's private life, they hadn't done a very good job.

Also percolating in his brain was the knowledge that Gail Hatcher's money lure had escalated with each turndown. Jimmy Barone had said she dangled twenty-five thousand in front of him, and—less than an hour later—Beau Prince was offered *fifty* grand. And for all Blake knew, there might have been an unknown third private investigator who turned down seventy-five before Hatcher got to E&O. The money had increased quickly and dramatically, as if Hatcher had known she was in a time crunch and needed to get someone—anyone—on the job fast.

Blake clearly recalled her promise to him, that the entire amount was his to keep even if the investigation took only a day. Barone and Prince had both confirmed she used the one-day-only hook on them, too. And wouldn't you know it, the job had taken Blake and Maureen *exactly* one day.

The more experienced PIs had noticed the fish hook sticking out of the worm, apparently, and not gone for the bait.

Charlie walked Denice as far as the security checkpoint at Burbank Airport, then hung around until the Arrivals-Departures board showed the 6:00 o'clock flight to Las Vegas had departed. Denice was now able to extend her every-other-weekend visits to three nights, as she had turned over a bit more responsibility to Cindy, her most reliable waitress.

Cindy had the haircut, clothing, piercings and attitude of a 1990's punk grrrl, but she was also a twenty-one-year-old single mom with a solid work ethic and no fear of long hours. Charlie had wondered out loud if Cindy might be entrusted to do the day-to-day running of Dolly's Diner to free up Denice for a move to LA, but his sweetheart had squelched the idea: too young, too inexperienced, too soon. Denice-speak for no way.

And yet, they were great together. His alternating weekend stays in Nevada had now extended to four nights, during which time he spent virtually every minute with Denice, while Cindy ran the diner smoothly and efficiently. He knew Denice loved him as much as he loved her, but he also understood her reluctance to be less hands-on with the business she had built from a showgirl's nest egg and a cheeseburger recipe. Understanding it and liking it were two different things, however, and he was tiring of the plane flights and living out of a carry-on.

Charlie checked the time as the valet retrieved his car. He was meeting Maureen at Spago for a dinner celebrating her imminent return home. His campaign had been successful, and after less than two weeks away from the nest, Maureen was coming back. Now, if he could only be that persuasive with Denice.

When Lt. Rhee heard his office door close none-too-gently, he looked up. Keesha Beale, his assistant for the past eleven years, glared at him from across the room, arms folded over her substantial chest. "And when *exactly* were you planning to tell me?"

Laying down the papers he had been reading, the lieutenant said, "How did you hear about it?"

"You know I never reveal my sources, and don't go answering my question with another damn question."

He sighed. "Okay, sit down."

"I'll stand; I mean, if that's all right with *you*," Keesha replied, challenge lacing her words.

"Fine, stand if you want."

She sat.

"We'll make the official announcement at the end of the day tomorrow."

"We. Meaning you and Det. Johnson."

"Well, she *had* to know, for God's sake. She's my replacement. And if this is about your job, don't worry.

Libby's going to need a strong right hand, and I praised you to the rooftop. Not that she needed to hear it from me; every cop in this building knows how good you are."

Rhee wasn't blowing smoke. He had learned early on that Keesha had an eidetic memory, and after two catastrophic power failures a decade ago, he asked her to skim each file—from cover to cover—as the case developed. The original plan was to use her as backup when the computers went down after an earthquake, but she had gradually become the go-to girl for detectives too busy or too lazy to look up something for themselves.

"And yet, I'm *not* good enough to be told up front that you're moving to Springfield-damn-Missouri."

Lt. Rhee opened the bottom drawer on the left side of his desk, pulling out two squatty glasses and a bottle of Chivas. "You want ice?"

"Don't you go tryin' to serve me any watered-down scotch."

And so, the two old friends reminisced, ignoring the occasional knock on the door and ring of his phone. He made the offer, but she declined, preferring LA's more dependable tolerance for alternate lifestyles.

Keesha understood why he had to leave, that what had looked like a temporary career plateau a few years ago was crystallizing into a professional dead end. The police chief's job in Springfield, Missouri, was a big step up, and Keesha was proud of him for having the sac to go after it. No need to all get weepy about it, though. "So those three trips to Branson were *not* because you're such a fan of The Mandrell Sisters and Jim Stafford."

"Stafford, yes. Have you seen that bit with the talking guitar?" As lights began coming on all over the city they both surfed a mild scotch mellow.

"I'm really going to miss you, Aldin Rhee."

"And I you, Keesha Beale."

His boring surveillance over, Blake went back to the office late Tuesday afternoon. Maureen was still there, along with the mysterious roses. Blake flopped into his chair, while Maureen wrapped up the call she was on. "I'll email you a profile of our agency, as well as CVs on my partner and myself. We'd love to bid on the job. Thank you, Mr. Fairchild."

"Since when does our agency have a *profile?*"

"Since Charlie wrote one. How was the stakeout?"

"Paint drying."

"Well, it'll only be for two weeks," Maureen said. "And it could lead to a nice contract. Although, if we start taking on private security gigs, we'll need to hire some freelancers to work on an hourly deal."

"In this economy they shouldn't be hard to find." Blake watched Maureen check off the next number on her roster and pick up the phone again. "Listen," he said, "I'm still not sure everything was kosher on that job for Hatcher."

Maureen put the phone down. "What doesn't add up for you?"

"I thought about what you said, how a clean-up crew of family, friends or co-workers might have gone in to remove any personally embarrassing items. That would explain why the 911 call didn't come in until after Hatcher was mobilizing, but there was plenty of iffy stuff found in Mason's house."

"Such as?"

"According to Keesha, there was a large collection of Asian teen pornography and enough Cialis to raise the Titanic. Isn't that the kind of material a friend would have removed to protect the guy's reputation?"

"Yes."

"So, if it *wasn't* cleared out, and no one delayed the call until the house was sanitized, how did Micah know so early to call Gail Hatcher? And why was *she* so sure exonerating proof would be found in one day?"

Maureen thought it over, realizing he had uncovered, at the very least, an inconsistency. "What about Micah's place? Did Keesha say if anything suspect turned up there?"

"Nada. No porn, drugs, sex toys, not even a tube of Preparation H or toupee adhesive. Not one thing the media could use to embarrass Micah."

"Well, the guy's as scummy as they come, so I find it hard to believe his house was vestal-pure, unless the sanitization was done for *him*, not Mason."

"If he knew the police would look at him first, he'd make sure there was nothing for them to find. Meaning, if he didn't kill Mason—"

"Which we have already proven he couldn't have done," Maureen interrupted.

"—then somehow he got a heads-up, enough time to hire a lawyer and get rid of anything he didn't want the police to find."

"Maybe you and I should go through his house."

"Libby already took it down to the insulation and dug up the entire back yard," Blake said. "Nothing's there."

"Correction. Nothing *was* there. Now that Frank Goodwin is about to be indicted, the proverbial coast is clear, so maybe anything that was temporarily removed from the house is back."

"And why would Micah allow us to search his place?"

"Oh, we're not going in when he's home."

That's when Blake learned that after getting dry-humped in Micah's security closet, Maureen had copied down the codes to override the system. Micah had foolishly taped them to the monitoring unit's housing, and while he was off searching for a blank SD card, she helped herself to the information that would give her access if she needed it.

They decided while Maureen pulled surveillance duty the next day, Blake would try to find out when the Deifenschlictor mansion would next be vacant.

At what point in Mary Shelley's novel did Dr. Frankenstein realize he had lost all control over his creation, and that he had birthed, not a miracle, but a monster?

As Dominic Briggs paced his luxurious office at Pinnacle Pictures, his thoughts didn't incline toward philosophy-laden literary horror, but to the disturbing prospect that the monster *he* had created was rapidly slip-sliding away. Ironically, the same strings Dom had used to bind Micah to him were now tugging the actor off into Looney Toons territory.

Pvt. Deifenschlictor had not been the brightest nor the dumbest recruit to survive Marine Corps basic training and turn up at Camp Smith on Oahu. Even though he had been in a few movies, Micah was kind of a goofy, wide-eyed kid back then, and Dominic had found it easy to establish himself as the alpha hound. At first he thought it was the presence of one extra stripe on his sleeve that had garnered the blind devotion of the T-rex with the heavy accent. That was long before Dom knew about Cody Mason, long before he realized he had almost perfectly replicated the big brother/little brother co-dependence the agent and the actor had developed years before Micah had met Dom.

The key to controlling Micah was to manipulate the big ox into thinking *he* was in control. Or at the very least, that he was an equal. The extra stripe had been an intimidating factor at first, but after a bar brawl in nearby Halawa Heights, in which Dominic was the instigator and a local man wound up in the hospital, the Marine Corps rescinded that stripe, so he and Micah were suddenly equals, at least by military standards. That's when Dominic had begun playing the head games that befuddled Micah into believing he had a friend.

Contraband, girls, weed: Micah felt like a bigshot securing them and magnanimously sharing with his buddy, never realizing how he had been maneuvered into doing all the work and taking all the risks. (Clarification: the word "magnanimously" would never have appeared on Micah's brain-screen. His I.Q. might have gotten him as far as M-A-G-N-A, but would have sputtered out at that point, leaving behind a vague image of molten rock spewing over the top of a volcano.)

The deal could not have been sweeter for Dom, and he had every intention of continuing the lopsided bromance in the civilian world. But the minute Micah was out of fatigues, Cody Mason got him the lead in an action film and sent him off to shoot in Costa Rica. Suddenly Dominic Briggs was a nobody, while Micah Deifenschlictor emerged as a movie star. Briggs had tried calling him, but numbers kept changing, officious little assistants kept assuring him that *of course*, his message had been given to Mr. Mason to pass along to Mr. Deifenschlictor, but he never heard back. Briggs knew the agent wasn't giving Micah the messages, or why else wouldn't the big lunk have contacted him? He had held sway over Micah for four years, and that could not have simply evaporated.

There was no way for Dom to understand he had been a substitute—and not a very good one. Cody Mason and Dominic Briggs had both used Micah, but where Dom's motives had been one hundred percent self-serving, Cody's were, if not completely altruistic, at least beneficial for both of them. That was the difference between a symbiotic relationship and a parasitic one.

Dominic kicked around a couple years, watching Micah's star continue to rise. He went to see those crap war movies, knowing in his heart he could do a better acting job in them than Micah, believing he could write a better script. So he bailed a Selectric typewriter out of a pawn shop for forty bucks, bought a ream of paper, and set about to prove his point.

Dominic believed his script for *Three Fists of Steel* had everything the previous two *Fist* movies didn't: gritty dialogue, heart-thumping action, sexy sex and bust-a-gut comedy. And it only took him four days to write it.

By calling every gym in Los Angeles and claiming he was Micah's assistant trying to track down the engraved Piaget watch the star thought he might have accidentally left in a locker, Briggs was able to find out where Micah worked out.

Dominic's plan was to scrape together the steep membership fee, "accidentally" run into his old Marine buddy, and then—for old times' sake—allow Micah to have a first look at the script several studios were supposedly about to make offers on. Then he would "let" the actor buy the project out from under everyone else. And it had happened exactly that way, right down to Micah's promise he would push hard for Dom to get the part of the one-armed sidekick.

But then Cody Mason had killed the deal. Briggs knew it had to have been Mason, protecting his turf, jealous that his client was being influenced by someone other than himself. Dominic was trying to come up with another way to get to Micah, when he finally caught a break. Micah must have mentioned around town how good the writing was in *Three Fists of Steel*, because out of nowhere, Briggs was offered $75,000 to do a rewrite on a World War II movie.

They gave him an office, a brand new Selectric, and they told him he could take all the time he needed to breathe realistic battle action into the flaccid script. Nobody ever bothered him, he ate lunch every day in a commissary alongside the rich and famous, and all the checks cleared. As far as Briggs was concerned, Micah Deifenschlictor could go fuck himself.

As the months went by, Dominic sent draft after Oscar-worthy draft over to the never-seen producers, always with the same result: a shitload of notes that made no sense. They wanted it changed from World War II to World War I, but balked when he deleted the now-historically inaccurate aerial fight scenes between RAF Spitfires and Messerschmitt 262s. They asked him to make it more *Saving Private Ryan*-ish, but with a general instead of a private, and with the squad trying to frag his ass, not save him. Then they returned his most recent draft with the note: *Dom, can you work in a platoon of midgets? Please check for military precedent. Also, give them a mascot...maybe a talking parrot. No rush on this.*

Briggs picked up the typewriter and hurled it through the closed window of his office, smashing the glass, doing to the Selectric what Bill Gates would do to *all* typewriters in a couple years, and unwittingly playing out a fantasy enjoyed by downtrodden Hollywood writers since the days of the first talkies.

Dominic still worked out at the overpriced gym. His life might be a hot mess, but he could at least keep his body in shape. He eventually ran into Micah there, and the action star congratulated him on landing the big rewrite, even apologizing for not being able to deliver on *Three Fists*. He helpfully suggested that a title change and the removal of all references to previous events in the *Fist* franchise would make the script attractive to Chuck Norris or Steven Segal, but Dom was done with the Hollywood bullshit. He knew now that even a mega-talent needed connections, and Cody Mason would always make sure Micah never played that role for him.

Briggs no longer sucked up to Micah, but they fell into a typical LA "friendship of opportunity," never meeting outside the gym, but occasionally chatting over wheatgrass smoothies or spotting each other on the bench presses. Their relationship might have gone on like that indefinitely, but two events rearranged the pieces on the chess board, giving Dominic a chance to get back in the game.

First, Cody and his client hit one of their rough patches. Insiders knew the brouhaha would pass and that, like two puppies going at it tooth and snarl, it looked more damaging than it really was. Dom read it differently. He recognized an opportunity to get a foothold, but would not have stuck his neck out if the second lucky break hadn't happened.

Micah's God-gifted, Marine-hardened body was becoming difficult to maintain, and his physique, more than his limited acting ability, kept him in the macho starring roles. He was forty-five years old and hated that his peak years were behind him, so he was easy prey for the pitch.

Cautious enough not to suggest steroids were *necessary*, Briggs presented their use as a natural adjunct to the healthy-diet-and-hard-workouts routine Micah was already on. This would only be a little something to even out the playing field when younger guys went out for the same roles Micah wanted. Dom became Micah's supplier of AAS and, although Micah thought they were *both* partaking, Briggs never shot anything but saline into his own rear end.

They bonded over the secret they had to keep from Cody, Micah instinctively knowing his agent would disapprove. And there was the extra benefit of Micah realizing he was bulking up at a much faster rate than his pal, even though he thought they were taking the same amount of juice. Micah felt good about himself, and he had Dom to thank for that.

Micah started throwing small parts in his movies to his old Marine buddy, and Dominic was gradually seduced into thinking he could run with the big dogs. But then Cody Mason had screened an advance print of *War Hogs*. As the soldiers stripped to their skivvies and crossed the leech-infested river with their M-1's held up above their heads, Cody realized Micah's body looked like one of the half-CG Spartan warriors in *The 300*. Except *War Hogs* wasn't computer-generating *any*thing.

Before you could say androgen anabolic steroids, Micah Deifenschlictor was out of his wet, clingy skivs and into a $6000 suit, out of acting and into running a small studio. And, even though he stopped taking steroids, the Stockholm Syndrome-like attachment to his dealer remained, and Briggs took advantage of it with a vengeance. Literally.

While Cody Mason was off playing big-deal show business agent, Dominic built a niche for himself at Pinnacle Pictures, slowly taking over the work Cody *thought* Micah was doing and quietly bringing in his own people—mostly guys from the old Marine unit on Oahu—for everything but the unionized studio jobs. After a lifetime of struggle and hard knocks, it was Dominic's turn in the driver's seat and designer suits, and he wasn't about to lose it all, no matter what he had to do to hold onto it.

Cody had been carefully monitoring Micah for

steroid use, so Briggs began ensuring his own control over the action hero with a different drug. And when Cody started talking about selling his agency and joining Micah in the running of Pinnacle—an event Dominic would never allow to happen—the former Marine used that leverage to force his monster to do the dirty, but necessary, deed.

Briggs assumed everything would be fine after Mason was taken out of the equation, that he would keep his profitable venture going balls-to-the-wall, and that he could maintain control of his meat puppet.

Without Cody's steadying hand on the rudder of his life, however, Micah, convinced himself he was wasting time playing executive, and that—even now, at age fifty-eight—he could shine in roles written for thirty-five year olds. With two illegal drugs coursing through his system, Micah's body wasn't the only thing easing out of the realm of reality. His brain was also being affected, and his periods of lucidity were almost equaled now by his periods of irrationality.

Briggs made an effort to wean Micah off the drug that had worked so well before the star stopped being merely a recreational user and began settling into a serious addiction. Dom claimed his source had dried up, but he knew the ploy had backfired when Micah said he would look for another source. The last thing Briggs wanted was for the dumb ox to try to score out on the street. A high-profile bust could bring everything Dom had built at Pinnacle crashing down.

To protect his profitable little operation, Briggs went back to feeding both of Micah's habits, hoping to maintain control until "Goody" Goodwin was convicted of murder. After that, Dr. Frankenstein would have to consider euthanizing his monstrous creation.

Blake called Maureen while she was yawning

through her last hour of surveillance, and when he said Micah would be gone all the following weekend, acting as the keynote shooter at a gun show in San Diego, they decided Saturday would be a lovely day for a Beverly Hills home tour.

Blake drove toward his own home, satisfied that he and Maureen would be digging deeper into what had *really* been going on the day they got that check from Gail Hatcher. Earlier he had met Keesha in a West Hollywood bar after she got off work, hoping to learn more about the case against Frank Goodwin, but she'd had her own agenda.

Keesha told him Lt. Rhee was quitting to take a job in Missouri, and that Liberty Johnson would be promoted to Rhee's position. Blake knew how long Keesha and the lieutenant had been a team and he sympathized with her unhappy response to the sudden change, but after she finished her second sorrow-drowning beverage, he slipped away to call Fran for a pick-up. She said she'd be there in ten minutes, so when he sat back down in the booth, Blake knew he had only a short time to get what he came for.

He flat-out asked for an update on the Goodwin case, not having time to waste on the usual banter and negotiating that pried loose a piece of information from Keesha. Maybe because she was on her third drink, or maybe because she, too, had questions about the case, Keesha waived the formalities and proceeded directly to the legume-spilling.

"The evidence against Goodwin is ironclad, not an inch of wiggle room for him or his lawyer. A skeptical person might even say the evidence is *too* perfect." When Blake asked her to explain what she meant, she told him about the cell phone in the trash can, the second knife, the button that conveniently tore off a jacket and fell in the grass under the alleged point of entry. "Even if he was an amateur, even if this was his debut homicide, didn't the guy ever see an episode of one of the CSI franchises? He dumps the victim's still-turned-on phone in the building where he works, and he 'hides' the knife behind the dumpster at his condo. Not to mention, who wears a blazer to climb over an eight-foot wall?"

By the time Fran arrived to drive her partner home, Blake was beginning to buy into her frame-up theory, especially since Keesha had said Goodwin's dry cleaner swore there was no blood visible on the blazer when it had been dropped off to be cleaned and have the button replaced. The lab had gone over the jacket fiber by fiber and found no trace of blood.

Blake pulled into his carport alongside his old car. When Cerise Marginata had "tipped" Maureen and him with a pair of Mercedes Benz 550SLs, Blake had given his own car to Jane. She had sold her Honda and sent the money to her parents in West Virginia. Blake knew he was lucky to have found a woman with such a sweet and generous spirit. As a wife, Jane brought joy and stability to his life, and he had no doubt she would also be a patient and loving mother. Right now, though, what he needed was her insight. The thing with Artie and Maureen still bothered him, and he wanted a little unbiased perspective.

Attempting nonchalance, Blake obliquely brought up the subject between the roast beef and the cherry cobbler. "Would you say Artie is attractive to women?"

"Our school librarian must think so; she's going out with him next Saturday."

"And it doesn't bother her that he was sloshed the night she met him?"

Jane laughed. "Artie wasn't drunk at our party."

"Are you *kidding* me? He was so hammered he had to be driven home."

"And you call yourself a detective?"

"Hey, I know what I saw."

She put down her fork, surprised by his challengy tone and thinking back to the original question about whether she thought Artie was attractive to women. There was a subtext she was missing, so Jane went after it with the logic and patience she used every day dealing with a classroom full of kindergartners. "What does Artie drink?"

"Beer," he said.

"Anything else?"

"Not really. Once or twice a year he might spend an evening with Mr. Jack Daniel, but Artie's basically a beer guy."

"A *one-brand* beer guy, right?"

"Yeah. St. Pauli Girl. That's why I asked you to pick some up for the party."

"And I bought one six-pack, four bottles of which were still in the cooler when I cleared it out the next morning."

Blake sat back, clearly surprised by this information. "Are you sure?"

"Look, I only met Artie eighteen months ago, and you rode with him for five years, but I definitely know he's a guy who talks big and drinks small."

Blake had always thought of Artie as a hard drinker. Not an alcoholic, but one of those burly men who can put it away with few side effects. Now that Jane had forced him to reconsider this belief, however, he could only recall Artie being drunk twice: once when he was still wallowing in grief after his previous partner was gunned down in a store robbery, and once when he and Blake were in Las Vegas on somebody else's dime. Six years had passed between those two events.

Artie always had a beer in his hand at parties, cop

gatherings at Roy's Ranchero and other social events. Could it be that one beer was half his intake for the evening? And if so, was he *playing* at being louder, looser and more wasted? Blake looked at Jane, who waited patiently for him to catch up and ask the obvious question: *why?* He caught up and asked.

"I think somewhere along the line, maybe after he lost his wife and then his partner, Artie decided to redefine himself as the lovable good-time guy, the bigger-than-life person people talk about the morning after. I mean, heck, who knew he could *dance* like that?" Jane then outlined her unified field theory of Artie Lassiter. He was too solid and responsible to blow it out to the walls, so the next best thing was to bluster and pose as if he had.

This brought Jane back around to Blake's original question about Artie's attractiveness, vis-à-vis women. "Artie's one of those rare men you just *know* will wrap you in a big bear hug and protect you when you're afraid everything is spinning out of control. He's someone a woman could depend on and feel safe with. Think about it; in all the time you've known him, has he even once let you down?"

"No. But, thank God, he's never tried to bear hug me, either."

"That's a shame; it feels pretty darn good." Jane forked up a dainty bite of cherry cobbler and popped it into her mouth, leaving Blake to wonder how much he really knew about *any* of his partners.

No driving techno-crap pumped out of wall-mounted speakers; no citrusy air freshener vied with the smell of exertion; and no Zumba class full of spandexed bitches ever rocked the well-equipped gym at Pinnacle Pictures. The sounds here were simple, pure: the clang of metal on metal as a bar holding a hundred pounds at either end settled back onto the steel uprights flanking the press bench. Loud grunts forced from bodies pushed to their limits. The near-orgasmic cry of release as someone surpassed his personal best and dropped a massive weight onto the floor. This was a *man's* gym.

The sweat slicking Micah's body contributed to the acrid funk of the enclosed space, and he breathed it in: the aroma of strength and power. He tensed his sculpted quads, slowly emptying his lungs as he pushed his shoulders against the leather pads of the hack-squat machine. Three hundred pounds inched upward as his legs straightened for the eighth and last time in this final set of squats. With his knees soft, he reached the top and relaxed his quadriceps, bringing the weight back down its short slide, inhaling deeply as he did.

Pivoting on the seat and grabbing a towel, Micah felt pain in his hips and knees. What was it Cody had said? *You're getting too old for this shit.* He pressed his face into the soft terry cloth, wicking away the salty film, trying not to think of Cody, his so-called best friend. But best friends don't give up on your acting career. And they don't stick you in a suit that makes you blend in with all the other executives in Hollywood.

Dominic Briggs was his *real* friend. It was Dom who had reassured Micah he could still be the action star America loved. And Dominic was the one who provided Micah with the equalizing injections that amped his muscle-building, giving him an edge over guys twenty years younger. He had even volunteered to take over many of the boring duties involved in running the studio so Micah could focus on his workouts and a redeployment of his movie career. Over time, all the busywork had been foisted onto

Dominic's shoulders, and Micah wondered if his old Marine buddy realized he was being taken advantage of. Well, if he did, the fat salary he was getting made up for it. Everything had been going so smoothly. Pinnacle was about to produce its first feature film, and Micah was set to direct it. But then goddamn Cody had started talking about selling his agency and moving over to help run the studio. Micah knew Cody would shit a brick if he found out Dominic Briggs was doing the *actual* day-to-day stuff. And, by then, Dom had convinced him he still had the chops to handle the lead in *The Devil's Platoon*, a great role that Cody thought should be offered to Matt Damon. With Cody out of the way, Micah could take the role for himself and hand off the directing job to Briggs.

Micah stood, the pain in his knees knifing him. He glanced around to make sure none of the other guys—all fellow Marines from Camp Smith—had seen him wince. He had lived with pain all his adult life, the price tag for his magnificent physique. Drinking a liter of water during workouts had always diluted the lactic acid in the stressed muscles, dialing down the hurt to manageable, but this new pain wouldn't let him go. His knees, hips, shoulders, elbows, even his ankles hurt, but he couldn't afford to let up on the workouts, not if he was going to prove Cody wrong. Not if he was going to shine as Capt. Luther Hardy in *The Devil's Platoon*. He made his way to the locker room, observed by a grizzled vet who noted Micah's slow and careful dismount from the hack-squat.

When Micah came out of the shower he felt a little better, the hot water having eased both muscles *and* joints, but he was still aware that nothing in his body worked as well as it had two decades ago.

One other person was in the area when Micah crossed to his locker: an older dude he recalled being introduced to several months back. Micah couldn't remember the guy's name, but Dom had said he was a lifer who had mustered out of the Corps a year ago and needed work. Micah nodded at the guy, making nanosecond-brief eye contact before continuing to towel his shoulders and arms. The guy acknowledged Micah with a *"hey"* (the AARP version of *"s'up?"*).

Micah finished drying off, then got dressed. The older dude sat there, rubbing the back of his neck and turning his head from side to side as if loosening a kink. Finally, he reached into his gym bag and pulled out a prescription bottle. Micah looked over to see two pills slide onto the man's palm. "Young guy like you can work out for hours without batting an eye, but I'm sixty-one and I flat-out ache all the time."

Micah was pleased somebody three years older would see him as a "young guy," more proof that Dom was right and Cody had been wrong. "Oh, I get the occasional twinge myself," he graciously admitted.

"Seriously?" the man asked, disingenuously. He was a lousy actor, but then Micah had never been able to differentiate between his own wooden performances and the luminous acting skills of a Morgan Freeman or a Ben Kingsley, so he took him at face value. "You should try these, then. They keep me going when all I want is to curl up and howl."

"What are they?"

"Salvation for weight-lifters. Tell you what, I'll give you a couple and you try'em next time you push too many pounds and get one of those twinges."

Out of politeness Micah accepted six of the pills, not questioning the fact that the guy conveniently had a small, glassine envelope in his pocket to hold the free samples.

Maureen and Blake continued their alternating

shifts of tedium, realizing with each passing day that their client had misread the situation. His business partner was guilty of nothing more than slipping away to dine secretly in gourmet restaurants. Secrecy was imperative, as the two were building a commercial empire based on the hawking of pre-packaged weight-loss meals containing ingredients like quinoa and kale, but tasting like they were full of cardboard and rug fuzz.

The two ex-fatties were not only the owners and creators of the business, but its chief TV spokespeople. Since their infomercial claimed they had svelted-down on their own slimming recipes, it wouldn't do for one of them to be caught shoving Frenched lamb chops and crème brulée into his face. An astute observer might then deduce he had not achieved his trim figure by eating rug-fuzz carbonara, but by leaning over a toilet with a finger down his throat and upchucking. Hence his elaborate disguises, the discovery of which had triggered his partner's original suspicions.

By Friday Blake and Maureen decided to call off the surveillance, ostensibly to save their client some money, but really because they were both bored silly. Surveillance is *not* the most stimulating investigative activity, and they both looked forward to checking out Micah's house while he was away.

Micah looked forward to the San Diego gun show, his first public appearance since Cody's death. It would give him an opportunity to strut around in his custom-tailored fatigues, show off his physique, and talk up *The Devil's Platoon*, which was scheduled to begin shooting in two months.

He felt good, thanks in part to the pills that had banished his joint pains and made him feel as limber and confident as a twenty year old. He sought out the older man—whose name he learned was Joey—and asked for a few more freebies to get him through the weekend. Once again, Joey pilled a glassine envelope, this time even more generously, knowing he would make it back many times over in the coming months.

Frank Goodwin wasn't looking forward to *any-thing*. He kept claiming his innocence, while racking his brain to come up with the name of anyone who might hate him enough to frame him for Cody Mason's murder. As a talent agent he had made plenty of enemies, but they were the kind who blackballed your membership app to an exclusive golf club, or pulled strings to get you seated at the crummiest table at a prestige event. Hollywood revenge was bitchy and petty, but almost never deadly.

Lt. Rhee of the Beverly Hills Police Department turned over his office to Libby Johnson, free-floating for the rest of the week to ensure a smooth transition of power before he left. Libby, riding the crest of success for her quick arrest in the Mason homicide, slipped easily into her role as lieutenant.

Garrett Smythe-Whitt, having checked out of his sumptuous suite at Chateau Marmont in advance of the inevitable pulling of the plug by Lloyd's, sat in a ratty motel room on Sunset, a stone's throw from The Comedy Store. The low-end digs were the choice of stand-up comics too broke to own a car, and aging hookers too skanky to rake in the big bucks. The comics tried their material out on the Brit, but got no laughs. Maybe it was the language barrier, but more likely it was the combination of their lack of funds to hire writers and GS-W's all-consuming worry about being fired. The hookers tried out their own material on the fastidious gent with the funny accent, but Little Willy remained limp.

Charlie O'Brien spent the week searching for the

perfect gift for Denice, a gift he hoped would convince her to turn over the running of her diner to punk-Cindy and relocate to his home in Los Angeles. Once he found what he was looking for, Charlie began making phone calls to set everything in motion.

In Madison, Nevada, Denice Cantrell thought long and hard about Charlie's marriage proposal. Yes, he had bungled it, but she knew he had been under pressure because of his daughter's departure, so she had let him off the hook. But Denice was certain he would propose again, this time with the romantic setting, the perfect ring and the classic knee-drop. It was time for her to make a decision.

Over the years she had been offered increasingly larger amounts for the Dolly's Diner franchise and her secret cheeseburger recipe, the most recent being five million dollars. If she took the offer she would go to Charlie with enough independent wealth to avoid any hint of gold-diggerism. Not that *he* would think her capable of such a ploy, but his daughter was an entirely different kettle of prickly, suspicious fish.

As much as Denice loved Charlie, as much as she knew he loved her, the thought of giving up her baby was scary. Holding onto the diner guaranteed she'd have something to fall back on if things didn't work out with Charlie. She had seen enough bitter divorces to know she would never be one of those women fighting over the financial carcass of a dead marriage. No, if she and Charlie couldn't make it, she'd walk away with her head high and her dignity intact. But to do that, you need something to go back to.

And so, she had turned down the buy-out offer, deciding instead to promote Cindy to assistant manager and get her more involved in the ordering, the bookkeeping, the payroll, the advertising, virtually every aspect of the running of Dolly's Diner. The secret recipe? Well, that would remain secret until Charlie made his move.

Denice had decided all that last night, Thursday, but she never got the chance to surprise Cindy with the promotion today. Instead, punk-grrrl had asked to speak with Dolly after the lunch crush, at which time she had given a week's notice.

Denice had already called Charlie to tell him not to fly in tonight, as she would be scrambling all week-end to place help-wanted ads and interview the walk-ins responding to the Now Hiring sign in the window. The decision about a move to LA went on hold.

A phone call to the convention center hosting the gun show confirmed Micah had checked-in the night before and would be speaking at the sold-out luncheon in a little over an hour. Blake and Maureen cruised the house twice, unnoticed among Saturday morning's normal traffic. On the third pass they pulled up to the gate, where Blake entered the number Maureen gave him. As the gate opened, they pulled onto Micah's property, both aware they were now officially on the wrong side of the law. Blake parked the Mercedes at the far end of the closed garage, making it less likely the car would be noticed by a Security Pro drive-by or a passing jogger.

Maureen's gloved fingers tapped the code onto the keypad, and when she heard the beep signaling the system was disabled, she pulled out her Buffy the Vampire Slayer lock-picking kit and went to work. Blake tried to look nonchalant as he blocked her from the view of anyone walking past the gate.

"We're in," she said, standing up.

They worked in total silence for the first twenty minutes as they checked for bugs. Whatever devices had been there the night of the murder were gone.

"It makes sense," Maureen said. "Once we told Hatcher about the paparazzo's recordings, she would have advised Micah to have the bugs cleared out."

"Yeah, I guess that's one explanation." They were standing in the kitchen, ready to begin their second search.

"And another would be?"

"That they had served their purpose and could go. Don't you think it's strange that tabloid creep just *happened* to get an anonymous tip the night Mason was killed, guaranteeing there'd be someone recording Micah's alibi?"

"Anonymous tips come in to the cops all the time."

"Right," Blake said. "Like that unknown caller who led the police to the murder weapon."

"Let's not head down an Area 51 conspiracy path here. Did Keesha give you an inventory?"

"No, she wouldn't go that far out on a limb."

"So we're looking for *any*thing incriminating that would have shown up on that list."

A few minutes later, Maureen called out to Blake from Micah's bedroom. "In here."

When he entered he saw his partner sitting on the bed next to the pulled-out drawer of the night stand. In one hand she held a small glass pipe; in the other a plastic bag containing a few glassy rocks of meth. "Is that all of it?" Blake asked.

"Yeah. Enough for the occasional crank ride, but not enough to prove he's a daily user."

"Something he wouldn't want found, though, and that suggests he got a heads-up about the murder."

After another hour of searching, Maureen went into the little utility closet housing the surveillance equipment and removed the SD card that had recorded their arrival at the gate.

Over a late lunch they brainstormed about where

Micah would stash the stash if he didn't want his drug usage to make headlines. The obvious choice was his office at Pinnacle Pictures.

Maureen was all low-cut, skin-tight, and well-above-the-knee as she pulled up to the guard gate at the entrance to the Pinnacle Pictures lot on Tuesday. She tossed her reddish-gold hair seductively and smiled through make-up that was heavy enough to scream: *I'm easy!* In her handbag was a dainty crack pipe and a small amount of lumpy brown powder in a plastic snack bag. It was light brown sugar, but Maureen hoped Mr. Big Stuff would think it was the real thing, only not top quality.

After she gave her name and said she was here to see Micah, the guard asked, "Is he expecting you?"

"You'd have to slip your hand down the front of his pants to make that call." The man turned away from her grin. He'd been a studio guard for nearly forty years, putting in time at Fox, MGM and United Artists before winding up here at Pinnacle, and he'd been waving in bimbos and mobile blow-jobs since before this one was even born. He was a religious man, and he had always disliked this part of his job, but a paycheck is a paycheck so he made the call that would give the slutty redhead access.

While he was on the phone, Maureen checked her rear view mirror. Blake was somewhere back there, pulled off the road, waiting in case she had to trigger the device that would tell him she was in trouble. She didn't expect to need the safety net, but she knew it made Blake feel easier about her going in alone.

Once she had private access to Micah—which her outfit and demeanor almost guaranteed—she would accidentally let the contents of her purse spill out. She assumed he would do the gentlemanly thing and offer to upgrade her shit-quality crystal when he saw they were sympatico on the meth front. Maybe he'd suggest firing up a bowl on the spot. Maureen had no doubt she could convince him she was smoking, too, but wasn't sure what to do after she got him high.

Blake had only some vague suspicions about Cody Mason's murder and their subsequent profitable work for Gail Hatcher. He *had* found a few inconsistencies, but Maureen wasn't sure they amounted to much. Still, she was willing to hear what Micah might give up under the influence.

The direct gate-line on Dominic's desk buzzed, interrupting Micah's tedious recap of the weekend's gun show. "Briggs."

"Sir, it's Roy. There's a lady here named Maureen O'Brien wanting to get in to see Mr. D. She's not on my list."

"Hold on, Roy." Dom turned to his computer and keyed in the sequence to pull up the camera at the gate. "You know this woman?" he asked Micah, rotating the screen.

"Hell, yes! It's that bangin' piece of ass I told you about. The one Gail Hatcher brought in to get the cops off me."

"Wait, she's one of the *investigators?*"

"Yeah, tell Roy to send her to my office. You got any Tic-Tacs?"

"No way is she coming onto this lot."

Micah's eyes narrowed. "Do I need to remind you who *owns* this place? Who gave you your job?"

There was threat beneath the calm words, and Dominic knew to tread lightly. "I'm well aware I owe everything I have to you. That's why I feel I have to protect you."

Micah guffawed. "Are you kidding? She's only

another hummer in heels."

"Maybe you're right. You told me she could barely keep her hands off you the day you met, so maybe she *is* here for some knee work and a C-note. But what if she's not?"

"The fuck are you talking about? Why else would she be here?"

"Think, Micah. She's a PI. What if she's working for somebody else now? What if she's trying to get on the lot to take a look around?" Briggs could see he was at least getting Micah to consider the possibility, so he pushed ahead with the bullshit flattery that would swing the pendulum. "Listen, you're a major movie star. Fit, great-looking, rich. Naturally she wants you. But does it have to be here? I mean, until Frank Goodwin is convicted and put away, do you really want to take even the smallest risk?"

"Okay, okay. You made your point. But tell Roy to get her number. Unless, of course, you object to me getting laid at my own house."

Dominic swallowed any retort to Micah's snotty challenge, then politely asked Roy to get her number and call it in to Micah's cell.

Blake was surprised to see Maureen's car pull up alongside his own so soon. He rolled down his window as she cut her engine. "Am I not pulling off ho-bag today? 'Cause I couldn't get past the gate."

"Maybe he's not there."

Maureen heard her ring tone and checked her phone. "A text from Micah. He's there, but says he can't get out of a meeting. And he wants me to be at his house tonight at 8:00 so—oh, ick!"

"What?"

Maureen handed her phone to Blake, who read the text. "Classy guy," he commented with disgust, handing her phone back through the window.

After sending the text, Micah sat in his office brooding. He knew Dom was right about not taking any risk, but he didn't like having an employee trying to dictate his moves. He had put up with it from Cody all those years because they were more like equals. But then Cody had grown jealous, hadn't he? Hated that Micah was buff as a god and could still pass for thirty-five. *That's* the reason he tried to turn Micah into a dull executive; that's why he wanted the part of Capt. Luther Hardy to go to Matt Damon. Damon! Give me a break. That guy couldn't bench a hundred pounds if his life depended on it.

Micah's paranoia blew itself in three or four more directions before he wandered down to the gym. The grunts of other Marines, the clang of steel on steel, the smell of his own sweat: those were the things that would calm his mood.

And maybe he'd run into Joey.

Briggs paced his office. Micah Deifenschlictor had never been a brainiac, but he had always been easily manipulated and he had understood the need for caution in the wake of Cody's death. At least he had until now. And this was not the time to start playing fast and loose. Dominic had a major operation to run here. Serpent's Tooth was shooting their new death-rap video on Stage One all week; P&G was doing spots for Bounty Towels on Stage Two; and McCann Erickson was sending a man from Chicago to see if Pinnacle should go on their roster of facilities. McCann had a huge list of clients, and they could keep at least one of the three studios busy all year round, so Briggs was willing to lose money on the deal to keep production going.

Everything was clicking. Dom was set to direct *The Devil's Platoon*. He knew the script stunk and his star was twenty-five years too old to play the lead, but there was no talking Micah out of the role. Dominic had done way too good a job of blowing vanity-smoke up Micah's butt when he was turning him against Cody. No, this would be a multi-million-dollar bomb, but two good things would come out of it. Well, three, if you count the tax write-off. First, the critics would savage Micah, and not their standard arfing about his limited acting ability. This time they'd go after him for committing the cardinal sin of Hollywood: getting old and refusing to get out of the way. Mel Gibson's cringeworthy performance in *What Women Want* had turned a film that should have been a zany romp into a creepy tale of an old perv crawling around in young women's minds. A man with Clint Eastwood's chops could ride age and leathered looks to Oscar glory, but he was smart enough to choose roles like the trainer in *Million Dollar Baby*, not one of the vampires in the *Twilight* series.

Once *The Devil's Platoon* had put the kibosh on Micah's acting career, Dominic could ease the old has-been into retirement, maybe on a private island or in a foreign country. Then Dom would be free to run Pinnacle and get even richer.

Unless, of course, that little show of backbone a few minutes ago had been a sign of things to come. Dominic was perfectly willing to kill again to keep his empire intact.

What Dominic didn't have enough information to figure out, and what Micah didn't have the sense to realize, was that the liquid in which the action hero's brain floated was steadily morphing toxic. Years of juicing had not only pumped up his muscles to Shreklike unreality, but had left little land mines along his neural pathways, each one a potential explosion of homicidal rage.

Layered on top of the anabolic steroid damage was the leave-behind from the methamphetamine. The crack pipe had been Dominic's secret weapon in his tug-of-war with Cody Mason over Micah, but he hadn't anticipated Micah's growing dependence on the drug. Briggs' one attempt to wean Micah off rock had misfired, so for now he reluctantly supplied increasing amounts of it to the actor, while praying Micah could keep his shit together and not do anything that could jeopardize Pinnacle.

Micah's teeth were already showing signs of "meth mouth," although he didn't consider himself an addict, merely a recreational user. But the cerebral soup told a different tale. The two extra ingredients were not harmonizing well and with Micah adding more to the cauldron, the chance of a volatile reaction increased.

As his brain sloshed languidly in its warm broth, absorbing both nutrients and toxins, it harbored its own secret: whitish plaque deposits forming in its cortex and hippocampus, the signs of early-onset Alzheimer's. Micah had no inkling his father had suffered from the disease. He had been only nine when his mother told him his father would be living at the hospital from then on, and with a child's limited understanding of illness, Micah thought his dad must have a bad cold, or maybe that cancer disease. He had visited his father regularly and the times the man made no sense or didn't recognize his wife and child, Micah's mother explained away as resulting from all the medications the doctors were prescribing.

His father had died when Micah was sixteen, his mother ten years later from pneumonia. She had never told her son about the potential time bomb in his skull.

Micah's brain had been simmering for years in its cranial crockpot, never boiling over. One more bit of seasoning might spoil the broth, though, so it should be stirred in with a light hand.

The soup had begun to absorb its final ingredient: oxycodone. Mm-mmm good.

Back at the office on Sunset, Maureen finally agreed there was something fishy about the whole Micah situation.

Blake looked at her. "So, I show you a half dozen inconsistencies in Mason's homicide and you aren't convinced. But as soon as your looks can't get you on the lot, you're suddenly a believer. Do I have that about right?"

Maureen was still slutted-up, and she swept a hand to indicate her face and body. "Oh, please. Look at me. He's old, he's horny and he did everything but pee on my leg to mark his turf. Even if he *was* in a meeting, he'd have wanted me waiting in his office for when he was done. That's how these sleazebirds work."

"And you know this how?"

"As soon as I got old enough to hear the dirty stories as well as the funny ones, Max Keller laid them on me. I think it was his way of warning me away from actors." Maureen told Blake about two male stars of a top-ten sitcom from the 1970s. Both were married and past forty, but each had a "guest" waiting in his dressing room when the cast broke for lunch every day. A short time later, the guests left the lot and the men headed to the commissary. "This was a five-day-a-week thing, rarely the same girls, so the guards knew to wave in every tramp who drove up around 12:45."

Now that Maureen was on board and they had been denied access to Pinnacle, they focused their attention on the lot. What *didn't* Micah want them stumbling onto?

They researched Pinnacle Pictures, discovering nothing unusual in its history. Founded jointly by Cody Mason and Micah Deifenschlictor twelve years earlier as a less expensive alternative to the majors, Pinnacle had built up a clientele by doing military training videos, commercials, independent films and corporate rah-rah stuff. They kept busy, were turning a profit, and were set to begin shooting their first in-house production, a movie called *The Devil's Platoon.* Interestingly, it had originally been scheduled to be directed by Micah, and speculation was either Matt Damon or Jake Gyllenhaal would be playing the lead. Shortly after Cody Mason's death, however, a notice in *Variety* announced Micah would be starring, and a newcomer named Dominic Briggs would take the directing reins. People got screwed over in Hollywood power struggles every day. Had Mason been screwed to death over one?

Nothing jumped out at Blake and Maureen, but they believed the studio held at least one piece of the puzzle surrounding the death of Micah's agent. Maureen suggested they try to get onto the lot on Sunday, when there would be fewer people around.

"If they wouldn't let *you* on the lot in your hooker duds, why would they let us *both* in?"

"I was thinking we'd take an alternate route," she replied with an evil smile.

The Bates brothers were born under an unlucky star. Well, two, actually, as each had been conceived on a conjugal visit to the Texas State Penitentiary, and those visits had been fourteen months apart.

Daddy was doing life times four—home invasion, kidnap, rape; you name it, Clarence Bates had done it—and mommy, a seventh-grade drop-out who finally decided three kids and a jailbird spouse were *not* the life she wanted, ran off with a Bible salesman when the boys were nine and ten, leaving them to be raised by their seventeen-year-old sister.

Dallis and Ostin Bates didn't think they'd had a particularly bad childhood. There was always food to eat and an aluminum roof over their heads, thanks to mom's dirty dancing at a place called Big Rigs, one of hundreds of truck-stop strip-joints sprinkling the shoulders of I-10 across the Lone Star state like porno-dandruff. After momma Bates followed the Bible's instruction to pack it in and groove on down the highway (Matthew 6:24; or at least that's what *he* told her), Load-Eye took up her mother's old pole position at Big Rigs, raking in even more cash on account of boobs that could pass the pencil test and the rumor she was still a virgin.

Then one day when the boys were in the eleventh grade, Load-Eye climbed into the cab of a westbound semi driven by a sweet-talking man name of Lucky Wilcox, and Load-Eye, Lucky and those four thousand live chickens he was hauling never returned.

Dallis had flunked third grade—deliberately, he claimed—so he was in the same year as his younger brother Ostin. The boys, now fatherless, motherless and sisterless, managed to get by that last year and a half of high school by selling off everything that wasn't bolted down inside the trailer they had lived in all their lives. Load-Eye had generously endorsed and left behind her last two paychecks from Big Rigs, and the Bates brothers collected on a $10,000 lottery ticket they took off a wino they had rolled, so their cash problems didn't kick in for awhile.

The response to their '70s tribute band, "The Retro Bates," was tepid and the boys took it badly. They tried their hand at a couple other small, but legitimate endeavors, yet nothing clicked for them.

As their failures mounted, the brothers were more and more inclined to seek an easier path. Not a violent one like their father's, but a path of scamming and petty larceny. For a few years after high school they got by that way, but were eventually forced to flee Texas one step ahead of the law when a scam of theirs went bad. Highjacking a truck full of leather jackets made it an interstate crime, and counterfeiting documents claiming each jacket was the very one worn by Henry Winkler on *Happy Days,* added fraud to the mix.

They headed west, winding up as so many before them had, in The Golden State. Los Angeles was too big, too crowded and too intimidating after the slower pace of their small-town Texas upbringing, so the two gravitated to the community of Tujunga, less than an hour north of LA. People there wore cowboy boots and the bars played C&W, so the Bates boys fit right in.

Dallis and Ostin still had some cash left over from their Fonzie scheme, so they drank, relaxed and put off the day they'd have to start hustling again.

And then the miracle happened. A man named Diaz approached them in a bar, claiming he was a lawyer and that they had an inheritance coming from their great-aunt Taffy. Neither Dallis nor Ostin could recall a great-aunt Taffy, but Diaz wore a suit and carried a briefcase, so they believed everything he told them, especially after he drove them out to the wooded, five-acre parcel of land Taffy had willed to them. The deed was in their names, free and clear, and the land came with a brand-spanking-new sixty-foot double-wide.

They signed the papers Diaz put in front of them and moved into their new trailer, which was already furnished with everything they needed right down to a freezer full of steaks, a Weber grill, ten cases of Bud, a 50-inch flat screen and two La-Z-Boy loungers. The TV came with satellite and a full package of sports and porn. Diaz told them aunt Taffy had left a trust that would take care of property taxes, utilities, and the sports/porn menu indefinitely.

It was a real sweet deal, for sure. Everything had fallen into their laps except walking-around money, and Diaz had a suggestion for that, too.

One look at the diamond on Jane's finger and Maureen knew it was out of Blake's price range. "It's beautiful. Where did you guys get it?"

"A place in Beverly Hills your dad recommended," Jane said.

Blake entered from the hallway wearing jeans, hiking boots and a baggy long-sleeved pullover. He was surprised to see Jane still there. "I thought you were gone already." Every Sunday afternoon, Jane spent four hours working with an autistic boy from her kindergarten class.

"I'm leaving now, but I wanted to show my ring to Maureen."

"Yeah," Maureen said, "I was a little distracted at your party the other week, so I never got a look at the Ervansky diamond."

"Have fun on your spy adventure today." Jane crossed to Blake, who bent to give her a quick kiss. "Bye, Maureen." She grabbed her schoolbag and went out the door.

It's now or never, thought Blake. "Speaking of the party," he began, a rough segue even for him. "I never thanked you for running Artie home that night."

She stiffened. "Artie said I drove him home?"

Blake saw she was on alert, so he backpedaled. "No, I haven't talked to him since the party. But when I went out the next morning, I saw your car in the lot down the hill." If Blake thought a casual delivery would disarm her, he was wrong. Her face hardened as he limped to the finish line with the very lame: "Anyway, I wanted to say thanks. You have the map?"

Maureen pulled a map out of the back pocket of her jeans and for a brief moment Blake thought he was home free. But then, as she unfolded the map on the counter and flattened it out, Maureen stopped. "The first day we rode together you made a judgment about me on the basis of faulty information."

He knew what she was referring to, although he had hoped it was forgotten long ago. Before he knew Maureen lived with her father, Blake jumped to the conclusion she had a sugar daddy. It was not his finest hour, he had felt like an asshole, and yet here he was doing it again.

"I assumed you had learned a lesson from that," she said.

"Okay, okay. Fifty lashes with a wet noodle. But when you came into the office the following Monday all uppity-doo-dah happy, well, I couldn't help but put two and two together."

"I was happy because right before your party I learned all my ties to the CIA have now been severed. Permanently. They will not be a factor in either my personal or professional future."

"That's a relief. And I'm sorry I jumped to the wrong conclusion. Now, what do we have?"

The map showed the area around Tujunga, including portions of the Angeles National Forest. She had drawn a red line around the general perimeter of Pinnacle Pictures, a portion of which ran contiguously with the border of the forest. A dotted line connected two X's.

"We'll park here," Maureen said, pointing to the X farthest from Pinnacle. "Then we'll go over the fence here," she continued, tracing the dotted line to the second X.

Blake studied the map. "Kind of a long way to walk in a wilderness we're not familiar with."

"Oh, I have a passing familiarity with the area." She folded the map back into a flat square. "And we *won't* be on foot."

Less than an hour later, Maureen eased her Mercedes in between two battered pickup trucks in the crowded noon-time parking lot of an old Tujunga landmark. The Blind Pig had been serving greasy burgers and foamy beer to customers who proudly referred to themselves as left-coast rednecks for as long as anyone could remember. As they climbed out of the car, Blake noted the ramshackle structure had no windows.

"Are you buying me lunch?" he asked warily.

"Here? No, the catch of the day is probably crabs. And I don't mean the ones you eat. Let me do the talking, and try not to aggravate any drunk bikers."

"Always good advice," he murmured, hurrying to catch up with her.

As the door of The Blind Pig closed behind him, Blake stopped to let his eyes adjust to the semi-dark. Maureen was already ten feet in, obviously familiar with the floor plan, when she was saluted by the bartender. He looked to be at least seventy-five, a skinny bald guy with so many steel hoops in his ears you could have used him to whisk egg whites.

"Obi-Wan!" he croaked with a smile when he recognized Maureen.

"Hey, Fluffy. Gladys in the back?"

He checked a dry-erase board behind the bar, then said, "Number five."

Maureen headed toward the rear of the room, and Blake was about to follow, when a huge man with a Mohawk and an open leather vest stepped directly into Maureen's path. She looked up at his grin—the toothline of which had a couple vacancies—then side-stepped to go around him. He matched the move, blocking her again.

Blake stayed where he was, ready to step in if he had to, but suspecting he wouldn't be needed. He quickly scanned the shadowy figures in the booths and at the tables. The unsavory-looking group seemed to be focused on drinking beer and listening to Bonnie Raitt's deep, throaty moan from the jukebox, but he knew every last one of them was covertly eyeing his partner and the roadblock impeding her.

"Hey, there, pretty," the crested behemoth teased. "Whyn't me and you go back to your place and see if we can't find you something good to eat?"

A few snickers of amusement swept the crowd and, as a precaution, Blake positioned his right hand near the Glock under his pullover.

"I'd like that," she purred up at the big jerk. "But I'm kinda busy right now. Whyn't you come by my place tonight. Sevenish?"

In a million years, Mohawk hadn't expected this bodacious redhead to do anything more than try to slap his face, so he was stunned by the possibility of having at her. Wait, wait, she was still talking.

"You got a pencil to write down my address?"

A dozen hands shoved cocktail napkins and ball-point pens Mohawk's way. The dolt clicked a BiC and poised it over a napkin.

In a voice loud enough to be heard by everybody

over Bonnie Raitt, Maureen said, "My house is at the corner of Hit-the Road and No Fucking Way."

He had already begun scribbling when he heard snorts and guffaws all around him and realized what she had said. As he lowered the pen, she stepped around him and continued toward the back.

"You didn't have to be a bitch about it!" he called out, as Maureen disappeared through the back door.

The bartender smirked. "Dude, if she'd awanted to be a bitch about it, you'd be on the floor right now, cupping your jewels and calling for Jesus."

Humiliated, the big man looked for a target, finding one in the tall, thin guy crossing the room to follow the redhead. He stepped in Blake's path, going chest to chest and initiating hostile eye contact. "What're *you* lookin' at?" he challenged.

Blake took one step back, lifting the bottom of his pullover to reveal the gun in his waistband. "Don't even," he said levelly. Mohawk put up both hands and stepped aside, turning to the bartender as Blake made his way out the back door.

"Fluffy, this place is startin' to attract some rough damn clientele."

Blake stepped through the back door of The Blind Pig, entering what appeared to be a converted horse barn. Numbered stalls lined the two long walls of the structure, but where you'd expect to see bales of hay and wall-hung tack, there were piles of motorcycle parts and shelves of tools. Maureen swung open the gate of number five, and by the time Blake crossed to it she was dragging a canvas tarp off something the size of a small horse.

As the canvas fell away, light from the overhead fixture bounced off the black enamel finish of the most badass motorcycle Blake had ever seen, and Maureen stepped aside with a proud, "Ta-da!"

"Holy hell, what *is* that?"

"This, my friend, is a 1950 Vincent Black Shadow and there aren't a hundred of them left on the planet."

"Does it still run?"

"Like a mother," she replied with a smile. "Fluffy can't make drinks worth a damn, but he's a brilliant mechanic. Some say he's the reincarnation of Big Sid Biberman."

Blake was sure that name would mean something to a serious gear-head, but he didn't have a clue. He noted the name stenciled on what he assumed was the gas tank. "Gladys?"

"As in 'Gladys not a Goldwing.' Bike joke. This is how we're going to get around to the back of the studio." As Blake tried to absorb the facts that the motorcycle was Maureen's, she apparently knew how to drive the thing, and that she expected him to ride with her, Maureen saw his hesitation. "Unless you're up for walking seven or eight miles in and the same back out, Gladys here is our best bet." She told him there were hundreds of trails running through the dense forest, ranging from narrow deer paths to three-person-wide hiker routes, but not one of them was "official" and not one of them was marked.

"Then how do we keep from getting lost?"

"I've been riding those trails since I was five years old. And if I thought you knew how to handle a hog, I'd let you take my dad's Harley and follow me."

"*Charlie* has a bike too?!"

"Nothing as hot as my Vincent, but yes." She pointed toward a huddle of three motorcycles on the far side of the barn, all partially disassembled. "The Low-Rider on the left is C.H."

Blake looked at the bike. "C.H."

"Charlie's Harley. Fluffy managed the apartment

building where my dad lived his first year in LA. Later on Charlie gave him the cash he needed to buy The Pig in return for free bike maintenance and a permanent berth for his hog."

She took a can of tick spray from a shelf with assorted helmets on it, instructing him to mist his boots and pants legs, then went over to the double doors at the rear of the building, which she pushed open. After putting on her own helmet, she walked the Shadow through the doors, asked Blake to close them, fired up the 998-cc V-twin engine, and signaled for him to climb aboard behind her. He swapped the tick spray for a helmet, closed the doors and climbed on hesitantly.

"Where do I put my feet?" Blake yelled over the rumble of the engine, prompting Maureen to point down at the foot pegs on either side.

"There aren't any hand grips for the passenger," Maureen shouted. "So you're going to have to hold on to me." He slid his hands around her waist, grabbing his own wrist to hold himself in place, but keeping a few inches between his torso and her back.

"Unless you want to wind up in a ditch," she called over her shoulder, "you need to press closer. We have to move in unison on the turns."

Blake snugged up to her, making full contact with his chest and stomach. The last thing he heard before the bike leapt away and the engine's roar drowned out all other sound, was Maureen shouting, "Is that a Glock in your pants, or are you just happy to be riding with me?"

Dallis and Ostin Bates were drinking in a bar called Vanderbilt's, spending a little of the cash they had gotten yesterday when Diaz paid them for their latest batch of shake 'n' bake, and dropped off more pseudo-eph. It sure beat paying smurfers to buy up all the cold medicine in a twenty-mile radius.

They used to do their drinking at The Blind Pig, but that skinny old hippie who ran the place threw them out when he caught Dallis trying to sell a couple rocks to a parolee in the head. They weren't supposed to be freelancing, anyway. That was the deal with Diaz: he supplied all the raw materials, and he bought all the product. He had made it clear from the get-go that Dallis and Ostin were cooks, not salesmen. Even guys as dense as they were could see the wisdom of his system after Fluffy caught them and permanently barred them from The Pig. What if that ex-jailbird had been a narc?

No, life was good without going all independent on their business partner. Besides, Diaz didn't seem like the kind of guy you wanted to cross.

There were no flat straightaways for Blake to experience that famous racehorse-like gait of the Vincent, but he might not have noticed it anyway, hanging on for dear life as he was. The turns were tortuous, the trails uneven, and his face plate had been tagged by whippy branches a few dozen times. Compounding his discomfort was the fact that as Maureen leaned deeply forward to slip under the leafy canopy, Blake's body had to stay tight to hers, making him feel like a participant in a new sport: extreme spooning. After fifteen minutes of bumps, twists, turns and leaps forward, the bike slowed and pulled into a tiny clearing. When Maureen cut the engine, the forest silence was a welcome relief. "This is as close as we can get without running the risk of being heard by someone at the edge of the lot."

They dismounted, hung their helmets on the handlebars, and shook off the effects of the bone-jarring ride. Maureen checked the compass snapped to the zipper-pull of her jacket, then started walking.

Blake cast a concerned glance at the knee-deep foliage. "Are there snakes around here?"

Maureen knew the forest was home to scads of Western rattlesnakes, which is why she had told Blake to wear heavy hiking boots and sturdy jeans. No need to worry him unnecessarily, though. "Oh, maybe a few harmless king snakes, but they'll get out of our way when they feel us coming." Blake hoped she was right, as he plunged into the undergrowth to follow her.

Thirty minutes later, Maureen checked her compass. "Okay, if I've figured this right, we should get to the fence in a couple minutes of walking *that* way." She pointed to where even the last vestiges of a path had disappeared, and Blake hoped he had squirted on enough tick spray back at The Blind Pig. After only a hundred feet of breasting it through the tight, brambly flora, however, Maureen stopped again. "Well, *that* isn't supposed to be here."

Blake pushed up alongside her to see what she was looking at. A huge trailer sat in the middle of a clearing. No vehicles were there, but Maureen was not in the mood for a confrontation with a gun-toting home owner. "Let's circle around and keep going," she whispered. She began moving through the brush again, but as they got downwind of the trailer, she halted, wrinkling her nose. "Do you smell that?"

"What?"

"Wet diapers."

"Hey, don't look at me. I'm nervous out here, but not *that* nervous." He sniffed the air and realized he could smell it, too. They both noted the large pile of stuffed garbage bags at one end of the double-wide. "Have we stumbled on a small-batch lab?"

"I do believe we have."

The discovery of a probable methamphetamine manufacturing site took precedence over a wild goose chase at a movie studio, and Blake took his gun out as they moved forward.

Eleventeen Budweisers into the afternoon, the Bates brothers picked up a bag of Popeye's chicken and headed back to the trailer. Dallis was at the wheel of their F-150, trying not to hit any trees as he drunkenly weaved along the nine-foot-wide dirt road that picked up a quarter mile from where Chippewa Avenue ended and threaded through the woods all the way to their five acres at the base of Pipe Canyon. Ostin held the open bag of fried chicken on his lap, savoring the aroma and dozing peacefully, oblivious to the bumps and turns of the journey.

Dallis half-mumbled, half-sang his way through the second verse of "My Sharona" as he neared the final blind curve before the property. Suddenly he stomped the brake pedal with everything he had, sending his younger brother and a dozen pieces of chicken hurtling forward. The cushioning effect of a juicy thigh, which hit the dashboard a millisecond before Ostin's face did, kept his nose from being smashed flat, but the impact was violent enough to trigger a gushing nosebleed.

"Shit!" Ostin screamed in pain.

"Shit!" yelled Dallis. "The cops!" He slammed the truck into reverse, twisting in the seat to back away before the sheriff's car up ahead could make him. In his haste to swing around so he could see the road behind him, Dallis launched his right elbow into a wide arc that caught Ostin squarely in the face.

"Shit! My nose!"

"Fuck your nose! Didn't you hear me? There's

cops at the trailer!"

Ostin didn't really take in the words, though, distracted as he was by searing pain and a sploosh of blood and breading. The blood brought a metallic taste to his lips, the crispy breading more of a garlic and paprika flavor. Younger brothers spend their childhoods suffering Indian sunburns, wedgies and swirlies at the hands of their older siblings, but when they grow up they fight back.

While Dallis guided the lurching truck in reverse as fast as it would go, he caught a hot breast below his left eye hard enough to raise a welt. Then a pair of wings flew into his cheek and neck. But before he could bitch-slap his idiot brother, the flashing lights of a sheriff's car came rushing toward him from the rear. To avoid a collision Dallis stomped the brake again and Ostin pitched forward again. This time no greasy clod of poultry broke his momentum, and the bridge of his nose cracked loudly.

"Shit! My nose!"

Dallis slammed his open palm against the steering wheel as the 150 rocked to a stop and armed deputies swarmed the vehicle from both ends. "Shit," he muttered, right before Ostin's fist punched his face.

It was after 5:00 by the time Maureen and Blake had finished giving their statements and receiving thanks and handshakes from the local constabulary. By mutual agreement, the two detectives had not said they were kinda-sorta working on a case, instead claiming the afternoon's outing had been for pleasure. The sheriff and his deputies assumed they were a couple, an assumption bolstered when she straddled the Vincent Black Shadow and he climbed aboard and wrapped his arms around her.

They rode the short distance to The Blind Pig,

where Blake dismounted to open the double doors of the bike barn. Maureen wheeled the Shadow to its stall as Blake secured the doors and put his borrowed helmet back on the shelf. He grabbed the can of tick spray, dousing himself to discourage any hitch-hikers. After placing the can on the shelf, he saw Maureen tear a check out of her checkbook. "I'll give this to Fluffy and we're out of here."

"I thought you and your dad got free parking and maintenance."

"*He* does; I don't," she replied tersely.

Knowing Charlie's generous nature, Blake was surprised he let his daughter pay. "That doesn't sound like your dad."

Maureen sighed. "It's a long story not worth the telling, but the Black Shadow is a sore point between Charlie and me."

Blake didn't ask anything further, thinking the problem had to do with a father's worry over his daughter zooming around on a big, butch motorcycle. He had no way of guessing the rift between Maureen and Charlie was much more complex than that. In fact, if Maureen knew how deeply she had hurt her father because of the bike, she would have given it away to the first person she saw. Her interpersonal skills being what they were, however, it was unlikely she would ever move up to that enlightened plane. And Charlie, even with a gun to his head, would never tell Maureen what she had inadvertently done to him.

The Pig was rapidly filling up with the evening's diners and imbibers as Blake and Maureen entered through the back door. She pushed to the bar and held up the check for Fluffy to see. He had three glass mugs by the handles in one hand and was pulling the tap lever with the other, so he leaned forward toward Maureen. She hopped onto the foot rail, stretching over the bar to tuck the check into his shirt pocket.

"Thanks, Obi-Wan," he shouted over the din of the rowdy customers and the loud proclamation from the jukebox that Willie Nelson was on the road. *Again.*

"Next time," Maureen shouted back, blowing an air-kiss in his direction. Blake waited by the front door and they stepped out into the parking lot.

"Okay, I'll bite. Why does he call you Obi-Wan?"

"It's actually O.B. One. Charlie started bringing me up here on the Harley when I was in kindergarten, and Fluffy said I had to have my own handle. My dad was already O.B. for O'Brien. So I became O.B. One. With Fluffy's accent it sounded like Obi-Wan and over the years that's what it became."

It wasn't that the dinners served to the two men in the Tujunga sheriff's station holding cell were terrible; they weren't. Salisbury steak, peas, instant mashed potatoes and a large biscuit. But the brothers had had their hearts set on fried chicken. After all, it *was* Sunday.

They both looked like hell, even after a paramedic had done what she could for them. When they met their court-appointed attorney the next afternoon, he would try to use the injuries for a claim of police brutality, only to be shut down by the dash-cam videos showing Dallis and Ostin already beaten and bloody when they exited their truck, hands in the air.

Dallis poked at his "steak" with a plastic spork. "Don't worry," he said in a low tone so as not to be overheard by the deputy outside the cell. "When Diaz finds out what happened, he'll hire the best lawyer money can buy and get us out of this."

Having no reason to doubt his brother's insight on the matter, Ostin nodded while attempting to spread an icy pat of Butt-R-Twin on his splayed biscuit.

Brotherly sagacity notwithstanding, Dallis and Ostin Bates would never again see the man they knew only as Diaz.

Dominic Briggs was surprised to see the gate arm still down as he neared the guardhouse Monday morning. Roy always spotted him approaching and got the gate up in time for him to go through without slowing. Today, though, the old guard waved for him to stop. "What's up, Roy?" Dominic asked through his lowered window.

"'Morning, Mr. Briggs. I thought you might want a heads up that Sheriff Trainor got here about ten minutes ago."

Careful to let nothing more than normal curiosity show on his face, Dom asked, "Did he say what he wanted?"

"No sir. Said he was looking for you, so I sent him on over to your office."

"Probably wants a donation to some police charity or another. Thanks, Roy."

"You have a nice day, Mr. Briggs," the guard said, as his boss gunned the engine and zoomed under the rising gate arm.

Dominic tried not to panic, but he hardly breathed until he saw the sheriff's car parked in a guest spot in front of the bungalow. Okay, he thought, at least he's not wandering around the lot. Production was running on all three stages this week, and he didn't want anyone taking an *un*guided tour, least of all anyone in law enforcement.

Dominic pulled into his designated parking space and quickly made his way to the reception area. Sure enough, the sheriff was there, drinking coffee and chatting-up the front desk bimbo.

"Sheriff Trainor, good to see you again," Briggs

said, extending his hand. "Come on in." After the handshake, he led the sheriff into his private office and closed the door.

"Sorry to drop in unannounced," the sheriff said, "but it's a matter of some importance, so I thought I should talk directly to you."

Maureen noticed the door to the office slightly ajar. That was unusual, since Blake's car hadn't been in his spot when she pulled in a few minutes earlier. She had walked next door to pick up a bagel, so maybe he had arrived then. Now that her assassin problem had gone away, Maureen wasn't routinely carrying, so she put her fingertips on the door and began to push it open cautiously.

"Coffee's up, and I brought Danish," a female voice said from inside.

Maureen opened the door the rest of the way and saw a plump black woman at the reception desk. There was a computer in front of her, a small stack of files, a framed photo and a vase with a single orchid in it. She looked as though she'd worked at the desk forever, so Maureen cut her eyes to the name plate on the door to make sure she was in the right place.

"Uh, Keesha?" she asked, finally recognizing the woman she had met only a couple times during her short stay at the Beverly Hills Police Department.

"Good morning, Detective. As I said, coffee's on in the break room, so unless there's something else, I'm kind of busy here."

Too stunned to respond, Maureen watched Keesha punch in a phone number, then cheerily say, "Hi, Linda, it's Ms. Beale from E&O. I have that final quote for Mr. Fairchild if you don't mind putting me through."

Maureen heard a ding, so she stepped back into

the hallway in time to see the elevator doors hiss open. When Blake stepped out, she strode toward him. "You hired someone without telling me?"

Blake could see she was pissed-off, but didn't know why. "What are you talking about?"

"Our new receptionist."

"We don't have a receptionist."

"Oh, really?" Maureen turned and led him to their office, where Keesha was thanking someone on the phone. Blake's eyebrows shot up, so Maureen knew he was as confused as she was.

Keesha ended the call and beamed at the two detectives standing in the doorway. "Great news. We got the Fairchild security account."

"*We?*" Blake asked, not sure what was going on.

As she jotted down some information and flipped open the top file on the desk, Keesha explained. "Okay, I bid the job higher than your scribbled notes indicated you were about to. Fairchild countered, I countered, and the bottom line is we're still getting fifteen percent more than you thought he'd go for."

The bewildered detectives tried to keep up as their apparent receptionist barreled on without pause for breath. "The profit from the Fairchild business will cover a third of my salary every month. By this Friday I expect to have two more corporate security accounts nailed down, and at that point we're break-even, so anything I bring in afterwards is gravy. I also returned two calls inquiring about your services. One philandering husband, one possible stalker the police aren't taking seriously enough in the target's opinion. Details are on your desk. Now, if we're done here, I've only got till Wednesday to vet and hire six guards for the Fairchild job. As I keep saying, coffee's on in the break room." With that, she picked up the phone and dialed a number she read out of an open file.

Blake and Maureen slunk across to the archway at the rear of reception, turned left into the short hallway, then left again into the kitchenette that was suddenly the "break room."

"What in the bejeebers just happened?" Maureen asked, reaching for a coffee mug.

"Remember *Ghostbusters*, how people got slimed? I think we've been Keesh'd." Blake took down his own mug, a gift from Jane, and held it out so Maureen could fill it after her own cup was topped. It had "World's Greatest Boyfriend" crossed out, then "World's Greatest Fiancé" crossed out, then at the bottom, "World's Greatest Husband."

While Blake stirred sugar and half-and-half into his mug, Maureen took a sip of her own black coffee. "Yowza."

"What?" Blake asked.

"Taste it."

He did, then looked at his partner. "This can't be the same stuff we've been making." He opened the door of the sole cabinet, but the only coffee there was the bag they had bought themselves. "How did she do this?" he asked.

"I have no idea, but if she can bring in business and make *this* every morning, I vote we let her stay."

In reception, Keesha did initial phone interviews with potential security guards, mostly successful police academy grads who had not gone on to join the force for one reason or another. In the locked bottom drawer of her desk was a two-pound bag of freshly ground, super-premium coffee from a shop that traded in rare blends from Sumatra, Jamaica and Hawaii. It had cost her eighty dollars, but it had been worth it.

Dominic Briggs walked the sheriff to the door. "I appreciate your telling me all this, Dale. More than you can know."

"Well, with it being on a piece of property right up next to your lot, I thought it was the right thing to do. You've probably got celebrities and whatnot walking around here all the time. Wouldn't want some crank-addled tweak jumping your fence when he can't find his old dealer."

"You can say that again."

"Are you sure you don't want me to assign a few deputies to your perimeter?"

Briggs clapped a hand on the sheriff's shoulder, then lowered his voice so as not to be overheard by the receptionist. "Most of the guys from my old Marine unit are working here now, and they are no strangers to confrontation. If any meth head comes on *this* lot looking for trouble, I guarantee he's going to find it." He gave a conspiratorial wink to the sheriff. "Don't quote me on that to *The Hollywood Reporter* when you come to pick up the body."

Dale Trainor chuckled. "I hear you, man."

Once the sheriff had left the lot, Dominic sat down to think. What a clusterfuck. Those Bates clowns had always been expendable, but he had intended to dispose of them when it suited *him*.

Losing them was a problem, all right, but the bigger issue was the two people who discovered the trailer. He had easily gotten their names by saying he wanted to send them each a thank-you note and a fruit basket for doing their civic duty. The sheriff told him the two were hiking in the woods when they stumbled onto the little crack lab on the prairie, but Briggs knew better than that. He hadn't forgotten Maureen O'Brien's name.

This was a critical time in his master plan and he couldn't afford a misstep. He was already holding his breath until Frank Goodwin went away for Mason's murder, and he was dealing with an increasingly unstable Micah. The last thing he needed was two detectives sniffing around.

Before he scored the cushy berth on Oahu, Briggs had seen battle for six years. He had killed enemy combatants with the blessing of the U.S. government, and he knew his way around a strike mission. As with *all* combat strikes, this required swift and decisive action.

After Maureen left to pick up lunch from Ziggy's, Blake finally had a chance to speak privately with Keesha. "I cannot work with Libby Johnson," she said, in response to Blake's question about why she had left the BHPD after so many years. "She makes lieutenant and all of a sudden she gets a bad case of the high-and-mighties."

Blake seriously doubted Libby had done anything wrong, but he respected both women involved, so he knew to tread lightly. Each was strong and confident, with absolute control over her own domain. Keesha was used to being the guiding hand for the competent, but receptive Lt. Rhee, only Libby Johnson wasn't likely to appreciate "guidance." And Libby had always taken the lead with her long-time partner, Jim, so she wasn't going to be thrilled having an assistant who was such an independent thinker.

Nothing wrong with oil; nothing wrong with water; but don't expect to mix them successfully. And the BHPD's loss was E&O's gain.

All they had learned from their little adventure the day before, Maureen and Blake decided, was where Micah had been scoring meth. They wondered if he was careless enough to buy direct, or if he used an intermediary. And where would he look to find a new supplier?

With Keesha's fresh leads on clients, they tabled their freelance investigation for the moment, splitting up so Maureen could check out the possible stalker and Blake could follow the philandering husband. They decided to revisit the Cody Mason murder again at the end of the week, although Blake was *not* looking forward to another jaunt through the woods on the back of a motorcycle.

In the gym at Pinnacle, Micah pushed himself harder than ever before. He'd show the critics and the movie-going public he was still vital, strong, the boy with the Greek physique now grown into a man in his prime. He grunted and strained, putting in long hours with increasingly heavier weights, determined to sculpt his already magnificent body into masculine perfection before *The Devil's Platoon* began shooting.

Micah had never studied method acting, believing all his career that he was "a natural," but now, as he immersed himself in what would be his finest role, he let his mind drift easily from his own reality to the fictional life of Capt. Luther Hardy. He used subtle hints in the script as jumping off points to craft a back story for the Vietnam hero, then inserted himself into that narrative, that childhood, those months of boot camp at Parris Island, the dangerous missions deep in the Mekong Delta.

Despite the rigorous gym regimen, Micah didn't hurt. Not because he was the fit, thirty-two-year-old captain, but because he had sagely persuaded pal Joey to part with a substantial quantity of his life-saving pills for a fee. Two every four hours allowed Micah to work at the pace he had when he was training for the Olympics only a couple years earlier.

His muscles were bulking up dramatically. As

Dominic had gotten more cautious and sparing with the AAS, Micah had quietly found another ex-jarhead gym rat to help him out. Now he was getting steroid injections from *two* sources and the results were breathtaking—at least in his own mind.

If Micah noticed that his testicles were shrinking, he wrote it off as contrast. While his hamstrings and quadriceps responded to the punishing workouts, swelling to god-like proportions, of course his balls would appear smaller by comparison.

He didn't know that one of his recent conquests, a model from a not-very-discriminating porn site, had reported back to her fellow escorts that the creepy old action hero was "all meat and no potatoes." It's unlikely Micah would have even cared about the dis, focused as he was on becoming the valiant soldier from the pages of *The Devil's Platoon* script.

At the end of each day, with his grueling workout behind him, Micah took two more of Joey's miracle pills, insurance against an evening of joint or muscle pain, then lit up a pipe to reward himself for his hard work. And when he woke at 2:00 or 3:00 A.M., coming off his high and twinging with the aches of old age and overexertion, he doubled down on the oxy and the meth. At least Briggs wasn't being stingy with the crystal.

As Micah slept, the soup in his skull simmered, poaching his brain in the increasingly toxic broth of steroids, methamphetamine and oxycodone. And as the liquid gently basted the exterior of that wrinkled organ, the white plaque on the interior extended its reach and influence slowly, but relentlessly.

Bubble, bubble, here comes trouble.

Charlie spent the week putting everything in motion for the gift that would convince Denice to move to LA. He had missed her like crazy the last two weekends, but he understood why she couldn't come to see him. Cindy had been her most dependable employee, so Denice was scrambling to find and train a replacement.

He would fly into Las Vegas Friday night, drive down to Madison, then spend three days with her. Well, as much of the three days as she could spare him, given her temporary extra workload. Charlie knew it would be a challenge for him to keep the secret secret, but he was damned if he'd go off half-cocked and blow his proposal a second time.

No, he would wait patiently for Mr. Duval to build the engagement ring Charlie had designed himself. The central stone should arrive from Antwerp within the next ten days and Charlie would use that time to visit Denice and work on her big surprise.

A total of thirty-seven former Marine colleagues of Dominic Briggs now worked at Pinnacle Pictures, and all were loyal to him. Most of them came from his years at Camp Smith on Oahu, but three pre-dated his sand-and-surf Hawaiian gig. They were also loyal, but for reasons much deeper than gratitude for a steady job and a generous paycheck.

Briggs and the three men who made up his inner circle had been in combat together. That dark bond which forms among men who have hunted and killed as a team remains intact, regardless of how much time passes. All those shared wounds, shared fears, shared actions—no matter how disgraceful—bind in ways no marriage vow or familial tie ever can.

Dominic trusted these men with his life, now as he had in the past. Only he and these three knew what was really going on at Pinnacle Pictures, and it was their job to protect that information and run an op within an op. They shared equally in the bounty from that hidden operation, and the freshly laundered cash flowed steadily outward to four offshore accounts.

Highly motivated as the four were, they gathered their intel rapidly, chauvinistically assuming Blake Ervansky was the leader of the inquisitive pair, and making him the target. Their strike would be clean, quick and devastating, a virtual surety the two detectives would never again poke around in affairs that didn't concern them.

Dominic made the critical decision *not* to kill Ervansky. The death of an ex-cop would trigger a relentless investigation—cops were like Marines that way, they never forget and they never leave a fallen comrade on the battlefield. Luckily, the intel had turned up something Briggs could capitalize on. Blake Ervansky had a beautiful blonde wife.

By Thursday the two cases were wrapped and ready for Keesha to bill. The philandering husband had been blatantly cheating with *two* women, neither of whom was aware of the other, although both knew about the wife. Now, thanks to Blake, all three women knew the score and the missus had contacted a divorce lawyer. Easy-peasy-cheddar-cheesy.

The second case had been more challenging, a felon who had fallen in lust with a young singer he had seen on MTV back when he was doing eight to ten for aggravated assault. The woman had since married up, left the entertainment business and borne three children, but to the ex-con she was still the girl of his dreams. If she wouldn't return his love, he would make her pay.

Gomey Jeffers sauntered out of the Tex-Mex place around the corner from his flophouse, picking shreds of ropa vieja out of his yellowed teeth. He approached the group of homeless people waiting for a handout, but they stepped aside as Gomey entered the alleyway shortcut to his cruddy squat. He had previously made it clear what his brutal response would be to any pathetic request for spare change.

Looks like not everybody's learned their lesson, Gomey thought as a scruffy redhead came toward him, eyes beseeching and left hand held up for alms. As she got close enough for Gomey to register that she was cleaner and younger than the rest, her right hand darted to the SIG Sauer in his waistband, yanking it away. Before he could react, she had spun around and fired at one of the homeless men.

Red bloomed across the man's coat front as he fell, his friends rushing forward to help, their eyes turned to the shocked ex-con.

"We all saw you shoot him when he asked you for a dollar. Didn't we?" Maureen asked the witnesses. They all nodded with enthusiasm. "The police are already looking at you for your unhealthy interest in a certain singer, and now this. Seven of us ready to ID you as the one who killed poor Bradley."

Gomey took the Greyound ticket Maureen handed him with a warning not to return, then scrammed. He had less than an hour to pack his shit and catch the dog to Pittsburgh. Once he was gone, Maureen helped Bradley to his feet and passed around the twenty-dollar bills she had promised each of them for their participation in the charade.

Maureen pocketed the unfired P220. It was probably unregistered and untraceable, and you never know when a piece like that might come in handy.

Her own Browning Hi-Power, loaded with blanks, had gone out of sight as soon as it "shot" the homeless man. After Maureen said good-bye, the street people gathered around poor undead Bradley to admire his spiffy wound.

Maureen had always loved those blood squibs the special effects guys used on *The Brothers Gunn*. When she was ten, she nicked one and hid it under a tee-shirt on a camping trip she and her dad had gone on to Yellowstone. Smashing the squib over her heart, then loudly popping an air-filled paper bag in the echo-y campground loo, Maureen had staggered out of the facility, clutching her bloodied chest. Two women screamed, a park ranger fainted, and even Charlie only appreciated the performance in hindsight.

Maureen and Blake were finally ready to turn their attention back to Cody Mason's murder when Keesha handed them details on another potential case, a corporate whistle blower situation. The blower himself wanted to meet in secret and talk to them about protection. Keesha told them the man said he was still employed by the company involved and would have to meet them before work the next morning at a secure location.

The drive on the 101 hadn't been all that bad at 6:00 A.M. when Blake and Maureen had started across the San Fernando Valley for their meeting with the whistle blower, only the normal thirty-mile-an-hour crawl the radio guys like to call "Friday morning light" traffic. But now, almost three hours later, they were caught in a vehicular nightmare, creeping back the way they'd come.

The client hadn't shown by 7:30 so they tried the number Keesha had given them, but when they finally got enough bars for the call to go through, it went to voicemail and they never heard from him. After another half hour in the remote Topanga Canyon location, the detectives had given up.

Keesha wouldn't be in until 9:00—when she told

them her salary and job description, she had also mentioned what her hours would be—but Maureen left a message on the office phone at 8:45. "Hey, it's Maureen. Our whistler never showed, so we're on our way in. Should be there by 9:30." Blake snorted. "Or 10:00," Maureen added, ending the call.

"You think something happened to the guy?" Blake asked.

"I guess we'll have to wait and see."

They rode in silence until Maureen's phone sang out the opening notes of the theme song from *The Brothers Gunn* at two minutes after 9:00. "O'Brien Custom Glassworks. What can we blow for you?" She listened a moment, then: "She say why?" Another pause. "Okay, we'll meet her there. Thanks, Keesha."

"Did she hear something?"

"Not from our guy. Libby called and wants you to meet her at your house."

"What for?"

"No clue."

Blake passed the Van Nuys exit that would have taken them to Benedict Canyon and dropped them down to Sunset, instead going east until he got to Laurel Canyon. Traffic was thinning and they picked up speed once they crossed Mulholland Drive. At Lookout Mountain Blake made a right and started climbing the corkscrew toward his house, but as he approached the split where Wonderland veered to the right, he saw a police roadblock. An impossibly young officer was waving him off to Wonderland, but Blake sharp-lefted to parallel the barricade.

"Sir, you can't park here," the uniformed fetus was already saying as Blake and Maureen climbed out of the Mercedes. It was his first day on the job and he was full of his own badge-certified importance. "Sir? Ma'am? I said you—"

"We're with the BHPD," Blake said, fudging the truth for the sake of expedience. "Call Lt. Johnson and she'll verify. Ervansky and O'Brien."

The young officer brightened, now that he realized he was interacting with another member of the blue brotherhood. "Oh, the lieutenant's already up there at the scene."

"What's going on?"

"You didn't hear on your radio?" he asked, happy for the opportunity to be their first contact. "Some cop's house burned down. They found a body, too."

Blake was over the barrier and running up the hill before the pleased expression had left the kid's face.

"You asshole!" Maureen yelled, grabbing the front of his new uniform and jerking him closer. "If they had been stupid enough to issue you a gun, I would use it to shoot off your dick!"

She roughly pushed him backwards, then started running after her partner.

Well! The Academy certainly hadn't prepared him for *that*.

As soon as the fire fighters found the body, they called the Hollywood precinct. As soon as the Hollywood responders learned from a neighbor that the house was owned by a Beverly Hills cop, they called Libby Johnson. And as soon as Libby heard it was arson, she called Artie Lassiter. He and Blake had partnered for five years, and if this was payback by some scumbag they had put away, Artie could be next in line. As soon as Libby and Artie heard there was a body, they braced for the worst.

When she couldn't get through to Blake's cell phone, Libby had left word on the E&O office number, hoping Blake was out on an early errand. She and

Artie huddled by one of the three fire trucks that had saved the entire neighborhood, possibly the whole mountain, by drenching the foliage surrounding the house, and preventing the blaze from hop-scotching to any of the nearby homes. Unfortunately, they hadn't been able to save anything of Blake's house, and early findings indicated multiple accelerants had been used. Someone had wanted the house to drop fast, and had set the incendiaries in graduated stages to achieve the hottest, quickest burn, crafting an almost surgical excision of one dwelling among many.

The body chained to a chair inside had not yet been identified, so when Libby saw Blake pounding up the hill toward the scene, her moment of relief turned to agony in a heartbeat. "Oh, Jesus," she whispered. Artie turned to see what had caught her attention, but Libby was already racing down the hill toward Blake.

"Where's Jane?" he shouted.

"Blake—"

She stepped in his path, but he had no intention of stopping. Playing basketball for LSU, Libby had caught deliberately thrown elbows and shoulders all the time, but nothing had ever hit her with the intensity of the six-foot-four cannonball that clocked her when she didn't step out of its trajectory.

"Wait, Blake!" Libby stumbled from the impact, and when she straightened she saw Maureen O'Brien legging it up the hill, a hundred feet back in her partner's wake.

Artie watched the hit on Libby and moved forward to intercept Blake, but Blake put his shoulder down, prepared to flatten anyone who got in his way. Libby Johnson was as tall as Blake, but much lighter, so she had been no match for the ferocity of his attack. But Artie Lassiter was a solid wall of don't-even-think-about-it, taking a half-step to the side right before impact, then grabbing Blake so that the younger man's forward momentum was deflected into a staggering spin that brought both men crashing to the pavement. Artie's elbow smashed into the asphalt under the weight of Blake's body, but he never released his hold.

"Get off me!"

Artie kept his arms locked tight around Blake's chest, pinning him as he struggled to break free. As they rolled to a stop, Artie banged his forehead hard into Blake's, trying to get his attention.

"Jane! Jane!" Blake screamed, and Artie spoke into his ear, lips close enough to brush the dark hair surrounding it.

"She's gone, buddy. She's gone."

Libby and a panting Maureen came toward the downed men, but halted twenty feet away when they heard the tortured wail.

"No-o-o-o-o!"

Work was finally getting back to normal at the diner in Madison, Nevada. The new waitress learned quickly and rarely screwed up, so Denice had decided she could take a little time off to spend with Charlie over the weekend. She felt bad about having cancelled two back-to-back trips to LA, and she looked forward to making it up to him when he arrived this evening.

Busy as she was, setting up for the Friday lunch crowd, Denice didn't check her phone until 11:00, and when she did her spirits fell.

Charlie's voice, tight and curt, said, "I can't make it this weekend. I'll call when I get a chance." She listened to the message several times, stepping into the cubicle off the kitchen for privacy. He sounded different, distracted, and the casually tossed-off "when I get a chance" was unlike him.

Denice sat on the cot where she took her nap between the lunch rush and the dinner crunch, wondering if she had played it too casually with him. A man like Charlie O'Brien doesn't come along every day; hell, a man like him might not come around in a lifetime. And when he shows up, there's going to be a line of women waiting for him. She had rebuffed his proposal, then wavered on a move to LA, and for what? A small town cheeseburger joint? Had Charlie lost interest and given up? Had she blown the best thing that had ever happened to her?

Charlie O'Brien wasn't thinking about Denice, but it was *not* because he had lost interest or didn't want to spend the weekend with her. Since Maureen's call he had been scrambling, first telling Mrs. Taylor to make up one of the guest rooms, then going out to shop for Blake.

Unless Maureen was exaggerating—and that had never been her style—Blake would have nothing but the clothes he was wearing when she brought him to the house, so Charlie picked out jeans, shirts, socks and underwear, making guesses on size and inseam length. His housekeeper would stock the guest bath with the usual toiletries, but Blake would need a comb, razor, toothbrush and probably a dozen other things Charlie was forgetting. The items he had bought, though, would be a start, would get Blake through the first couple days.

The busy-ness of the shopping had kept Charlie's mind from going where he desperately didn't want to go: to thoughts of Jane.

If you dangled Charlie O'Brien over a precipice, threatening to let him fall to his death unless he told you *one* thing he didn't like about his own daughter, he would steadfastly maintain that he loved Maureen unconditionally, that not a single thing about her was a disappointment. And he would convince you, too, even at the cost of his life.

But Charlie knew in his secret heart it wasn't true. Maureen *had* disappointed him, *did* disappoint him, simply by the fact that she didn't really need him. He had never understood the appeal of clingy, helpless women who deferred all decisions to the man in their lives, and he had avoided women like that since his brief, disastrous marriage to Maureen's mother. He respected independence; he was thrilled by a challenging intellect; and he was proud of Maureen's successes. *But.* Somewhere deep in his heart was an ache for what he never had, a daddy's-little-girl, a daughter who would allow herself to be pampered by a loving father right up until the day she left to begin a life with the man of her dreams.

Yes, Maureen enjoyed the life Charlie's money had provided, but he never saw delight in her eyes. When she turned twenty-one, he had given her a magnificent diamond necklace to mark the milestone, proud he could afford to lavish such a lovely gift on his only child.

Her face had lit up when she saw Mr. Duval's exquisite creation and she breathlessly asked, "Is it *really* mine?" Charlie had felt a moment of pure happiness, knowing he had made Maureen happy, not realizing he had misread her excitement when he assured her the beautiful piece was all hers. In less than twenty-four hours, the necklace went on e-Bay, and with the money from the sale, Maureen had bought a motorcycle.

Charlie and Jane had been thrown together on Maureen and Blake's first big case. He had gotten to know her a bit as she played assistant to his movie producer. Again, on the second major case for E&O

Investigations, Charlie and Jane were left together for long periods of time, notably a drive from Los Angeles to a small town in Nevada. Jane had been terrified on that drive, knowing someone had tried to kill Blake, and she siphoned off her fear by telling Charlie about her family and her childhood back in West Virginia.

Charlie had come to admire in Jane what he didn't see in Maureen, her delight and appreciation for the little things—and they were, indeed, only little things—that Charlie did for her. The Christmas gift he had bought Jane, an aerial photo of her home town, had brought tears to her eyes. And the grateful hug she had given him nearly brought tears to his own. A one-hundred-dollar framed photograph had bought him more of the feeling of being a dad than a one-hundred-*thousand*-dollar necklace had.

Charlie O'Brien didn't need effusive thank-yous, didn't even want them. What he needed was the assurance that he had brought joy to another person. He never got to see the engagement ring he had paid for, and Jane would never have learned of his participation in the purchase, but Gerard Duval's account of her reaction to the stone she chose was enough to make Charlie O'Brien feel like father of the year.

Artie had not left Blake's side, and had firmly supported the doctor's suggestion of a sedative. Blake was calm now, but limp and desolate as the two men sat in the back of the ambulance, legs dangling out through the open doors. The rig waited, and neither man wanted to think about what it waited for.

Down the hill, Maureen answered questions from Libby Johnson and a homicide detective from the Hollywood PD whose name she hadn't caught.

They had questioned her at length about any

cases she and Blake were working on, or had recently wrapped up, that might have brought this level of retaliation, but Maureen knew it had to have been from before, from when Blake and Artie had been detectives at the BHPD. Nothing she and Blake had taken on came close to this level.

"Are you *sure* you haven't looked into some big drug ring," the detective asked, for the third time in an hour. "Because this is the kind of fuckriot we expect when a cartel is threatened."

"Asked and answered," Maureen replied wearily, suddenly aware of what it feels to be on the wrong side of an official interrogation. She had already told him about tipping off the sheriff up in Tujunga last Sunday, but said it was only a bush-league, shake-and-bake crack lab run by two clueless boobs.

"Could the cooks you busted be connected? Maybe have friends in low places? Could they have possibly been a farm-out for a bigger operation?"

"Detective, with all due respect, from what I saw Tweedle-Dee and Tweedle-Dumb-Shit couldn't have found their own asses with a flashlight and a GPS. Shouldn't you be trying to find out which scumbag my partner and Artie Lassiter put away who recently got out of prison?"

Libby heard frustration and edge in Maureen's voice, realizing further pushing was pointless. She placed her hand on the other detective's arm, a completely uncharacteristic gesture for her, but one she hoped would establish rapport. Though this involved some of her people, it wasn't her case, and she wanted to be kept in the loop. "Mark, why don't we leave it for now. Ms. O'Brien knows to call you if she remembers anything that might help."

Artie saw them first, the two men carrying the gurney from the burned-out house. The black body bag didn't have even the remotest shape of a body; it was a zippered-shut mound on the stretcher. Artie stood, a move that caught Blake's attention. And when he saw what was approaching, he closed his eyes. Artie took Blake's arm and helped him to his feet so they could clear out of the way. "Come on, I'll take you home."

Maureen had expected he would come back with her to Charlie's, but Libby quietly informed her Artie was taking Blake to his house. "I guess I'll go get his car then," Maureen said, feeling helpless. "I'll drive it to my dad's and get it to him tomorrow."

When he got out of the car down at the barricade, Blake had left his keys in the ignition, so the young officer had pulled it up onto the edge of a lawn to get it out of the way. Now the poor cop was arguing with the driver of a delivery truck who insisted he had to get through for a drop-off further up on Lookout Mountain Avenue. When Officer Kidcop saw the potty-mouth redhead walking down the road toward him, he started rethinking the whole law enforcement career thing, and braced himself for whatever fresh hell she would unload on him. As she approached, though, all she said was, "Keys in the car?" He nodded, but before she could walk away, the delivery guy started yelling.

"Listen, I got four other stops to make, so let me through so I can drop off the goddamned furniture!" Maureen could see the young officer didn't know how to handle the situation, so she walked toward the truck, intending to intimidate the driver into leaving. Then she remembered Blake had started another of his home-improvement projects.

"Any chance this delivery is for 8816? Ervansky?" The driver checked his clipboard and said it was. "Okay, you know Acacia Drive in Nichols Canyon?"

"Yeah."

"Take it to the big Spanish house at the end of the cul-de-sac. I'll call the housekeeper and tell her to open the garage so you can unload it."

After the truck turned around and left, Maureen went to the silver Mercedes, carefully backing it onto the asphalt and driving away. Two minutes later, the young officer hauled aside the barricade to let the silent ambulance through, then a black sedan with a driver he didn't recognize and a passenger he did.

The medical examiner's report quantified the horror into prosaic data. Female, early twenties. Height between five-five and five-eight. Cause of death: one .45-caliber round to the back of the head. Maureen had obtained the unauthorized copy of the report after she had shown up to ID the body. Her claim that she was the dead woman's best friend, and that the woman's husband had asked her to do the viewing was met with surprise.

"Uh, were you not told? A visual ID won't be possible." The soft-spoken coroner's assistant braced himself to catch her if she fainted. "The deceased was burned beyond recognition."

Without flinching, Maureen responded with a whopper. "I realize it's a little unorthodox, but her husband asked me to do this for him. He doesn't have any idea how extensive the damage is, and if I see the body, I can soften the blow when I report back to him."

"Couldn't you do that *without* actually viewing the remains?" He was still trying to protect the young woman from a devastating shock.

She looked at him with a solemn and slightly puzzled expression. "But that would be lying to my friend's husband, and I'm not comfortable with that," Maureen lied.

Against his better judgment, he let her see the charred remains.

Maureen thought she knew what to expect, but nothing could have made the viewing less horrific. Fingers and toes had been burned away, and what remained of the hands and feet merely hinted at their former shape. The rest: a black, crusted nightmare.

And melted into the palm area of the left hand was a small amount of rose gold, still clinging to the pink, heart-shaped diamond that would be the only thing of Jane's returned to her husband.

Maureen had brought the coroner's report with her into the office Monday morning, where Keesha confirmed she hadn't heard from Blake, either, since the fire. Now Maureen sat at the desk she shared with him, going over every line of the report, hoping to find something—anything—to prove this wasn't Jane. She was unsuccessful, learning only that an attempt would be made to find dental records and, failing there, the M.E. would request a DNA sample from Jane's family in West Virginia.

All readily identifiable features like fingerprints, hair and face were gone, although the fire had burned out so fast after the initial inferno that many of the abdominal organs were virtually intact, as if a thick steak had been put on a too-hot grill, charring the outside, but leaving the interior bloody.

"Maureen?" She looked up to see Keesha in the doorway. "Artie Lassiter called. Jane's body is being released to Blake this morning and he's taking it back to West Virginia for burial."

"Did Artie say how he was doing?"

"Yeah. Not great."

Four days Blake was gone, and when he came back he didn't check in with Maureen. That stung.

She piddled around on nothing cases, referred the ones requiring any immediate detective work, and on Friday she signed paychecks for the people Keesha had hired to service their first security contract. Unable to stand the silence any longer, she called Artie and asked to meet.

He was already in a booth when Maureen got to the coffee shop, so she slid in across from him. "Artie. Thanks for meeting me."

"Hey, I could use the break."

"That bad?"

"The man lost his home and his wife. What do *you* think?"

The waitress took their meager order of two coffees—more a justification for taking up a booth, than a desire to drink anything—then left them to talk. "It's been a week and he hasn't even bothered to call."

"Look, O'Brien, I'm not saying I know how he feels, but before he and I rode together I had the same partner for almost fourteen years, and when he got killed I was incommunicado for months. Lt. Rhee was smart enough not to push me to snap out of it. He let the line play out until I was finally tired of feeling guilty and angry. Then, when it was time to reel me in, I didn't fight him."

The waitress set down the coffees and asked if there would be anything else. Artie smiled at her and shook his head, so she placed the bill on the table and walked away.

"I know you're not happy he hasn't called you, but hang in there. You've got to keep the agency going so he has something to come back to when he's ready. It'll all work out."

"I know you're right, but I hate that there isn't anything I can do for him."

"Your little cross to bear while he's shouldering his big one."

Maureen watched him check the bill, then pull a five out of his wallet, but she knew she couldn't let him leave yet. "Artie?"

"What?"

"Listen, I—" She spoke down into her cup. "I'm sorry I never got back to you after, uh—"

"Oh, hell, O'Brien. We're not gonna talk about the night of the party, are we?" Her embarrassment was his answer.

"I should have called. Especially after you sent flowers."

"That was a thank-you, not an encore request. I knew what was going on with you that night."

"Well, that makes *one* of us."

Artie pushed aside the bill and the five, then leaned in to make sure what was said in the booth, stayed in the booth. "A million years ago this cave-man got all pissy when he didn't kill something for dinner, so he went home and cooled off his frustration by porking his old lady. He was the first, but men have been working out their own garbage since then by sexing up the closest female. And I say God bless America that you women now have equal rights in that department. The difference is a man who uses someone walks away with a smile on his face, but a woman who does the same thing feels guilty and wants to *talk* about it."

Maureen lifted a skeptical auburn eyebrow. "Got it all figured out, huh, Lassiter?"

Artie slid his hand over to take hold of hers. "I didn't know if you were celebrating, suffering or blowing off steam, and frankly, I didn't care. But I was happy to be your one-night stand." The squeeze of his hand was quick and reassuring before he withdrew it and stood.

"Artie?" Maureen said, flashing a smile up at him. "They're *all* one-night stands until the second night."

The loud bark of his laugh drew the attention of several nearby patrons. Then he leaned down so only Maureen heard his next words. "You're so full of shit, O'Brien. No wonder Blake adores you."

He winked and left, leaving Maureen to realize she had not asked to meet with him to assuage her guilt, or even to check on Blake, but to be reassured by those last three words.

The following week Dominic Briggs and Micah gave an interview to *The Hollywood Report* about their upcoming movie. Briggs was not thrilled when Micah showed up for the photo in combat fatigues, but the reporter assumed it was part of the publicity for *The Devil's Platoon*. And Micah's wardrobe choice wasn't the only thing bothering Dominic.

He was alarmed by the escalating erraticism in the star, mood swings which had Dom speculating about possible underlying medical issues. Maybe Micah was bi-polar or something. Briggs couldn't afford to have a doctor check Micah without risking having the steroid and meth usage discovered, so he convinced himself the actor was only feeling a lot of pressure about the film he thought would herald his comeback. Dominic knew *The Devil's Platoon* would be the star's final movie...one way or another.

Then there was the issue of the teeth. Briggs was paying a fortune to a well-known cosmetic dentist for a full set of caps, crowns and bridges to hide the meth damage already noticeable in Micah's mouth. The dentist had signed a strongly worded confidentiality agreement, but every additional person who learned about Micah's little "problem" was a potential leak.

He cursed himself for having introduced Micah to the pipe in the first place, but at the time was the only way to maintain some control over him. Especially after Cody Mason had made the big jerk get off the steroids.

And what the hell was going on with the steroids? Dominic had been steadily decreasing the amount of AAS he was shooting into Micah's butt, making up the difference in saline solution so the actor would not notice. But a check with the wardrobe master had confirmed what Briggs already suspected—Micah's muscles were bulking up and roping under his skin at an alarming rate. Could it be from all those extra hours he was putting in at the gym? Or was a second "helper" slipping him a little extra something?

Micah needed to hold it together for another few months, long enough to finish shooting the movie, so Briggs had to come up with another way to keep the actor on a tight, short leash.

For weeks Maureen had kept thoughts of Blake out of her head while she tried to get back to work. Artie had told her on the phone a few days earlier that Blake disappeared right after dark every night, and didn't come back for hours. Maureen couldn't help but wonder where her partner was going. Not to visit a cemetery; Jane's grave was in West Virginia. She decided to follow him and find out.

Her Mercedes, fraternal twin to Blake's own car, would be spotted by him too easily, so Maureen swapped cars with Keesha for the night. The compact Toyota blended in with all the other cars parked in Artie's neighborhood, and she settled in to wait.

A half hour after sunset, Blake came out and got in his car. When he pulled away Maureen followed.

Rather than meandering on the aimless path of a

person clearing his head, Blake drove with purpose, the turns and straightaways taking him out of the quiet Santa Monica residential area and putting him in the Sunset Boulevard crush heading east. Maureen wondered if he was going to the office, but when he continued past it, she knew he would take a left on Crescent Heights. He was going back to his house.

It wouldn't be possible to follow Blake up the mountain without being seen, so she turned into the parking lot of the little restaurant that had catered Blake and Jane's party. Maureen assumed he would go by the property, torturing himself with what-ifs, then come down and continue his nocturnal street crawl, but twenty minutes passed with no sign of him.

When she cruised past Blake's address, Maureen saw his car parked on the concrete slab that was the only thing left of the former carport. Continuing up the hill, she rounded a few turns until she saw a bank foreclosure sign, turned into the drive of the vacant house and parked.

It was still early enough in the evening for there to be traffic as she made her way back down on foot, so Maureen was careful to step off into the shadows when a car went by. A hundred feet away she slowed, thinking Blake might be sitting in his car, but as she passed the charred foundation she could see the vehicle was not occupied.

Approaching the Mercedes, she was assailed by the reek still hanging in the air, an acrid, burnt-wood odor that coiled itself around the core of a smell much worse. She looked on the passenger side and saw what appeared to be a small pile of clothing on the seat. Moving over to allow as much of the streetlight's glow as possible to stream through the car's window, she peered inside. A pair of jeans, a crumpled shirt and jockey shorts made an almost invisible mound, topped by Blake's wallet. Loafers kicked off in haste pointed accusingly at each other on the floor. The only thing missing, besides the man himself, was his Glock.

Jesus, no, she thought. Her mother's suicide, when Maureen was nine, had left in its wake a thin wire of terror that anyone she cared about could disappear at any time by their own hand. That wire thrummed as Maureen pushed away from the car and looked around frantically. She darted in front of the Mercedes, stopping at the edge of the concrete ped that cantilevered over the long drop to the sunken back yard, eyes straining in the pallid light of a waning quarter moon filtering through the branches of the towering oleanders. A soft splash drew her attention to where she knew the pool was. Slowly, the dark rectangle came into focus, separated from the surrounding black lawn by its framing flagstone deck. As her night vision adjusted, Maureen saw him.

Blake swam from one end of the huge pool to the other, barely making a sound except when he touched the wall and turned, pushing forcefully in the opposite direction. Moonlight glinted off each ghostly arm as it lifted, knifed into the water and pulled him toward some imagined finish line he would never cross. His long, pale back rotated up and out of the water with each stroke, but his buttocks and legs were only a shimmery blur beneath the surface.

Maureen stilled, counting the crossings. Twenty. Fifty. Somewhere shy of her count of one hundred, Blake failed to push off when he reached one end, pulling himself up from the water instead. Maureen was prepared to disappear if he headed up the embankment—the wooden stairs had burned with the house—but Blake sat on the flagstone and pulled his knees to his chest. She watched him wrap his arms around his knees, then tilt his head forward until it rested on them.

The only sound she heard was the admonishing shush of the evening breeze whispering past a million shivering leaves. It was soon joined by a low keening, the agonized moan of uncut human grief. Below, the nude man rocked back and forth in his solitary hell, while the woman above backed into the shadows and slipped away.

Maureen got into Keesha's car, closing the door silently. The key was already in her hand but she did not put it in the ignition, slamming herself, instead, against the seat back and headrest.

The first gasp was barely audible, but as her safety valve blew, Maureen's shoulders shook and she sobbed without restraint, smacking her open palm again and again on the caramel and sienna burl of the faux wood steering wheel.

Maureen hadn't come out of her room by the time Charlie left for Beverly Hills, but he chalked it up to her ongoing funk about the fire three weeks ago. He knew she missed working with Blake every day and was hurt that he had not contacted her. Charlie understood—even if his daughter did not—that it might be a long time before Blake was ready to reclaim his friends, job and what remained of his life.

Denice would arrive that afternoon and, although he wanted nothing more than to finally spend time alone with her, Charlie decided he'd ask Maureen to join them for dinner. Maybe take her mind off things for a short time.

On his way to Gerard Duval's, Charlie stopped by Maureen's old apartment building to pick up the rent checks from Max and Ethel. They had done as he requested and brought in a third roommate to replace Maureen, and were eager for Charlie to meet him. "I brought bagels," he announced, holding up the bag from Canter's as Max swung the door open.

"Charlie," Max crowed, exuberant as he always was. "How's it hangin'?"

"White and tight."

Charlie entered to find Ethel Rosen having coffee with a balding man of about forty-five. "Hi, Charlie," she chirped. "Meet Harold. Sheldon's youngest boy."

Harold stood to shake hands. "Nice to meet you, Charlie."

"Same here. You're dad is one of the best comedy writers I ever worked with."

"I'll go toast those bagels," Harold said, reaching for the bag.

Once he was out of the room, Ethel patted the couch for Charlie to join her. When he did, she lowered her voice to keep the conversation private. "Harold's a writer, too, but he isn't very good."

Max grunted down onto the side chair to join their chat. "Yeah, not much of a chip off the old block, if you catch my drip."

"Well, those are some mighty big shoes to fill and I'm sure it isn't easy being compared to a legend."

"But he got a job a few months ago," Ethel said. "A staff gig, so he could finally move out of his mother's condo."

"I mentioned the sweet rent set-up here," Max added, "and bada-boom, bada-bing, we got our third roomie. Speaking of rent." He pulled an envelope of his velour running suit and handed it to Charlie.

Harold's voice called out from the kitchen. "Who wants plain cream cheese and who wants chives?"

Charlie left before serious brunching began, not wanting to be held up. The engagement ring was finished and he couldn't wait to see it. The second project was done, too, and it was perfect. Tomorrow he would propose again to Denice.

In Nevada, Denice Cantrell packed clothes for the weekend, still not sure how she felt about the irrevocable decision she had made the day before. She hadn't seen Charlie since the black-tie gala more than a month ago, and before that they'd only known each other for six weeks. Maybe what they'd had was never real, only the embodiment of the hope she had carried through most of her forty-nine years—that someone, someday, would cherish her.

Granted, she'd been the one to cancel several trips to LA, but she hadn't had much of a choice after Cindy quit. Then Charlie had punked out twice, leaving her in an uncomfortable limbo. Denice would terminate that limbo this weekend.

Maureen padded into the kitchen for coffee, finding the chipper note from Charlie saying he'd be back around lunch time. Her eyes were still puffy from last night's crying jag, her red-gold hair was a shoulder-length rat's nest, and she generally looked and felt like hell. Wrapping her hands around the hot mug, she closed her eyes and tried to find her way through the maze of emotions.

First, she was losing her dad. He would propose to the cheeseburger queen tomorrow, and if Denice had a brain in her head she'd say yes. All Maureen had heard about for the past week was the canary yellow diamond that was the center stone of the ring Charlie would dangle in front of Denice like a million bucks worth of bait to catch a two-dollar fish.

Even as Maureen entertained the uncharitable thoughts, she knew she was being a selfish brat. She had never seen her father happier than he had been since he'd met Denice.

Then there was Jane's death. Maureen had liked her; she really had. They weren't exactly BFF's, but the foundation was there for a potential friendship, something Maureen had never experienced with a woman. Growing up around a bunch of middle-aged comedy writers—all male—Maureen had not been expected to share feelings or offer support. All she had to do to belong to *that* club was curse like a sailor, keep up with the flying zingers, and learn to crack wise on her own.

Jane had turned out to be more interesting and complex than Maureen would have guessed when they met. It might have been nice to have a female friend. Maybe that's why Maureen was eaten-up with guilt about her feelings for Blake.

She had found him attractive from the start, but when she learned about the girlfriend a few days later, she shelved any thoughts of partnership beyond two cops riding together. And when the girlfriend became his fiancée and then wife, well, that was that.

Now Jane was gone. Maureen had believed any inchoate romantic feelings for Blake had faded away months before, but here she was feeling very wrong things about a man whose life had disintegrated.

She thought about the motorcycle ride in Tujunga, Blake's chest pressed against her back, his arms around her. He certainly wasn't the first guy she'd taken out on the Vincent, but he *was* the first one who hadn't jammed his junk up against her ass. Blake had maintained a discreet several inches between them below the belt, proof of his innate decency and the seriousness with which he took his wedding vows.

He was everything Maureen wasn't: honest, good and free of sin, so she knew even if Jane had never been part of his life, Blake would have been off limits.

When she signed up, Maureen had been too young

to understand the price she would be required to pay to fulfill the obligations of her work with the CIA, and by the time she knew the personal cost it was too late. She had crossed an invisible line, mortgaging her soul beyond redemption. Charlie knew what she had done multiple times, and still loved her. You had to love your own kid, right?

Blake had a vague idea about her dark past, and he *seemed* to have accepted it. If things between them ever heated up, however, how long would it take him to see her for the soiled, flawed specimen she knew herself to be? How long before he threw that in her face during an argument?

No flag-waving, America-first, anti-terror bullshit changed the fact that Maureen had been a hired killer. And when you take human lives deliberately, you join a very small club whose members you might not want to associate with, but it is only among their ranks you can ever hope to find a partner who won't bust your balls for what you have done. Or even worse, turn away from you in disgust.

Unless you're prepared to lie about your past. Too late for that; Blake already knew.

Unless you're prepared to live with the risk your chosen one might someday turn on you, decide late in the game to try you on criminal charges for which you are already serving time.

Blake would never willingly cross that moral line Maureen had stepped over years ago. Jane's purity, goodness, sweetness would form the yardstick by which he would measure all future women in his life, and Maureen knew she couldn't hope to compete.

The self-loathing was rudely interrupted by her cell phone rendition of *The Brothers Gunn* theme, so she yanked her own chain and put her glib on. "O'Brien Finial Finishers. Can we polish your knob?"

It was Keesha, reminding Maureen today was Friday and someone needed to sign seventeen paychecks.

Seventeen?! Maureen learned that while she was AWOL and Blake was grieving, Keesha had won another security contract for E&O Investigations.

Dominic Briggs expected Micah to arrive any minute for his Friday morning AAS injection and he intended to regain total control over his resident loose cannon. Dominic had met with his council of three earlier and they had all agreed the way to guarantee Micah didn't do or say anything to jeopardize all their hard work was to bring him into the loop, make him part of the team. That way he would have as much to lose as they did and might be persuaded to modify his recent jacked behavior. Or at least see the wisdom of cutting back on the meth.

The other three didn't know Micah had murdered Cody Mason, and Dominic needed to keep it that way. It wouldn't take a genius to figure out Micah didn't have the brains to have planned it himself, and then it would be a short leap to realize who had pulled the strings. That knowledge *could* give someone leverage over Briggs, a situation he would not allow to happen.

No, if they were all neck deep in the same game, everyone would have a vested interest in staying quiet. It was time for the so-called head of Pinnacle Pictures to find out what was happening on Stage Three. And what Dominic and his boys had done to that detective's wife. It was a risky choice, but the only one they had.

In the Pinnacle gym Capt. Luther Hardy did his last burning set of lat pulldowns, oily sweat beading on the muscular ridges of his back. His mind drifted back to 'Nam, to leading his men on those rain-soaked jungle strikes against the Viet Cong. To the feel of his bayonet ramming home between that dirty gook's ribs.

Oh, yeah. Soup's almost done.

As Maureen showered, she decided to make a run up to Tujunga after she signed paychecks. She and Blake both had misgivings about the handling of Cody Mason's murder and weren't convinced Frank Goodwin had done it. They had gotten sidetracked by the Bates brothers last time and hadn't made their little foray onto the Pinnacle lot. If Maureen could scrounge a bit of intel, she'd have a nice gift to hand Blake when he rejoined the living.

On the back porch of Artie Lassiter's Santa Monica home, Blake stared at what was left of Jane's ring. Artie had picked it up in Hollywood and brought it to him an hour ago. The heart-shaped diamond she had loved so much was intact, but was now wrapped in the melty grip of the reconfigured rose-gold setting.

For twenty-one days he had made no decisions. The burial had been in West Virginia because, when he called to tell Jane's parents what had happened, Janice Larsen asked to have her daughter brought home. Artie had booked the flights and the room at the Cobalt Motel. Even the clothes he wore were not purchases of his own; Charlie O'Brien had sent them over.

Looking at the pink diamond, recalling how Jane's eyes had lit up when she held it, Blake made his first decision in three weeks, the kind of decision a man only makes when in extremis.

He would take the ring to the nearest jeweler and have the remains of the setting detached from the stone. Then he would have the tiny heart put on a chain he could wear around his neck for the rest of his life, a reminder over his own heart of the woman he had loved.

The Blind Pig was nearly empty, the hard-drinking lunchers having started at 11:00 A.M. and staggered out by 2:30, and the hard-drinking supper crowd not due until 4:00. Those few hardy souls who liked drunklunch to ease into drunksupper, nodded over their steins or shot glasses.

Fluffy Bennigen sat on the customer side of his bar eating a late lunch of The Pig's interpretation of boneless hot wings. As he picked up a deep-fried clump, he bit through almost an inch of crispy batter and spat it into the wax paper-lined plastic serving basket, unveiling the match stick of chicken cradled in its lard-and-carb sarcophagus.

At least Fluffy *hoped* it was chicken. The guy who delivered it claimed it was, but Fluffy had once taken a look inside the back of the refrigerated van and seen a couple traps big enough to hold a badger.

Deftly, he plucked out the sliver of—well, let's just say "meat" to be on the safe side—and popped it into his mouth. As Fluffy prepared to excavate the next fist-sized clod for its tiny treasure, he saw Maureen O'Brien walk in, her shapely little body backlit by the bright afternoon sun for that few seconds before the door closed behind her. Not for the first time, he thought: God, if she wasn't Charlie's kid, followed immediately by: and if I wasn't a seventy-four year old with a dick that's been nothing more than a water-spout for the last decade.

"Obi-Wan," he said in greeting.

"Hey, Fluff, you got a minute?" she asked, sliding onto the stool next to him.

"The doc says I got six whole months, so fire

away." When he saw the look of alarm on her face, he realized the joke hadn't been very good. "Kidding. I'm still in remission." He knocked twice on a bar surface that was as far removed from wood as his wings were from chicken. "What's up?"

Her questions about Pinnacle Pictures brought no new information. Fluffy was aware of the studio only seven or eight miles north of The Blind Pig, but said the folks on the lot mostly kept to themselves, didn't patronize the local watering holes.

Once in a while a crew from back east would wrap their day of shooting some dog food or Greek yogurt commercial and head into the Tujunga bars for drinks before going back to their various motels and motor lodges for the night, but all they talked about was the usual advertising/showbiz/production blah-blah-blah.

Without even a shred of gossip to show for her trip, Maureen tried a different angle. "You ever see a couple of good ol' boys named Dallis and Ostin Bates drinking in here?"

Fluffy snorted dismissively before allowing as how once upon a time those two assholes were tolerated at The Pig, but that was before he had walked into the shitter and found one of them trying to off-load a bag of crack to a former jailbird. And no, he hadn't been shocked to hear about their trailer lab getting busted a couple weeks back. "By the by, they bonded out."

So, Micah's suppliers were back on the street. Maureen wondered if they would try to set up and cook somewhere else.

Ed Vick of Vick's Jewelry, Pawn and Consignment wasn't surprised to see the homeless man enter his shop late Friday afternoon. Almost every day street people wandered in with shiny objects they had picked up off the ground, sometimes nothing more than a silver gum wrapper. They held their pathetic finds out to Ed, hoping for a few dollars, and he almost always "appraised" the goods at enough for a sub sandwich or a hamburger.

What the tall, gaunt man showed Ed, however, was a genuine, fancy-cut diamond. Way out of Ed's league and worth maybe a couple hundred grand. Ed Vick humored the guy as he described what he wanted, then said he would go in the back and bring out a nice selection of chains to choose from.

A short time later, Blake Ervansky was roughly cuffed by two officers from the Santa Monica PD.

To be fair to Ed Vick and the arresting officers, Blake hadn't bathed in a week, unless you count pool water. His clothes looked like they'd been slept in (they had), he couldn't produce a receipt for the diamond, and the stubble on his face owed more to Mickey Rourke than Bradley Cooper.

His one phone call was to Artie Lassiter.

Capt. Luther Hardy woke up. No, no, it was Micah. He shook his head, trying to sort out the memories. Vietnam slowly became Hawaii. A strong thirty-two resolved into a tired fifty-eight. Cody was alive. Wait, maybe he was dead.

That realization was shoved down immediately, buried again where Micah didn't have to face what he had done. But it didn't matter how much crystal he smoked, how deep he pushed the memory down, the truth kept crawling out of its grave. Micah had killed his best friend, his business partner, his brother. Why? Dominic said—what was it again Dom had said? Why was it Cody had to die? No, forget it. The past is the past. Focus on the now, the movie, the rebooted career.

And yesterday. How could he have forgotten

about them shooting that woman in the head, burning her body? Dom said Micah was there, Micah knew. Said Micah knew about the other, too. Why couldn't he remember? Thank God for Dom. He kept track of things, just like Cody used to.

Cody. Oh, Christ. That knife ramming into his scrawny little body. Wait, wait. Luther remembered now. It wasn't Cody. It was some dirty gook. They had splashed around in that rice paddy until Luther shoved the bayonet in. The pipe. Where's my pipe?

Charlie O'Brien woke up happy. A glance to his left confirmed what he had dreamed all night, that Denice Cantrell was in his house, in his bed, in his life. And today he would seal the deal.

Slipping quietly out of the covers so as not to wake her—she so rarely had the chance to sleep in—Charlie pulled on yesterday's jeans and padded off to the kitchen to make coffee. Maureen perched on a stool at the island, wearing her usual sleep ensemble of tank top and boxer shorts, this pair featuring Tweety Bird and Sylvester. He saw the cup in front of her. "Hey, thanks for making the coffee."

"I figured you two might not be up for a while. Otherwise engaged, don'cha know." She shot him a knowing, undaughterly smirk.

"Mind out of the gutter, snipe," he said, reaching for a mug. "I wouldn't *dream* of having carnal relations with a lady to whom I had not already plighted my troth."

"So, today the big day?"

Charlie nodded while pouring his coffee. "I will propose on the sidewalk along Ventura Boulevard between Hazeltine and Van Nuys."

"And is it the pushy pedestrians, the noisy traffic or the ground fog of carbon monoxide that you think will cinch an affirmative?"

He smiled at her over the rim of his mug and was about to make a quip when something slammed hard against the front door, jolting the two of them.

"What the hell?" Charlie said, setting down his coffee mug. The loud slam repeated and, as he and Maureen hurried down the short hall to the foyer, it picked up both speed and intensity, like a lunatic smacking his hands against the wall of a cell.

Charlie got to the door first and looked through the peephole. "It's Blake." Maureen unlocked the door and swung it open, her father barely moving back in time to get out of the way. She had waited almost a month for her partner to reconnect with her, to begin plugging in to his life again.

But Blake wasn't there for Maureen, and he blew right by her, slamming his open hands hard into Charlie's chest, sending the older man staggering backwards.

"Hey!" Maureen shouted, rushing to intervene. She was stopped by the hand Charlie put up at her before he had even regained his balance.

"You son of a bitch!" Blake shouted, slamming Charlie's chest again. This time, though, Charlie was ready, taking a step back to lessen the impact, putting up both hands to show he wasn't going to fight.

"Blake, what the fuck do you think you're doing?" Maureen demanded.

But she was ignored and cut-off by Blake's laser-focus on Charlie. "You always have to be the big shot, don't you? Always have to dick around with other people's lives."

Maureen couldn't understand what was going on. Why was Blake so angry with her father? Why didn't Charlie say something? But Charlie knew nothing he could say would quell the storm raging in Blake, so he stood and let the younger man's fury play itself out.

"The one thing, the one *goddamned thing* I have left of Jane and I find out I didn't even buy it for her! *You* did! Were you two laughing about it behind my back? 'Poor, pathetic Ervansky. Can't even afford a decent ring. We'll step in and take up the slack.' And your stooge of a jeweler must've been yucking it up over this one."

Maureen looked from her partner to her father, realizing what Charlie must have done, tensing when Blake moved in close to snarl in Charlie's face.

"Newsflash, Charlie, I'm *keeping* the diamond. And I'm going to pay you back every last dime of that money. I don't care if I have to flip burgers, scrub toilets or live in a crate."

The open hand became a fist with an extended index finger that jabbed into Charlie's sternum. "I don't care if it takes me the next fifty years to pay it off, but someday, *someday*, I'll know it was *me* who made her happy!"

Blake abruptly withdrew, turning and leaving without another word. Maureen noticed a bewildered Denice, wearing a sky-blue peignoir and standing on the side of the foyer leading back to the bedroom.

Charlie stepped forward and gently pushed the door closed, muffling the slam of a car door and the squeal of tires. "Well," he said, addressing the two women. "I guess we know which stage of grief *he's* in."

While Charlie and Denice had a quiet breakfast in the kitchen, Maureen stomped around her bedroom, a swarm of "how-dare-he's" buzzing in her mind. Most were Blake-centric: how dare he attack my father; how dare he storm in here and ignore me. But some had to do with Charlie, and those were the ones that would have devastated her, had she let them come front and center in her thoughts.

Aiming her anger at Blake was easier than questioning why her father had spent more than two hundred thousand dollars on a ring for Jane. She was gradually—if not graciously—coming to accept that she would be taking a back seat to Denice in Charlie's affection, but she could not wrap her brain around the idea that, had Jane lived, Maureen might have been relegated to the number three position.

No, much easier to mentally savage Blake, even realizing she was angry with him for doing precisely what she would do if she let her thoughts run wild: blame Charlie for the generosity he showed everyone.

Not willing to deal with her own pettiness—after all, Maureen had been the primary beneficiary of that generosity for nearly twenty-eight years—or the disturbing idea she might be jealous of her father's feelings for a woman who was now dead, she aimed her fire power at Blake.

A smile of amusement crept in, however, when she wondered how Charlie was explaining to Denice why he'd bought an engagement ring for someone else.

Blowing up about the ring was the first sign of life Blake had shown since the fire, and Artie had been hopeful when he saw his ex-partner react to the information about the pink diamond's worth last night. From firsthand experience, Artie knew this anger was the initial baby step back toward normal.

The second step was reclaiming personal hygiene, so Artie had been relieved to see Blake head for the shower after he returned from his confrontation with Maureen's father. And the shower was still running fifteen minutes later. It takes time to scrub off that much indignation and humiliation—not to mention more than a weeks' worth of body odor.

Artie's cell phone rang and he wasn't surprised when he saw the name on the screen. "Lassiter."

"Artie, it's Maureen."

"He can't come to the phone right now."

"I have no desire to speak with him. I'm calling so you can tell him we're going to have a third car here very soon, so we need his crap out of our garage."

Whoa! Apparently Ervansky wasn't the *only* one all pissy today. "How much crap we talking about?"

"Two trips with an SUV, one with a small truck."

"Okay, I'll set it up for Monday morning. You gonna be around at 10:00 or 11:00?"

"I'll tell the housekeeper to open the garage for you," she stated flatly.

Artie sighed. He really didn't feel qualified to deal with more than one person's bullshit at a time, but she was obviously hurting in her own way as much as Blake. "Thanks. And O'Brien? He's doing better."

Artie waited through the long pause, then heard her waffle off with a stiff: "Well, I'm happy for him."

As he put the cell phone back in his pocket, he realized he could no longer hear the shower running. Then the bathroom door opened a crack and Blake called out, "Hey, Lassiter? Where do you hide the shaving cream?"

Charlie tugged Denice through the crowded mid-day foot traffic along Ventura Boulevard. "We only ate breakfast a little while ago," she protested. "I'm not sure I could eat another bite no matter *how* good the food is at this place."

But Charlie wasn't taking her to the lunch he had fabricated. He stopped in front of a small junk-slash-antiques shop on the south side of the busy road that bifurcated the San Fernando Valley, then looked all around. Traffic whizzed by, tourists ambled and a bus idling across the street emitted malodorous diesel farts. It was perfect.

Letting go of Denice's hand, while simultaneously drawing out a small velvet box from his pocket, Charlie lowered himself to one knee, getting approving nods from women, and you've-got-to-be-kidding looks from men, as the tide of pedestrians parted and went around the romantic tableau. The only face Charlie focused on, though, was Denice's.

"Damn, but I love you, girl, and if you say the word, I'll spend the rest of my life proving it. By the way, that word is *yes*." He flipped open the lid of the tiny box, revealing the ring he had designed himself.

Three tiers of brilliant-cut, VVSI white diamonds surrounded the main stone, descending in size as they fell away—15 points closest to the middle, 10 points in the next circle, and two dozen 5-point sparklers at the outer rim. In the noonday sun, their hundreds of facets threw fire in all directions. The hair-fine prongs of yellow gold that held each perfect stone in place contributed their own satiny gleam to the piece, but it was the breathtaking jewel in the center that caught your attention.

At almost 129 carats, the Tiffany Diamond is the largest, finest canary diamond in existence and, side-by-side, would dwarf the 4-carat gem at the heart of Charlie's offering, but he had searched the world for an uncut stone that matched the deep golden yellow of The Tiffany. Unlike its bigger, cushion-cut cousin, the diamond Charlie held out had no facets. He had commissioned it to be cut cabochon-style, its round shape doming up gently to intensify the sunny glow at its heart, and giving the piece the look of a medieval tribute for a beloved queen.

Unable to speak, and with tears spilling over with love for his man, Denice nodded, then extended her trembling hand. As he slipped the exquisite ring on her finger, he said, "Madame, I present you with the one-of-a-kind jewel to be known henceforward as The Cheeseburger Diamond."

The crowd of people that had gathered behind Denice broke into applause. Charlie stood, but instead of giving her the kiss she was expecting, he waved to silence the applause, then spoke at Denice like an infomercial pitchman. "But wait! There's more!"

With his arm around her waist, he turned to look across Ventura Boulevard at the idling bus stinking-up the air with diesel fumes. He raised his hand, and when he dropped it the gathered crowd joined him in their pre-rehearsed chant.

"MOVE! THAT! BUS!"

Blake's angry attack had changed everything for Maureen. No more waiting around for her partner to get his head back in the game. Monday morning she'd go into E&O Investigations and start kicking ass and taking names. *Some*body had to keep the place afloat. She had already left a message on the office phone for Keesha to see if she could track down that missing whistle blower through his phone number. And there were several other pending investigations into which she could throw herself.

But right now it was Saturday and she had nothing to do, no one to be with. Charlie was up in the valley "plighting his troth," Blake was off being an asshole, and she had already made her bitchy phone call to Artie. Maureen decided since she'd made such a big deal about getting Blake's stuff out of the garage, she should probably go make sure it was stacked and ready for pickup.

Boxes and paint cans were haphazardly scattered at the far end of the three-car garage, evidence of how thrilled that driver had been about making an extra stop, so Maureen started organizing. She grouped the one-gallon cans of paint in a cluster up front, nearest to the garage door. Next, she dragged over a long, heavy box labeled wallpaper, but when she let it drop heavily onto the concrete behind the paint cans, the seam of the flimsy cardboard container split open and the tightly wound cylinder of wallpaper rolled out.

Maureen stared at the pattern. Teddy bears and bunnies looked back at her with big, happy eyes set in furry faces. Her own eyes darted to the paint cans as she realized they were all pastels: lemon yellow, baby blue, pale pink. She turned toward the two largest cartons, finally noticing the words stencilled on them. *Changing table. Crib set.*

The sudden elopement now made sense. Maureen sank to the concrete floor in shock, one hand on the playful wallpaper. Jane had been pregnant.

The huge bus passed gas one last noisy time, then pulled out of its noxious cloud to join the other motorized lemmings heading west. As Charlie held tight to Denice's hand, she experienced the reveal of a diner on the opposite side of Venture Boulevard—a replica of the one back in Madison, Nevada. The word "west" followed Dolly's Diner on the sign, but otherwise, the exterior was identical.

"Oh, my God," she had time to blurt out, before Charlie jaywalked her through a break in the traffic to the other side. Once across, Charlie opened the door, then made a bow and a sweeping hand gesture to invite her inside. Denice stepped into a newer, fresher incarnation of the diner she had run for more than a decade and immediately recognized the only other person there besides Charlie.

"Surprise!" punk Cindy shouted.

"Don't be mad at her," Charlie said before Denice could react. "It was all my idea and I bribed her to quit and come help me set up everything. All the permits and licenses are in place, so all you have to do is order the food."

"Charlie—" Denice began.

"Cindy can be back there on a plane tomorrow," he interrupted. "She'll manage the mother ship and you can run this one. Your only real competition is Fatburger a few blocks away, but if—"

Denice finally stopped the flow of words by grabbing Charlie's ears and kissing him. "Shh, quit babbling," she said when she released him.

Cindy and Charlie watched as Denice's eyes took in the room. The booths, tables, chairs, even the napkin holders were spot-on; Cindy had done her homework and deserved the managerial position back in Madison. Deserved it, but wouldn't get it.

"Oh, Charlie," Denice said, sadness in her voice. "You have to get that sign taken down ASAP. There's never going to be a Dolly's Diner West. And Cindy can't run the one in Madison because the mother ship is gone."

"What?!" If Charlie was shocked, then Cindy was devastated. She darted her eyes toward the man who had promised her she'd still have a job when this was over, a job with better pay. They both turned at the sound of Denice's laugh.

She had sat in one of the familiar booths and was looking fondly at the laminated, one-sheet menu. Her gentle laugh quickly rolled into a raucous outburst, the kind you have when you are desperately trying to hold something in. Her shoulders shook and her eyes squeezed shut, while Cindy and Charlie nervously watched.

"I sold it," Denice choked out between gasps of

snorting laughter. "I'm now contractually barred from using the name on a business, and I can never make my cheeseburger recipe again."

Maureen sat on her bed, scanning the pages of the medical examiner's report, searching for the words she only half-recalled from her initial reading of the document. When she found them, she took a sharp breath and closed her eyes.

As she let the breath out and opened her eyes, she picked up a highlighter and leaned forward to spread neon sunshine over the two words that changed everything: *menstruating female*.

Jane was alive.

Cindy chewed the cuticle of her thumbnail in a very un-punklike way as she watched Charlie and Denice talk quietly in a booth across the diner. It had all sounded like such a romantic, wonderful idea when he approached her a month ago. As a single mother without a GED, Cindy knew a chance to manage an ongoing business would give her the security most other girls in her situation only dream of.

Charlie had virtually guaranteed her she would manage Dolly's Diner in Madison if he got a yes on his proposal. And on the outside chance the answer was no, he had said he would be her money man while she got Dolly's Diner West up and running. It had been presented in a way that sounded like she couldn't lose.

Neither had anticipated Denice's selling of Dolly's, along with the recipe for the second best cheeseburger in America (according to the Food Channel).

In the booth, meanwhile, Denice absently stroked the smooth, convex surface of The Cheeseburger Diamond as she told Charlie the whole story.

She had turned down five million dollars, but then

began worrying she was losing Charlie after four consecutive weekends cancelled—two by her, two by him. So, when the corporation that had made the original offer came back last week with a figure of *seven* million, Denice had pulled the trigger, hoping he still wanted her. "I love you, Charlie, and I want to marry you, but I'm not sure I'm cut out to be a lady of leisure. I've earned my own living since I was sixteen."

"We'll get this thing up and running under a different name, then Cindy'll handle the day-to-day operation and you can participate as much or as little as you like."

She looked down at the beautiful ring, aware now that her stroking finger had smudged the surface of the golden-yellow center stone. As she pulled a paper napkin from the dispenser and polished away traces of body oil dulling the diamond, she shook her head. "It wouldn't be the same without the recipe. That was the one thing in my life I ever did that set me apart, made me special."

Charlie disagreed, but said nothing. He reached across to take both her hands, not caring if a million-dollar diamond got a little schmutz on it. He wanted to protect this jewel of a woman, instead. His mind raced as he rewrote their script. If he were crafting this scene as the ending of a romantic comedy, how would he save it? How would he push the star-crossed lovers past their Gift-of-The-Magi impasse and into a happily-ever-after?

Charlie O'Brien had written hundreds of hours of television, had come up with tricky, satisfying plot endings for sitcoms and cop dramas, and he knew TV writers never have the luxury of slacking off until an unpredictable muse delivers inspiration. As he had explained to more than a few classes of aspiring young scribes, sitting with your thumb up your butt doesn't get you anywhere. Like a shark, you've got to keep moving forward.

So, as he had always done with *Dewey's View*, *The Badge* and *The Brothers Gunn*, Charlie came up with a fix. "Tell me *exactly* what the contract says about your secret recipe."

Denice was alerted by his change of demeanor, but didn't know what he was excited about. "Don't get your hopes up; it's right there in legal mumbo-jumbo. I can never make that recipe and sell the product for profit again."

"Yes!" he shouted, pulling one hand away from hers and pumping it in the air. Cindy watched from across the room, hoping this was an indication her future would not be as bleak as she had been imagining for the last half hour.

"Charlie, what?"

"Okay, here's the deal. I'm very rich. Maybe not Warren Buffet rich, but definitely *Jimmy* Buffet rich. And now you're a millionairess, so the bottom line is neither of us *needs* to make any money."

"But I told you I'm not sure I want to sit around doing nothing just because I can suddenly afford to."

"Oh, you're not going to be eating bon-bons and reading bodice-rippers, doll. In fact, you'll be working your sweet ass off, making those cheeseburgers and *giving* them away. Free. Gratis. No charge, Sarge.

Over the next ten minutes, with Cindy invited into their enthusiastic pitch session, they laid out plans for what would soon become C&D Diner, a place with no prices on the menu and no requirement to pay. A donation box would be set up near the door, and those who could afford to pay would drop money inside, while those who couldn't would be able to leave with a full belly and their dignity intact.

Given Charlie's deep pockets, it was foolproof, an opportunity for some of the one percent to help out the ninety-nine percent. It was Denice's belief, though, that they'd break even, that the people who have would give generously to feed the ones who have not.

He said he'd call his attorney on Monday, but he was certain by giving the food away they'd be within the letter of the law. Charlie would turn out to be right about the contract, and Denice would be right about people's willingness to give. Against all odds, C&D Diner would turn a profit from day one.

Maureen couldn't prove Jane was alive; the only thing she *might* be able to say for sure was that it hadn't been Jane who died in the fire. Anxious as she was to bring some relief to Blake, she knew going off with only a fragment of the story might exacerbate his suffering, because if the crispy critter wasn't Jane, then she had been missing for twenty-two days.

She opened the top drawer of her desk and found the card of the Hollywood detective who had worked the fire scene and interviewed her. She jotted down his name and phone number, then tried to recall the name of the coroner's assistant who had let her view the body. Maureen came up blank, but knew she'd recognize him on sight, so she wrote down "morgue guy." The last name she put on her short list was Libby Johnson, whose home number she took from the laptop on Blake's side of the desk.

Maureen noted the time, a little past 2:00 o'clock. She would use the rest of the weekend to double-check the M.E.'s findings, learn where Hollywood was on the arson investigation, and see if Libby Johnson had turned up any likely suspects from Blake and Artie's old case files.

Keesha arrived at the office a couple minutes before 9:00 Monday morning and immediately took out the bag of super-premium coffee she kept locked in her desk drawer. Moving quickly to the kitchenette, she set up the coffee machine to brew the good stuff, then opened the cabinet and grabbed the bag of garden-variety java Blake and Maureen always bought. She took a Baggie, filled it with a few scoops of ho-hum, then stashed it in her purse. No reason she and Fran shouldn't put the coffee to good use at home.

Her tracks now covered, Keesha returned to her desk, locked away the primo grind and prepared to go to work. Her plan to rough out the schedules for the security guards she had hired was ditched when she picked up Maureen's phone message asking her to try to locate the whistle-blower who had never shown for their meeting.

Keesha called the man's number, but it was no longer in service. Turning to her computer, she then keyed in Lt. Rhee's old access code—which she knew he had transferred to Lt. Johnson—and searched for who had that number. Several minutes later she knew it was an untraceable burner, but she wasn't surprised. If I were ratting out a major corporation, she thought, I wouldn't use my regular phone, either.

Stymied about what to do next, she stared at the number, realizing she had seen it somewhere before. As she scanned her memory, Blake stormed in.

"Where's Maureen?" he barked. Keesha would have normally barked right back, but given his recent bereavement, she bit off her smart-ass rejoinder. "I expect her any minute. Can I get you some coffee?"

"Tell her I'm in the conference room," he said, as he strode through the archway at the rear of the lobby. While Keesha debated whether or not to bring him coffee, Maureen entered, a bag from Ziggy's in her hand and an eager look on her face.

"I saw Blake's car downstairs."

"Yeah, well don't get too giddy about his being here. He is P.O.'d with a capital F."

"Why?"

"He didn't say, but he's waiting for you in the conference room."

Leaving the deli bag on Keesha's desk, Maureen hurried through the archway and into the short hall bordered on her right by the conference room she and Blake referred to as the fishbowl.

He was staring out at the view of the LA basin, but turned at the sound of her entrance.

"Blake—"

"What the hell have you been doing?" he snarled, cutting her off.

"I don't know what you're talking about," Maureen said, taken aback by his ferocity.

"No? Here's a clue. I had a visit this morning from that cop out of Hollywood. Wanted to know if Jane and I were having any marital problems, if she owned a gun, if I knew any reason for her to fake her own death. He wanted to know about insurance we had on the house. And each other. So, what *exactly* have you been telling people?"

Maureen had thought her inquiries yesterday were subtle, never suspecting that idiot detective would suddenly start running with a Blake-and-Jane conspiracy theory, instead of adding the possibility of kidnapping to the arson and homicide angles.

"I'm sorry. I should have come to you first with the information."

"What information?"

Never one to use a pebble when a boulder was at hand, Maureen asked, "Was Jane pregnant when you got married?"

The shock on Blake's face changed into pain. "Jesus," he breathed, stunned that intimate details of his private life were being put into play. He sank into a chair with his shoulders slumped.

Maureen explained about discovering the baby furniture stored in Charlie's garage. She revealed the pertinent contents of the M.E.'s report that indicated the victim had been having her period when she died.

Blake tried to surface from the lake of grief in which he had been struggling not to drown, latching on to the lifeline Maureen was throwing out to him. For the first time since the fire he felt something other than pain or anger, and he asked her the questions a detective working the case would ask. Had Libby found any possibles from Artie's and his old busts? Was the M.E. positive about his findings?

Maureen provided what few answers she had gleaned from her weekend queries. Libby had pulled in several bottom-feeders who had run afoul of Blake when he was still a detective with the Beverly Hills PD, but nothing had panned out. Not one of them had the means, brains or motive to pull off something of this magnitude. Blake began to compartmentalize Jane, his wife, into the corner of his mind where he still curled up naked and howled with grief, differentiating her from Jane, the potential kidnap victim his law enforcement skills would have to home in on. And a thin, thin thread of hope linked the two.

As they spitballed on the big question—*who had motive to do this?*—Keesha entered, carrying a tray with three cups of coffee. "You two have a problem."

"It's all right, Keesh," Blake said, taking his cup. "We worked it out and we won't need a referee." They were the first light words he had spoken since the fire.

Ignoring him, Keesha sat at the table and put her own cup in front of her. "Maureen asked me to try to find our missing whistle-blower so she could pick up the case. The number he called from turned out to be a burner, so I couldn't trace him, but it rang a bell in my memory. Anyway, I cross-reffed it with numbers in the files Lt. Rhee had, plus all the ones active with Lt. Johnson."

"Did you get a match?" Blake asked.

"Yes and no. I can't tell you *who* has the number, but that same phone was used to point the cops in the direction of Frank Goodwin."

By 9:00 o'clock Monday morning, Briggs had been at work for hours. Rehearsals for *The Devil's Platoon* would begin next week, and shooting two weeks after that, so he ordered the flooding of K-6. Micah might never have been the highest-wattage bulb in the fixture, but he'd had the brilliant idea twelve years ago—when he and Cody first bought the land for Pinnacle Pictures—of doing specialized planting in a number of five-acre sections of the property. The studio was then able to offer low-cost "location" shoots for select geographical profiles. K-5 and K-6 were Louisiana bayou and sub-tropical Asia respectively. Cypress trees, water tupelo and dwarf palmetto bordered one mile of the man-made, two-mile-long river that ran through the two parcels, with rice paddies, bamboo and sedge flanking the other.

After barely a decade of growth, foliage in the specialized areas had not yet reached maturity, but was tall and dense enough to give verisimilitude to all but the longest camera shots. Post-production CGI filled in canopies and taller background greenery.

An underground water system maintained the lush vegetation of K-5 and K-6 year round, but pre-shoot flooding—mirroring the effects of hurricanes, monsoons and rainy seasons—would dramatically pop the green factor. When Dominic started directing the movie in a few weeks, rice paddies would be dense with shoots, vines would twine seductively on host trees, and the river would flow with the same brown, sluggish water as did its cousin across the globe.

Bookings for Stages One and Two were solid for the next month. A Christian rock group was making music videos for the two hits they expected from their next CD, and McCann-Erickson was halfway through their deeply discounted, eight-week booking, shooting commercials for a number of clients. Production on Stage Three hummed along as always.

Briggs was weary from spending the weekend as wing man and baby-sitter. He had been embarrassed to bull his way into clubs where the music made absolutely no sense to him and the sweet young things writhing on the dance floor were, literally, one-third his age. While Dom nursed a beer at the bar, Micah preened for the ladies—well, the girls—unaware they were laughing *at* him, not *with* him.

At last call, long after the prettiest ones had been whisked away, Micah and Dom gathered a few of the tired, the poor, the huddled lasses and brought them back to the mansion.

Dom poured liberally for the gals, hoping a large intake of premium-label beverages would dull their memories of what had *not* happened with action-hero Micah. And, fans being fans, they could be counted on to lord it over their sisters in star-fucking, inventing tales of prodigious size, screamy sex, tender promises.

When dawn neared and Micah was so wasted he was likely to soil his pants, Briggs called for cabs, then gently herded those unsmelled blossoms into their rides, discreetly tucking a couple hundreds into the purse or pocket of each one—an avuncular gesture done in such a way as to make each girl feel less like a drunken hooker and more like a favorite niece. He wanted no ill-will from anyone who might be tempted to go to the tabloids.

Afternoons, Briggs had gone over the details of the shooting and fire again and again until Micah began boldly boasting of his part in it, too dim-witted and too meth-addled to realize he hadn't known about the fire until afterwards. Dominic didn't dare go so far as to lead Micah to believe he had put the bullet in the back of the woman's head himself, but he counted on the muscled oaf to get there on his own. If complicity in a murder and an arson didn't temper Micah's behavior, nothing would.

The news over the weekend offered nothing more on Cody Mason's murder, but Dominic assumed the legal system was trudging ahead on its mandate to convict Frank Goodwin and put him away for life.

He had no qualms about setting-up Goody to take the fall. When Dom had been seeking representation for *Three Fists of Steel*, that son of a bitch had told him the script was laughable, a total piece of shit.

Yeah? Who's the piece of shit now, asshole?

It wasn't much of a jumping-off point, but it was enough to reanimate Blake. If the same cell had been used to phone in the tip that led to Frank Goodwin's arrest *and* to lure him away from his house long enough for it to be torched, might it have been used for something else? They left Keesha with the task of bringing their storyboard to the office from Charlie's house, then went to call on their favorite paparazzo.

They were in the bar at Casa Vega when Greg Wartham arrived, but they waited until he had ordered his lunch before sliding into the booth from either side, trapping him as they had on their first encounter.

"Hi," Maureen said brightly. "Remember us?"

Of course, he remembered. He had stiffed them for two grand on some worthless recordings. Praying the two weren't here to get their money back, he cautiously responded. "Sure."

"We need some more information," Blake said.

Greg relaxed. *They aren't here to shake me down for the cash?* Relief turned instantly to calculation: they'd paid a fortune for absolutely nothing last time; how much could he squeeze out of them now? "Well, I *am* the info guy. What are you looking for?"

The red-haired knockout asked him if he kept records of his phone tips, and Greg went all coy on her. "Sometimes," he answered, with what he hoped was a mysterious smile. The smile turned to a grimace of pain as Maureen's hand snaked under the table and put a death-grip on Greg's prides and joy. Then, before he could pull his own hands away from his beer and prevent her from neutering him, the tall guy jabbed something hard into his ribs.

"Keep those hands on the table," Blake said, as Greg gasped. "I guess we haven't made ourselves clear. If you don't want the cops to know about those recordings you made *very* illegally, you're going to tell us what we want."

"Jee-*zuss*! Make her let go!"

Blake nodded at Maureen, who eased up the nut cracking but left her hand in place to remind him what kind of hurt was only a split-second away if he got cute.

"Now," said Blake, pulling back the finger that had stood in for the Glock he wasn't carrying. "We're looking for the number on that phone tip you got on March twenty-fifth. The one about the extra-marital partying supposedly going on at Micah's house that night."

Greg Wartham *did* keep a list of all incoming tip numbers, mostly so he wouldn't fall for the bad ones a second time. He walked them out to his car, where he retrieved his iPad and found the number they wanted.

Blake and Maureen were not surprised that it matched the number used by their fake whistle-blower and the one that had led police to the knife behind the dumpster at Frank Goodwin's condo building. While they still had Greg's full attention, they asked him how he had gotten his listening devices into the house in the first place.

"Hey, don't go looking to pin a B&E on me. I got approached by one of his housekeeping staff, a girl named Rosa."

"How long ago?" Blake asked.

"Maybe a week, ten days, before Micah's agent was killed."

Maureen and Blake exchanged a knowing glance. Then she asked, "Rosa have a last name?"

"Probably. Only she didn't share it with me. She met me at the house one night after the staff was gone for the day and Micah was at a club. I stuck a half-dozen bugs where I thought I'd catch the best stuff, paid Rosa her fifty bucks and was out of there in less than an hour. You mind if I go have my lunch now?"

Blake and Maureen began putting it together the next day. He had spent a rough night balancing hope against skepticism where Jane was concerned. If—*big* if—the woman who died in the fire wasn't Jane, then the logical conclusion was that whoever did the execution and arson had taken her. But where? And why?

He set aside his fears as a husband, fears about her being in the hands of someone brutal enough and calculating enough to pull off the crime. Instead,

Blake thought analytically, the way he always had as a police detective. First, gather as many facts as you can. Follow where they lead and invariably you make a good arrest.

He and Maureen put cards on their storyboard, not sure what the three separate calls from the same unidentified phone meant, but realizing they formed an initial tenuous connection between Cody Mason's murder and the torching of Blake's house.

The next two orders of business were to find out why Micah's employee would risk her job for a lousy fifty dollars and to conclusively rule out Jane as the shooting victim.

Keesha wasn't overjoyed about having to wear a maid's uniform, but she promised to be at the bus stop down the road from Micah's place that evening when his housekeeping staff left for the day.

There were no dental records to exclude Jane as the woman who had died in the fire. Like millions of American kids growing up below the poverty line, she had received virtually no dental care throughout her childhood. Waitressing to put herself through college had barely covered books and food, so even routine check-ups were out of reach. And as a second-year kindergarten teacher at a public school, Jane made only a modest starting salary, much of which she regularly sent back to her family in West Virginia.

That left DNA identification. Nothing of Jane's had survived the fire to provide a comparison with the DNA of the victim.

Blake called the medical examiner, acting the part of widower, rather than cop, and confirmed there *was* DNA from the woman who had died. Having heard many relatives grasp at improbable straws during his career, the M.E. was gentle with Blake, promising only that he would run the results if a family member could be found to provide sample DNA.

It was late afternoon and Blake did not relish making that call to Jane's mother, so he put if off until tomorrow. By then Keesha might have befriended Rosa and found another piece of the puzzle. As they prepared to close up their office for the night, Maureen hesitated. "I know you're all settled in with Artie, but if you two start getting sick of each other, well, we set up a room for you weeks ago. Just in case."

Blake wasn't ready to face Charlie again after the scene he'd made at the house. "Thanks. Tell Charlie I appreciate it and I'll let you guys know."

Keesha was too late. When she pulled into the underground lot a few minutes before 9:00 Tuesday morning, she saw two Mercedes' taking up half the allotted spaces of E&O Investigations. And when she walked into the office she could already smell coffee. Leaving her purse on her desk, she went back to the kitchenette cum break room.

Blake and Maureen took up what space there was in the glorified alcove, so Keesha stopped in the doorway and crossed her arms over her chest, assuming a confrontational stance. "So whose bright idea was it to try to do *my* job?"

"It won't happen again," Blake said, wrinkling his nose at the coffee in his cup.

"Yeah, what do you use anyway?" Maureen asked. "Some kind of bottled water, a special filter or what?"

Keesha snorted. "Like I'm giving away my secrets to you two so you can ease me right on out of here."

She took their cups, shoo'd them from the room, and said she would meet them in the fishbowl with fresh coffee and a report on Rosa.

Blake and Maureen studied the few filled-in cards up on the big board while they waited. The numerous remaining blanks reminded them they were a long way from figuring out what was going on and who was behind it. Keesha entered, carrying a tray with three cups of coffee.

"So," Blake said, turning from the board, "were you able to talk to her?"

"No, because Rosa is gone. *Supposedly* back to Guatemala to open her own dressmaking business."

"Supposedly?" asked Blake.

"Well, she shared an apartment with three other maids, and none of them has more money than the pitiful salaries their wealthy employers pay." She then repeated what the head housekeeper had been eager to share at the bus stop and on the long ride to east LA. Rosa, a girl none of them knew to have ever purchased a lottery ticket before, must have decided to spend a few dollars and try her luck, because she recently showed the other maids a winning lottery ticket for fourteen million dollars.

They had all looked in the newspaper to double-check the numbers before congratulating Rosa on her good fortune. "She showed off the ticket on Thursday, April 26th, then told them all she was thinking about going back to Guatemala. She also promised to give each of the other women on staff ten thousand dollars when she collected her money."

"And did she?" Blake asked.

"Rosa never showed for work on Friday, the 27th, and they haven't heard from her since. The house-keeper thinks she had second thoughts about sharing her windfall."

The two detectives, however, didn't believe for a second Rosa had changed her mind about helping her friends. April 27th was the day Blake's house was torched, the day the body was found.

Blake made the uncomfortable call to Jane's mother, unconsciously touching his shirt front over the spot where the pink diamond rested against his chest. Now that he had a potential identification on the body, he felt less ridiculous suggesting they had buried the wrong woman. Like Blake, Janice Larsen was willing to grasp at the flimsiest of straws. He told her Keesha would make all the arrangements for taking the DNA sample, and that he would let her know the minute there was any news.

While Keesha tried to locate a lab near the town in West Virginia where Jane's family lived, Maureen wrote on a card: *Rosa Padilla-victim?* She pinned it up between the blue index cards representing the call that had tipped the police about Frank Goodwin and the one that had led Blake and Maureen off on a wild goose chase the morning of the fire.

"Okay," Blake began, "whoever murdered Mason presumably relaxes once Goodwin is arrested for the crime. Thinks he's home free."

"Until you and I start nosing around in the case."

"Right. And my house is torched five days after we get within a hundred yards of Pinnacle Pictures."

"It wouldn't be unusual for surveillance cameras to be all over the lot," Maureen volunteered. "Theft at those places is rampant. But I can't believe they'd have eyes in the adjacent forest."

"Maybe we were outted some other way. Like busting the Bates brothers. Tujunga's not a big place and word might have drifted back to the killer. If he's connected with Pinnacle, he might've felt threatened that we were so close to the studio."

Before leaving to visit the Bates boys they asked Keesha to dig deeper into Pinnacle. And Maureen flipped through issues of *The Hollywood Reporter* until she found the photo she was looking for: Micah, dressed in fatigues to promote his upcoming movie.

They went to the Tujunga sheriff's station first, ostensibly to say hi to Dale Trainor and ask if he'd had any luck locating Dallis and Ostin's supplier. "We'd like to feel safe riding the trails up here," Maureen said, aiming helpless, innocent eyes at the sheriff.

Dale knew she was already spoken for—her tall boyfriend leaned in the doorway—but the smile she gave him made him feel like an awkward twelve year old looking for a way to impress a girl. "Whoever it was is long gone, I'm sure, and we never stood much chance of finding him anyway."

"Why not?" Blake asked from across the room.

"No evidence, no real name, no idea what he even looks like."

"Didn't you have a sketch artist work with those two guys to get a likeness?"

The sheriff gave Blake an amused smile. "Yeah. Want to see what she came up with?" He pulled out a drawer in his desk and scrabbled through papers, finally grabbing a page which he handed to Maureen. Blake crossed the room to look over her shoulder.

Back in the 1950's and 60's, long before smoking became a moral failing and cheap butane lighters were available at every gas station, Americans used books of paper matches to ignite their coffin nails. One of the most popular ads to appear on those match books was the "Draw Me" enticement, promising to train you for a career in commercial art if you could freehand replicate the cartoon character featured on the inside cover. Often it was a clown, sometimes a squirrel and, occasionally, in those days before ethnic sensitivity, a caricature Mexican, complete with floppy mustache, bushy brows, sleepy eyes and a big sombrero. If you lost the sombrero, you'd have something very close to the police artist sketch Maureen held in her hand.

"I deduced from this," the sheriff said, still hoping to impress Maureen, "that the Bates brothers were jacking us around."

Maureen studied the drawing. "I don't know. Maybe Diaz's parents were Chiquita Banana and Speedy Gonzalez."

"Don't start the car yet," Maureen said, pulling out a pen. Blake watched as she laid the page from *The Hollywood Reporter* against the dashboard and drew bushy eyebrows and a 'stache on the photo of Micah. Once shaggy black hair covered his buzz-cut, she held up the page for Blake to see. "He's an actor, right? With access to make-up and wigs. Maybe Micah himself is the elusive Señor Diaz."

Finding the trailer was easy, now that they knew there was a road of sorts leading to it, and while they drove the seven miles into the forest, they discussed Rosa Padilla.

"Do you think she won the lottery?" Blake asked.

"Not a chance. It was a set-up so the other maids would think she blew town. That way no one would report her missing."

"But Keesha said the housekeeper saw the ticket and matched it to the numbers in the LA Times."

Maureen shook her head. "It's a trick I once saw Max Keller play on the stage manager of *The Brothers Gunn*. We all knew the guy bought a lottery quick-pick every week and pinned the ticket to the bulletin board in his cubicle. Max waits until there's a big jackpot, then he buys a ticket with the same numbers that were pulled the night before. He goes in early to swap it for the ticket on the stage manager's bulletin board, and when the guy came in and checked his numbers, he about had a coronary."

"So someone gave her the ticket or made sure she 'accidentally' found it."

"And in the heat of the moment, with fourteen million bucks brightening your future, how closely are you going to study the date on that ticket?"

Blake mulled it over as he negotiated the narrow, unpaved road through the forest. Maureen noticed that several times he took one hand from the steering wheel and lightly touched his upper chest, a gesture she had never seen him make before.

Dallis and Ostin Bates were sitting in nylon-webbed lawn chairs in front of the trailer, getting the only exercise they ever did: curling 12-ounce cans of Bud. They had been working out for some time, so they were too drunk to be more than mildly surprised when the 550SL emerged from the trees and pulled into their yard.

"Hey, Dallis; hey, Ostin," the beautiful redhead called out as she approached. She looked vaguely familiar to the brothers, and they both assumed she must be an actress they had seen in a movie. Maybe she had gotten lost on her way to that big studio over yonder. They were too hammered to wonder how a movie actress knew their names. To paraphrase the Romans: *in vino stupitas.*

"Howdy-do, Miss," Dallis said, his suave greeting marred only by the belch punctuating *do* and pre-ceeding *Miss.* "Can we offer you a cold libration?"

"Don't mind if I do," Maureen purred, taking the dripping can Ostin lifted from the ice chest that rested alongside a huge pile of crushed aluminum.

She declined to sit in the lawn chair Dallis hastily cleared of leaves and a running shoe with dog poop on the bottom, choosing to remain standing while she raised the beer and tilted back her head, giving the boys an extry-good look at her perfect body stretching up like a cat in the sun. She drained the can without stopping, crushed it with one hand, then dropped it onto the metallic slope of Budweiser Mountain. She gave a ladylike burp and the Bates boys fell in love.

Five minutes later, watching her sashay back to the waiting car, Dallis and Ostin began arguing about who would call her tomorrow. Dallis thought it should be him, since he was the one she had handed her phone number to. "Yeah, but she was smiling at *me* when she did," Ostin insisted. They finally decided to make the call together, and so both would be disappointed the next day when the number on the scrap of paper connected them with the Los Angeles County bible scripture hotline. Numbers 14:12. *I will smite them with pestilence and will dispossess them.*

"Jackpot," Maureen said, climbing into the car and waving through the windshield at the smitten drunks.

"They identified Micah as their buyer?"

"Not *exactly*. When I flashed the photo at them, they got all excited about seeing their ol' pal Diaz, but they pointed to another guy in the picture." She tried to read the caption under the photo while the car bounced along the uneven road. "His name is Dominic Briggs and he's directing Micah's next film."

"Why is a movie director mixed up with bottom-of-the-food-chain meth cooks?"

"Trying to keep his star supplied and happy would be my guess." Then she suggested a stop at The Blind Pig to see if Fluffy had heard anything new.

It wasn't lunchtime yet, so the lot at The Pig was nearly empty when they pulled in and parked. "Is it safe to use the men's room?" Blake asked, getting out of the Mercedes.

"As long as the only thing you touch is your dick," Maureen said cheerily.

She wasn't kidding. Blake headed back toward the restroom while his partner hopped up on a bar stool to talk to her hippie pal. He pushed the door open with one elbow and entered a stench all the urinal cakes on earth couldn't knock down. Wishing he had taken a deep breath before entering, Blake breathed shallowly through his mouth as he stepped up to the stained porcelain trough and freed himself as quickly as possible. While he tried to put a rush on it, his eyes skipped over the graffiti straight ahead. It was dominated by the predictably crude boobs-and-hair-pie motif, but at least one of The Pig's resident artists had been marginally literate, leaving behind in No. 3 pencil lead the following warning: *Please don't throw swizzle sticks in the urinal. The crabs here can pole vault.*

With a glance downward, Blake decided he had peed enough. Flick, zip, exit stage left, thankful he had Wet Wipes in his glove compartment.

Meanwhile, Fluffy was telling Maureen he hadn't heard anything more on Dallis and Ostin Bates. He assumed the two morons were making sure to stay clean until their trial. "Although I'm not convinced they have enough brain between 'em to realize they should."

"I know what you mean. We can't figure out how those idiots produced such high-grade meth."

Fluffy gave her a funny look, just as Blake joined them. "What are you talking about? That crank I took off 'em was shit. You'd have to be one desperate tweak to settle for the brown crumbles they were trying to pass off as rock."

Maureen and Blake exchanged a glance, remembering what they had found in Micah's night stand, pristine, glassy crystals. So if Frick and Frack weren't supplying Micah, who was?

Keesha looked up from her lunch when they entered the office. "I need a credit card to prepay a lab tech to drive to Cobalt for that DNA. The closest guy's three hours away."

While Maureen took out her wallet and handed over a VISA, Blake said, "You find anything suspicious on Pinnacle?"

"Not really. But I did discover an inconsistency between how they describe the property in their promo material and what the county tax assessor shows. Pinnacle claims a hundred acres, but the tax base is predicated on ninety-five."

"You checked the original purchase?" he asked.

"It was for a hundred. But a few years ago a five-acre parcel was surveyed and transferred to a holding group with no money changing hands. I'm still looking into who and why. Any luck in Rednecktown?"

"Maybe," Maureen volunteered. "Can you check with the Directors' Guild for anything on a guy named Dominic Briggs?"

By 6:00 P.M. they had learned Briggs was not a member of the DGA, although Keesha did manage to link him to the holding company that received the five-acre gift parcel several years ago. That company held it only a few weeks before transferring it again, so tomorrow she would try to track down the name of the ultimate owner.

Keesha left for the day, and Maureen offered to ride down to the underground lot with Blake. "I think I'll hang for a while. Stare at these index cards and see if I get any brainstorms."

Maureen hesitated. "Uh, you want me to stay?"

Blake shook his head. "Thanks, but I'm okay. Really."

After she left he went over to the glass wall that opened onto the view of the Los Angeles basin, sorting out his feelings while the sun eased down into the last minutes of its slow-motion dive into the Pacific Ocean.

Each time he tried to comfort himself with the idea that Jane could still be alive, he was immediately gut-checked by visions of what might be happening to her. Blake didn't need any imagination at all to put the gruesome images is his mind; six years on the police force had given him an advanced degree in the magnitude of the cruelty one human being is capable of inflicting on another. And so, to keep that horrific speculation at bay he also held back on embracing the possibility of her being alive.

He wondered if it was a betrayal on his part, this unwillingness to bring Jane back to life—if only in his head—but then dismissed the idea. If he wallowed in fear, grief *or* hope he'd be useless as a detective. And who was going to find and rescue her if not him? And Maureen.

Blake wouldn't have started searching, wouldn't have a shred of hope if it hadn't been for Maureen. He'd rather have her on the case with him than a dozen guys like that detective from Hollywood. Blake might have trusted Libby, but the BHPD didn't have jurisdiction, and her new job shouldn't be jeopardized by an old friend asking for a favor.

No, it was only Maureen and him. And as much as he'd like to emulate the heroes of those popular blockbuster movies and the detective thrillers he read—storming into the basement/warehouse/isolated mountain cabin where she was held, spraying the bad guys with bullets, defeating the main thug in violent hand-to-hand combat before rescuing his wife—Blake knew that was cliché melodrama.

This would play out with a slow grind of down-and-dirty detective work, so he holstered any thoughts of heroic rescues. Patience and diligent investigation were the keys. He and Maureen had to work smoothly as a team, Blake realized, if they were going to run down every slim lead. So he had to stop pushing her away; he had to admit he needed her more than ever.

Turning from the wall of glass, he decided to tell Artie he was moving out. He would accept Charlie's offer to let him move into the big Spanish house on Acacia Drive.

Thursday morning Dominic Briggs looked over the legal document in his hand. Once Micah's signature was on it and witnessed, Briggs would own a big share of Pinnacle Pictures. Not a controlling interest—yet—but a nice chunk.

One of Cody Mason's not-very-grieving ex-wives had been happy to cash out her inherited piece of the studio for nearly double what it was worth, giving Dominic his first slice of the pie. He had also been making subtle inroads with the mother of Micah's only child, ostensibly to commiserate with Mrs. D-number-three about the state of Micah's mental health and possible chemical dependence. Deidre Deifenschlictor was shrewd enough to know Micah couldn't earn money if he couldn't get insured to do movies. And if he didn't earn money, how would she get her fair share of it? She wasn't as concerned about Micah, Jr.'s future as she was about maintaining the lavish lifestyle of her own present.

Deidre had already rounded the Horn, age-wise, and could no longer securely hold the attention of any of the impossibly attractive boy-men who migrated annually to LA with the predictability of swallows to

Capistrano, unless she was able to supply all the first-class perks of the private-jet set. Such are the harsh trickle-down economics of Hollywood. Luckily, Dom had met with her a week ago and assured her over mimosas in the Polo Lounge that Micah *would* pass the physical to do *The Devil's Platoon.*

"I found a doctor willing to overlook certain, let's call them *inconsistencies* in Micah's medical profile, in return for a generous bonus. Paid, of course, out of my pocket and under the table, so there'll be no record of it to come back and haunt us should anything—God forbid—happen to incapacitate Micah before the picture is wrapped."

Her Latisse-lengthened lashes flapped over twice-tightened lids as she reached across the table to take his hand. "Thank you for looking out for Micah, Jr."

Deidre had departed from the bubbly breakfast with Dominic's promise to buy Micah, Jr.'s interest in the studio for double its value if Micah, Sr. passed away. God forbid. She had been thrilled to realize she still had the kind of sex appeal that could persuade a smart guy like Briggs to overpay for something. But promises in Los Angeles are as plentiful as movie ideas, with as few of them coming to fruition, so Deidre wondered if it might be better to unload the kid's legacy right now. Gliding through the doors of Neiman-Marcus she decided to buy the kind of killer outfit that would, at their next tête-á-tête, convince Briggs to make her a cash offer now.

Dominic had left their last meeting confident he had planted that double-or-nothing seed, knowing it would take root in her greedy mind. Their next champagne summit was set for the following Monday morning, and he was gambling on her bringing up the idea of an early sale.

But first he had to get through another weekend

of baby-sitting Micah. Briggs had already warned him the partying would have to stop once they started shooting, and Micah had agreed. He wanted one last balls-to-the wall blow-out, though, and Dominic was tired even *thinking* about a repeat of the clubs, booze and bimbos that had filled his recent weekends.

Somewhere between Micah's Friday lucidity, such as it was, and Sunday's late night pants-crapping drug stupor, Briggs would get the action star to sign on the dotted line. By this time next month, he intended to have controlling interest in Pinnacle Pictures.

Maureen said good-morning to Keesha, then went straight back to the fishbowl, where Blake was attempting to crush a Pepsi can with one hand. He had obviously raided the recycle bin, because cans in varying stages of squish dotted the conference table.

"How did you do that?" he asked. "Your hands are maybe half the size of mine," he asked.

"It's a little skill Fluffy taught me when I was in my teens. Took months to learn how to position the can in my hand so it crunched flat every time."

"So *that's* why our paparazzo was gasping when you had him by the cojones."

"Oh, that isn't an acquired skill; crushing gonads comes naturally to me." She flashed him her evil grin.

He told Maureen that Artie and the librarian wanted a little privacy—to read to each other, Blake speculated—so he asked if the offer of a room was still good. When she confirmed it was, he said he'd move in that night.

"Will you need any help with your stuff?"

He gave her a curious look. "Everything I own except my car fits into one box now."

The awkward moment was broken when Keesha entered. "I found out who wound up with that acreage carved off Pinnacle. Two guys named Dallis and Ostin Bates."

The board now had another card of information, but none if it jelled in a cohesive fashion. All they knew was that everything somehow connected back to Pinnacle Pictures, and they were unlikely to get onto the lot to learn more.

Blake and Maureen decided to farm out the job to the one guy who might be able to get past that gate.

Blake wasn't sure how to greet Charlie when he showed up at the front door with a cardboard box and the suit he'd been wearing the day of the fire.

"Does being a jackass preclude my taking you up on your hospitality?" Blake asked sheepishly.

"I've worked with actors," Charlie said, stepping aside to let him in. "On a scale of son-of-a-bitch to son-of-God, jackass is way up there."

Blake hadn't had Denice's cheeseburgers since he was in Nevada working on their last big case, but, knowing he would be coming over, Maureen had asked Denice if she would mind making them for dinner. Blake said they were as delicious cooked on the big Viking stove's griddle as the ones at Dolly's Diner, and he did not demur when seconds were offered. Pickings at Artie's house had been bachelor-slim, and Blake had not had much of an appetite until now.

Sensitive to Blake's situation, Charlie and Denice did not talk about their engagement. Charlie already knew from Maureen that she and her partner were working on the theory that Jane was still alive—or at least had not been the woman in the house fire.

After they ate dinner Denice excused herself, claiming she needed time to complete her order list for the grand opening in a few weeks. Once she left, Maureen asked her father if there were any legitimate way he could get onto the Pinnacle Pictures lot.

Sammy Greenbaum had never had an original idea in his life, but he was a genius at taking other people's ideas and packaging them in new ways. Instinctively sensing what the public would want next, he approached the creative forces behind a complementary product. He did not necessarily go for schlock but he never reached for the moon either. As a result, Sammy had packaged more than two dozen projects—some TV, a lot of movies, even a Broadway musical featuring giant puppets that talked dirty and had simulated sex with each other on stage. Nobody ever lost money on a Sammy Greenbaum production.

Because of his track record, he was bombarded with pitches from washed-up actors, hack writers and would-be producers, all trying to get him to wrap *his* magic around *their* ventures. He had his pick of what was out there to be re-branded, and he chose several projects a year to follow through on, but there was one he had never been able to land.

Sammy Greenbaum had done everything short of dropping to his knees and begging the owner/creator for a chance to turn the product into a buddy-comedy feature film, but he had been turned down each time.

It was with genuine delight, then, that Sammy took the call from Charlie O'Brien that evening and listened to the words he'd wanted to hear for more than a decade: "Sammy, why don't you and I turn *The Brothers Gunn* into a movie?"

Blake and Maureen stared at the newest card on the storyboard Friday morning, trying to figure out how two guys as I.Q.-challenged as Dallis and Otis Bates came to be so ass-deep in whatever was going on.

"Maybe they did a favor for Micah in the past," Maureen suggested. "And for whatever reason, they wanted their reward in land rather than cash."

"But Micah owns the studio, and Briggs's name is connected with the land deal," Blake said.

"So? Briggs wants to get in good with Micah, maybe wants a shot at directing a movie. Celebs often delegate their dirty work to someone else. And there's no shortage of volunteers, suck-ups hoping to gain leverage and turn it into showbiz gold."

Keesha walked into the fishbowl and plopped a stack of checks onto the conference table. "I need some John Hancocks here so people can get paid."

Blake took out a pen. "Good lord," he said, noting the size of the stack. "How many employees do we have now?"

"Twenty-nine, counting me."

"Can we afford to pay all of them?"

"M-mm, not really. But I'll send out invoices on the first to those four companies we're now providing security services to. You might not want to write any large checks out of the E&O account till they pay."

Maureen heard the opening notes of the theme from *The Brothers Gunn*, and saw it was her dad calling. "Cannibal Café. How may we serve you?" She listened while Blake signed checks. "Okay, that's great. We'll see you at home tonight." She then turned to her partner. "Charlie's having lunch with a guy who can get him into Pinnacle."

Once the checks were signed, Blake left. He had put off dealing with the insurance agency and taking care of the other dozen things that followed in the wake of his house burning to the ground. He had also ignored calls from the principal of the San Fernando Valley school where Jane had taught kindergarten. Her first call had been an invitation to attend the memorial service the children and faculty held weeks ago. The next few calls had been requests for him to pick up Jane's things.

Maureen spent the afternoon checking on lottery amounts over the last few months. She found two in the fourteen-million-dollar range, but there was no winner either time, bolstering her belief that Rosa Padilla was conned. She and Keesha brainstormed on how to get more Rosa intel without tipping anyone off that inquiries were being made. Maureen was sharply aware of the fatal response to their last look into the Cody Mason murder.

Late in the day Keesha heard from the DNA tech in West Virginia, telling her he would drive to Cobalt on Tuesday to get a sample from Jane's mother. And how fast did they want the results? Maureen handed over her credit card and Keesha read the number to him. By next Thursday they would know for sure if it was Jane's body that had been found in the fire.

"What exactly am I supposed to be looking for?" Charlie asked.

It was only the three of them for dinner, as Denice had flown back to Nevada to put her house on the market and to start packing for her move to LA.

"We aren't sure," Blake said. "We know Pinnacle figures into this whole mess, but we don't know how."

"Try to get a feel for the place. See if it seems legitimate," suggested Maureen. "I mean, if you're supposedly going to film there, you should have the right to ask a lot of questions."

Charlie's lunch with Sammy Greenbaum had gone very well, not unusual when both parties are getting precisely what they want. If Sammy was surprised by how quickly Charlie proposed they move ahead—you don't go looking at studios before a script exists—he didn't show it. For all Sammy knew, Charlie could have money problems and might need to make this all happen fast. And Pinnacle Pictures wasn't the first facility that popped into Sammy's head when he thought about where to shoot, but if that's what it took to keep Charlie on board, so be it. While still at the table at The Ivy, Sammy had made the call to book their tour of the lot next week.

Maureen and Blake retired to their rooms, while Charlie worked on wedding plans. Denice wanted it plain and simple, and he wanted it sooner, rather than later, in case she had a change of heart.

Maureen lay awake, aware that Blake was down the hall. With the very real possibility Jane was still alive, she knew any lingering romantic feelings she harbored toward him had to be killed, buried and have heavy rocks piled onto the grave.

In his own room, Blake tried to work up the nerve to look into the box he had collected from the school where Jane had taught for the past two years. He wanted to hold things she had touched and look at things she had seen, but it felt like an invasion of her privacy, as if he were contemplating opening her mail or going through her drawers at home.

Home. The insurance agent had gone over the figures: rebuilding, replacing personal possessions; Blake had only half-listened, not sure he had it in him to start over. If you could put that much effort into something—as he had done with his house—only to have it disappear in a flash, what was the point?

He looked at the sealed box. If he believed Jane was alive, that he would find her, he had to respect her privacy. Blake left the box where it was and turned off the bedside lamp, unconsciously touching the heart laying over his own.

Key word: atrophy. His muscles were bigger than ever, striated meat pumped up to almost comical proportions, but the gray-matter matzo ball floating in its salty broth shrinky-dinked more every hour—in both weight and efficiency. As brain cells fell to the advancing beta amyloids, dementia settling into its future home, Micah's real memories flickered out and were replaced by new ones. The memories of Capt. Luther Hardy, Vietnam war hero, freshened each day as Micah struggled to memorize his lines, and as he worked with a retired gunnery sergeant to master the smooth operation of the M-14. Occasionally a genuine memory sighed its final presence before departing forever, leaving a confused Micah to wonder why the stock of his M-16—the model he had carried on Oahu—felt unfamiliar.

This out-with-the-old-in-with-the-new continued as Dominic Briggs reminded Micah daily about the fire, the killing of that woman and his participation in all of it. Dominic never drilled it home the way the script girl did with the lines Micah couldn't seem to fix in his mind. Instead, Dom offered Cosacos cigars, swapped dirty jokes with Micah, supplied the AAS and the crystal, and made the actor believe he had a friend, a brother.

That feeling was so familiar. Didn't there used to be someone else who...? No, it must be Dom because we fought together in 'Nam.

And so, Micah's memories guttered out, replaced by the fictional memories of Capt. Luther Hardy and the ones supplied by Briggs. Halfway through their debauched weekend, Dominic had Micah sign some papers.

"Is this the purchase order for that new crane we're getting? The one you mentioned last week?"

"Yes. And if you can remember little production

details like that, I don't think you need to worry about forgetting stuff every once in a while. You're a busy man with a lot on your plate. Now, are we hitting the clubs or what?"

Micah smiled. Dominic always reassured him, kept him on track, always had his six. "Let's go nail some tail. Oo-rah!"

Maureen and Blake realized everything had started the day they got the evidence ruling out Micah as Cody Mason's killer, so they decided to spend the weekend revisiting that evidence. Maureen had kept a copy of the recordings the paparazzo made the night of the murder. She also was able to obtain, with her secret access code, transcripts of what the police had of those three calls. They had both sides of the first call, the normal nightly call from Cody's cell to Micah's cell. Well, they had all but the last eighteen seconds of Cody's side of the conversation. That's when Micah said he had realized he was inadvertently recording the call and hit the stop button. They also had Micah's cell-to-cell call-back checking in on Cody and his follow-up cell-to-land-line call, the one in which he threatened to come over and kick Mason's ass.

They listened to the recordings in Charlie's home studio, not sure what they were listening for. They searched the transcripts for clues. Charlie came into the room to get their take-out order for lunch, entering as they played back the second part of Transcript #1 for the umpteenth time. He listened, then snorted derisively. "Bad writing."

"What?" Maureen turned in her chair, seeing her father in the doorway. Blake lowered the sound on the recording.

"It's an amateur's mistake. You have to write one side of a telephone conversation, but you need the audience to get what the whole conversation is about. So you overcorrect and put in TMI."

"This isn't a movie soundtrack," Blake said. "It's an actual recording of a call."

"I don't think so." Charlie crossed to them, his hand out. "Let me see the script. Oops! I mean the *tran*script." Maureen gave him the page covering the last eighteen seconds of that first call, the part where only Micah's voice was heard. "Okay, you start with a pause, presumably the guy on the other end saying something like 'I just heard a noise downstairs' or 'what was that?' Right?"

"Yeah," Blake replied, unsure where Charlie was headed.

"Then the guy you *can* hear says: 'probably your cat knocking over something in the kitchen.' See what he's doing? He's supplying the *what* and the *where*. So maybe we buy that much, but then there's another pause, and after it your guy says: 'so go downstairs and check it out.' Again, he tells us the where. So, where *was* your victim found?"

"Downstairs. In the kitchen," Maureen said, realization dawning.

"And here's the maraschino on the sundae. Read me that last recorded line," Charlie said, handing the transcript back to Blake.

Blake shrugged and read out loud: "'You're right. It's probably nothing, but give me a call back anyway.'"

"Now think. What was the line before that, the one you can't hear?"

Blake and Maureen exchanged a glance, then she took a guess. "I don't know. Maybe Cody said 'it's probably nothing.'"

"Good guess. But if someone said that to you on the phone, what you would say in response?"

"'You're right?'" Blake said. "To reassure him?'"

"Bingo! But why would you bother to repeat 'it's probably nothing?' I'll tell you why. Because you're a lousy writer and you can't figure out another way to hint at the other side of the phone conversation. So all you do is parrot it."

Before Charlie left to pick up Thai food for lunch, he gave them an exercise: try to fill in the other half of the dialogue in the one-sided transcript. "Then read the two parts out loud."

"But we're not writers," Blake protested.

"Yeah? Well, neither was the guy who came up with *this* shit," Charlie said, tapping the transcript.

Once Charlie left, Blake and Maureen did what he had suggested and soon they could see the difference between the first half of Transcript #1, where both men were heard speaking, and its other half. In the first part of the conversation, Cody and Micah spoke in the shorthand they had naturally developed over a forty-year relationship. But in the second part, and in the two other calls where Micah's was the only voice heard, he repeated what Cody was supposedly saying, and he mentioned both the cat and downstairs twice, as if to make sure the listener got the point. Micah also established his expectation of a call-back.

Blake and Maureen remembered their first case together, when actress Ali Garland mentioned two times in her initial interview that the man she had shot was wearing the same outfit as the mugger who had tried to rob her. She also hammered home a tiny detail about a can of paint.

Ali had led them where she needed them to go, and she had done it well enough to trick Maureen and Blake, as well as the grand jury that let her walk free on a homicide charge.

By the time Charlie returned in a redolent cloud

of Pad Thai and beef Panang, the two detectives had found another peculiarity in the transcripts.

"Hey, you old cocksucker, whussup?"
"Uh...please hold for Mr Mason."

For twenty-two years, the length of time she was Cody Mason's assistant, Karen Chapel had listened to disgusting phone openers of that type. If she had been shocked or offended at the beginning when she was first out of college, Karen had gotten over it long ago. All Mr. Mason's *other* business associates—even his enemies—were respectful on the telephone, but he and Micah played rough with each other, at least verbally. Karen had waited years for the action star to realize it was always going to be *her* on the line when he got a call from Cody's office. That way he could save his filthy talk until she had connected him to his agent. But Micah was too dense to figure that out.

Karen had heard one side of those calls since her first day on the job; Cody made up for his smallish size by speaking in a loud voice, and he never closed his office door. She adored her boss, but was well aware he could match Micah, crudity for crudity.

On each call, after a few minutes of battering each other with sexual, scatological and mental-deficiency innuendo, they finally got down to business. And every call ended the same way, with one of them saying, "Piranha sends her love," then hanging up before the other could respond. Karen never knew who Piranha was, because the incident pre-dated her employment. While Micah wrapped his last months of military service to his adopted country, Cody hooked up with a beautiful starlet. She had a generous Julia Roberts mouth chock full of gleaming Marie Osmond teeth. Her smile made her face even more appealing, and agents sniffed her out for both professional *and* personal reasons.

Hoping to add to his talent roster, Cody wined and dined her then took her back to his starter mansion clinging to the side of a Hollywood hill. And when the inevitable transpired, Cody experienced the downside of those big choppers, feeling lucky to come away from the encounter with his manhood still intact.

He didn't sign the starlet, claiming with tongue in cheek they "weren't a good fit." But they remained on cordial enough terms for him to fix her up with Micah the day he came home from the Marines, a last one-finger salute to the actor for having abandoned the career Cody had worked so hard to build.

Piranha passed into the mists of their personal mythology, and neither man knew what had become of her. But she lived on in their phone sign-offs, the only part of the legend familiar to Karen Chapel.

When the two investigators showed up at her apartment Saturday afternoon, Karen was surprised. She told them she thought the man who killed her boss was already in jail.

"He is," Blake explained. "But we've been hired by one of Mr. Mason's clients who's so heartsick he wants us to go back over everything connected with the case."

Maureen was impressed; Blake wasn't usually an adept liar. Maybe this whole situation has pulled him slightly toward the dark side, she thought, before he said, "The night of Cody Mason's death, on the last call he made, he said the word 'piranha,' and was cut off. Do you have any idea what that means?"

Karen told them what she knew, that every call between Cody and Micah ended the same way: one of them said "Piranha sends her love," then hung up.

"They never kept talking after that?" Maureen asked.

"No. One of them only said it when the conversation was done."

"Piranha sends her love, that's all?"

"That was all for the twenty-two years *I* worked for him."

As Maureen's car pulled away from the apartment building, she said, "I think she may have given us the break we've been looking for."

"Well, don't keep me in suspense."

"If Cody Mason was signing off on that first call, and he only got the word piranha out before Micah hit the stop-record button, how much longer would he have talked before hanging up?"

"Long enough to say 'sends her love.'"

"Exactly. Maybe two or three seconds. But that conversation went on for another eighteen seconds according to the transcript."

"Proving what exactly?"

"Possibly proving Cody was already off the phone and Micah kept talking to begin setting up a timeline and an alibi."

Blake nodded thoughtfully. "He was counting on the paparazzo's bugs to pick up every word he said after he disengaged the cell's recording mode."

When they got back to the house, they checked the transcript against the cell tower hit and the length of the call. Sure enough, the call had been disconnected two seconds after Cody said piranha, but Micah had kept talking for another sixteen seconds, long enough to establish the suggestion of a possible intruder.

Charlie offered to take them out for champagne brunch in Century City on Sunday morning, but Blake and Maureen wanted to work, so it was only Denice and him who went. Now that Charlie had pointed out the clumsiness of the dialogue in the transcripts, and now that they had discovered the sixteen-second discrepancy, both detectives knew for sure Micah was up to his eyeball muscles in Cody Mason's murder.

The calls indicated he was establishing an alibi for the window of time in which Cody was killed, but even if they were fake, they put him two miles from the crime scene when it all went down. They figured that must mean he had an accomplice, the person who did the actual knifing.

Blake shook his head as he looked at the blue cards up on the board. "But isn't it a long way to go to cover your ass, when a small dinner party or the overnight stay of a lover would do the same job? And wouldn't he have given his accomplice the gate and security codes to get in?"

Maureen reminded him doing that would have shrunk the list of suspects to Micah, Cody's assistant and his housekeeping staff. By staging a climb over the wall and breaking a window to get in the house, the killer threw suspicion in a wider circle.

They went over the police report, soon agreeing with Keesha that the method of entry felt too perfect. A conveniently bent shrub leads police to a broken branch, under which is one torn-off button. And a look at the top of the wall behind the shrub reveals a disturbance of dust and leaves.

The button had been positively matched to a jacket belonging to Frank Goodwin, and the receipt from the dry cleaner proved when the missing button had been replaced: two days after the murder. Was Goody too lame to ditch the jacket in a distant Dumpster when he discovered the missing button? Or was this, like the calls and the break-in, as authentic as the script of a Hollywood movie?

While Charlie toured Pinnacle the next day, Blake and Maureen would see if they could get face time with Frank Goodwin.

Lying awake in the O'Brien house that night, Blake calmed himself with the knowledge that only this kind of investigative work, grind-pace digging, would lead him to Jane. He was now convinced her disappearance was connected to Mason's murder and Pinnacle Pictures. When Maureen tried to get onto the lot in her hooker outfit, and then when the two of them stumbled onto that crack lab near the Pinnacle fence, they had unknowingly sent up a red flag about their continuing interest. And someone had decided to shut them down.

Maybe tomorrow Charlie would find the puzzle piece that would clarify the entire picture, Blake thought, his fingers unconsciously stroking the pink diamond on his chest.

"Mr. Greenbaum, good to meet you. Dominic Briggs."

"A pleasure, Dominic. But please call me Sammy. This is Charlie; he's my number two on the movie."

"Charlie," Briggs said, extending his hand while keeping his focus on the more important guy. Charlie nodded and shook the proffered extremity.

Sammy Greenbaum didn't know why Charlie had insisted on being introduced by only his first name, and frankly, he didn't care. Sammy was used to the eccentricities of creative people, and had learned early on to work within the parameters of their quirks to get what he wanted. And what Sammy wanted was to make *The Brothers Gunn* into a feature film. So, if Charlie O'Brien wanted to remain incognito, if he wanted a full studio tour instead of the usual quick look at facilities, amenities, availability and price, that was okay by Sammy.

"Micah really wanted to be here, but he's in final prep for his new movie, so I'll be taking you around myself." Micah was actually sleeping off the effects of his last-hurrah weekend of irresponsible and reprehensible behavior.

Last night, when the action star had been unable to get any action out of his own equipment, the young lady awaiting his ministrations made the near-fatal mistake of rolling her eyes with impatience. As soon as Briggs heard the scream, he crashed into the bedroom and found a naked Micah pulling back his fist to land a second blow on the cowering girl.

Dominic knew he couldn't take the actor down by himself, as Micah was as ripped as a human being can get and trembling with rage. Briggs barked out an order in his most commanding drill-sergeant voice: "Marine! Stand down!"

The words shot past the dead spots in Micah's brain until they hit still-functioning dendrites and registered. The shaking stopped and Micah looked around, confused about where—and who—he was.

"As you were, Marine." Briggs spoke less harshly, now that his words were getting through. He draped a sheet around the whimpering girl and hustled her off to another bedroom. Clearly her jaw was broken, so he told her he would drive her to the hospital. Going back to Micah's room for her clothes, he found the actor sitting on the bed, already sucking on a meth pipe. He would be out of it for hours, giving Dominic time to clean up the mess.

While the girl got dressed, he called for three cabs; he didn't want the remaining trio to have a chance to talk among themselves on the ride home. Briggs gave each of them $500 and his card, assuring them there would be parts for them in Pinnacle's upcoming romantic comedy to be filmed in Bermuda.

Assuming, of course, they knew how to be discreet.

He phoned a doctor he trusted and said he'd be bringing an injured woman by the house. The usual off-the-books remuneration would pay for the MD's annual family vacation in Europe.

After checking to make sure Micah had already nodded off, Briggs drove the girl to the doc's house, negotiating the whole way. She wasn't holding *all* the cards, he admonished her, as she had been a more-than-willing participant in sketchy activities that wouldn't look good on her résumé. Also, a word from him in certain circles, and her status would instantly go from ingénue-wannabe to prostitute.

In exchange for her silence Dom offered to pay for breast augmentation and a rhinoplasty after her jaw healed. Any plastic surgeon she chose.

It was a strong opening offer and he could see her weighing his deal against her leverage. Too many seconds passed, though, so he upped the ante. "I can also guarantee you a co-starring role in our upcoming romantic comedy to be filmed in Rome."

"Wait," she mumbled through her swelling lips. "Didden you tell thosh other girlsh it wash gonna de shot in Dernuda?"

Shit. It was 3:00 A.M. and he was having to keep multiple lies going. "They're getting bit parts in one location. You, as the co-star, will do *all* the locations, and that includes Singapore and Rio de Janeiro." She gave him a skeptical look. "No, really. It's the story of a guy pursuing a beautiful girl—that would be you—all over the world trying to win her heart. And did I mention who's playing the male lead?" Briggs wondered, who the hell would someone her age think is hot? He wished he had kept up with the names of the younger red-carpet crawlers. "Okay, you know that great-looking actor from *The Hunger Games*?"

Her eyes lit up. "Leen Hezwerk?"

The lower half of her face was ballooning rapidly, but Briggs assumed she had said a man's name. "That's the guy. Only it's all very hush-hush because he has another movie to shoot before we get him. So, are you in?"

She considered the impact on her career of a less Semitic nose and a more marketable rack. Plus, the chance to work with Liam Hemsworth. It was a good deal, but hey, maybe she could make it better. "Throw in a Drazilian dutt-lift, dude and we're in dusiness. Agreed?"

Dominic *thought* he heard her say she wanted a million to go to Radcliffe and get a business degree, but she could have asked for the moon and he still would have said yes.

Briggs climbed into the golf cart drivers' seat, as Sammy and Charlie got in the back for the studio tour. Putting aside his concerns about possible lawsuits, Micah's dodgy mental state, and his weariness after only four hours' sleep, Dominic sucked it up and delivered his spiel with all the verve of a Disneyland tour boat operator taking the rubes through the fake rain forest.

An hour later, back in Dom's office, Sammy got down to talking money and was surprised by the very competitive rates. Maybe Charlie *had* known what he was doing, insisting on coming here first. Briggs showed them the production calendar for the last twelve months. All satisfied customers, he assured them, handing Charlie promotional material and rate sheets to put in his briefcase.

They walked out to Sammy Greenbaum's car, where Charlie stopped and said, "Damn it, I left my briefcase in your office." He ducked back inside while Sammy tempted Dom with a few other projects he had going. Interested, Dominic began telling him about the specially-planted and landscaped parts of the lot that could double for different foreign locations, a real money-saver for a producer.

Once inside, Charlie flashed his winning smile at the receptionist. "I'm such a doofus. Left my briefcase in Mr. Briggs' office. My boss," and here he jerked his thumb back over his shoulder toward the door, "will have a hissy fit if I forget all the paperwork *your* boss gave him." She nodded in sympathy. Her boss could be a real jerk, too.

Charlie darted into Dominic's office, grabbing the leather satchel from the floor, then picking up the production calendar from the desk.

Once back in reception, he sheepishly handed her the calendar. "Man, I don't know what's wrong with me today. I was supposed to get a copy of the last two years' production schedules before we left."

She made a zipping gesture across her lips, glanced at the door to make sure her boss was still outside, then hurried over to the copy machine.

A few minutes later, Charlie joined the two men at the car. "Got it," he said, hoisting the briefcase.

As they drove off the lot, Sammy congratulated Charlie on finding the studio. "I don't think that guy has a clue what other places are charging, so I'm going to nail down our deal before he figures it out."

Charlie only half-listened to Sammy's enthusiastic monologue. During the tour, as Briggs walked them through the small office building that housed what he called "support personnel," Charlie had seen a face he recognized.

Blake went alone to see Goodwin, figuring if he had a problem getting in, one of the guards at the lock-up could be persuaded to bend the rules. After all, they'd seen him regularly during his years as a cop. Whether Goodwin would consent to see him was another question, so Blake had sent a note in to him: *I know you didn't kill Cody Mason. Help me prove it.* A few minutes later Blake sat at a laminate-topped table heavily pocked with cigarette burns in a room that could have induced Mary Poppins to hang herself. Goodwin was brought in, ankle chains shuffling and hands cuffed before him. He looked like an aging flyweight fighter fallen on hard times.

Once Goodwin's ankles were secured to the chair and they were alone, he asked, "So, who are you?"

"Blake Ervansky. Used to be a cop, but now I'm in the private sector. And before you ask, I'm not working for anyone and nobody's paying me a cent."

"Indy prods," Goody murmured with a smile.

"Beg pardon?"

"Nothing, I'm only amusing myself. Now, what makes you think I didn't kill Mason?"

The question caught Blake off guard. With raised eyebrows, he asked, "*Did* you?"

"Hell, no. That's what I've been telling anyone who'd listen since the day I was arrested. Yet here I sit, public enemy numero uno, waiting around for a jury's stamp of approval before I fry."

"If it's any consolation, it takes an average of twenty years to get through the appeals process before an execution."

"What a relief," Goodwin said sarcastically. "Only *two* decades sharing a cell with some ass-grabby skeev named Maggot."

Blake couldn't really blame him for being bitter, especially if he wasn't guilty, but the meter was running. "Mr. Goodwin, did you keep that jacket—the one with the incriminating button—in your office?"

"I always keep several jackets at work. That one

rotated in and out."

"And could Micah have gotten access to your office any time in the month before the murder?"

"Like I told that bald lady detective, he showed up unannounced one afternoon, telling me he was ready to quit Cody. That big jockstrap might have zilch in the talent department, but his movies make money so, yeah, I took the meeting."

Goody couldn't recall if the incriminating jacket was hanging in his office that day, or if he had left Micah alone in there during the meeting. Luckily, his assistant had a much better memory for details, and Maureen was talking to him in Playa del Rey at that very minute.

"Charlie, you bloodsucker! The rent's not due for another two weeks!" Max Keller, in a powder-blue track suit, swung the door open for Charlie.

"Social call. I want to make sure you didn't kill Ethel for her Social Security checks. Harold around?"

Max looked at his watch. "Unless the traffic from Tujunga is worse than usual he should be here any minute."

When Harold Tishman came in a short time later he looked sweaty and nervous. "Oh, my God! You're here," he said, seeing Charlie on the couch with Ethel. "I was going to call you as soon as I got home."

"Can we talk privately?" Charlie asked.

"Hey, babe, let's go watch last night's America's Got Talent," Max said, helping Ethel to her feet. "I wanna see if that guy who juggles the live hamsters makes it to the next round."

As they left the room, Harold thudded onto the couch. Charlie opened. "First, thanks for not saying anything when Sammy and I came through the building today."

"The look you shot me made it abundantly clear you didn't want to be acknowledged. What were you doing at Pinnacle?"

"Checking out studio space for a movie."

Harold put his head in his hands. "No, Charlie, you do *not* want to shoot on that lot. Anywhere but Pinnacle."

"Why do you say that?"

"Because my father always told me you were a mensch, and I don't want to see you get caught up in what's going on there."

When Charlie asked him what *was* going on there, Harold couldn't give a definitive answer, only that something wasn't right. Micah was supposedly the head of the studio, but when he wasn't grunting and strutting in that homoerotic dumbell-pit they called a gym, he was trotting around the lot in camo fatigues, carrying a gun and looking for Viet Cong. "They *say* he's getting into character for the movie he's about to shoot, but I don't buy it."

"Do you ever talk to him?"

"Yeah, and he even comes across as lucid once in a while. Asks me how the rewrites are coming, has a perfectly normal conversation. But five minutes later, he's lurking behind some bush, muttering about the 'goddamn gooks.' Pardon my French."

"Well, if the head of the studio is losing it who's running things?"

"The guy who was showing you around, Dominic Briggs." He described the slow takeover of the lot by Micah's old Marine buddies. As far as Harold knew, Briggs didn't have a title or official position *per se*, but he had a luxurious office, acted the part of the man in charge, and seemingly pulled strings behind the scene. He also exerted absolute control over Micah.

"Is the place legit?"

"Far as I can tell. Production companies come in and out all the time and the stages are apparently always booked."

"Why would you say *apparently?*"

"Because I don't know for sure. We peons are discouraged from roaming the lot. All those jarheads with sidearms creep me out anyway, so I'm happy to sit in my office and keep my head down."

Charlie kept asking questions, hoping to get a piece of information that might help Maureen and Blake. It took another half hour of pumping, but he finally scored.

Blake and Maureen met at the office, where they went over their separate findings for the day, posting cards on the storyboard. There were a few blue ones, representing provable facts. Most of the rest were white: not-quite-provable "facts," informed guesses, and wild-ass speculation. But a picture was beginning to form.

Frank Goodwin's assistant had told Maureen he dropped off the incriminating jacket at the dry cleaner's, along with the others hanging in Goody's office, but said that was routine for the last week of the month. He also confirmed the date of the meeting with Micah, saying it wasn't on the day-planner the police had confiscated because the star had shown up with no appointment and no call beforehand.

Charlie arrived at E&O Investigations with three new puzzle pieces: an aerial view of the Pinnacle lot, a list of all production for the last two years, and the tale of a script not produced. Blake handed Keesha the production schedule. "Tomorrow morning start calling the clients on this list. Gather whatever data you can and look for inconsistencies. Tell them you're the owner of a business looking to do commercials and you'd like feedback on their Pinnacle experience before you commit."

Before she left with the schedule, Keesha smiled at Charlie, a man she had met ten minutes earlier. "Last week I was wearing a maid's uniform and today I'm the owner of a business. *America!*"

Maureen was already unfolding and spreading out the bird's-eye view of Pinnacle, the flip side of which had all the usual facilities shots and promotional copy, but Charlie put a hand out to stop her. "Before we look at that, there's something you need to know. The big buzz at Pinnacle right now is that they're about to start shooting their first in-house film."

"Old news," said Blake. "It's a war movie starring Micah."

"*The Devil's Platoon,* I know. I spoke to the guy who wrote it, and he says it was a real rush job."

"Isn't that story as old as Hollywood?" Maureen asked.

"It is. But this particular rush job was given to the writer the day Cody Mason's body was found. A piece of crap war movie idea Micah came up with over that prior weekend. What makes things interesting, though, is the script that got bumped for this turkey.

The week after Harold Tishman was hired at Pinnacle, Dominic Briggs stopped by his tiny office, ostensibly to welcome the writer to the lot. After flopping down in a chair, Briggs shot the breeze for a few minutes with the nervous newbie, then started throwing out suggestions about the kind of projects the studio wanted to do in the future, movies that Harold would script, of course, for a Writers' Guild approved amount above and beyond his weekly salary.

Harold had been scrabbling for work since he hit forty, and would have penned "9/11: *The Musical*" with pleasure if Briggs had asked, but was relieved that his first assignment would be much more aligned with his skill set. Some people made the mistake of thinking Harold Tishman was a mediocre writer because he couldn't churn out brilliant comedy like his legendary father. But Harold knew how to plot a mystery, and had been responsible for some of the most memorable episodes of *Murder, She Wrote, Monk* and several of the old shows on CBS's "Crime Time After Prime Time" line-up.

Harold felt confident he could give Briggs what he was asking for, a script about committing the perfect murder.

When Libby Johnson found out her access code had been used to download all the information in the Cody Mason homicide file, she assumed Lt. Rhee must be following up on his last case at the BHPD. A call to Springfield, Missouri—supposedly to see how he was settling into his new job—quickly disabused her of that notion. Next on her suspect list was Keesha Beale, Rhee's former assistant.

Stepping out of her office, she signaled to the detective who seemingly kept tabs on all departmental gossip. "Hey, Willis. A word?"

He guiltily shut his laptop, making Libby wonder if he was porn surfing again. Twice he had been reprimanded, and she knew she should do something about it, but he was a good detective. He had even saved her life last year, knocking her aside and taking a bullet in the chest that had been meant for her.

"You rang, Loo?"

"Yes. Do you happen to know where Ms. Beale went to work after she left here?"

"Sure. Keesh got hired by Ervansky and that redhead. You know, to work at their *detective agency*."

Willis put big air-quotes around the last two words, and his smirk communicated what he thought about civilian investigators.

"Thanks. Now you can go back to the online *case* you were researching." The air-quotes she put around the word "case" and the look on her face told Willis she was aware of what he'd been doing. With a sheepish nod, he went back to his desk.

The first thing Libby did was cancel Lt. Rhee's old access code, cursing herself for not getting a new one as soon as she came onto the job. Then she put in a call to that dick detective at the Hollywood division, learning Maureen O'Brien had gone there more than a week ago. She had been asking for updates on the investigation into the house fire and homicide, but even a lightweight like Det. Hollywood sensed there was more to the story.

"Why didn't you give me a heads-up on all this?" Libby asked.

"All due respect, Lt. Johnson, but this isn't your case. Sure, the torched house belonged to a former cop at BH, but that doesn't automatically put it in *your* jurisdiction."

Her mind snarled *you stupid little prick*, but her voice remained calm and respectful. "I'm aware of that, but we suspect some possible overlap with a homicide that *is* in our jurisdiction."

"Yeah? Tell you what, you bring me evidence that connects them and I'll splice you into the loop. Now if you don't mind, I got work to do."

Libby seethed. Should she ask her captain to talk to the captain at Hollywood, maybe risk a turf war? No, she decided, best to knock Ervansky and company out of the ring before they compromised an important operation. She called Artie Lassiter to find out where Blake was living these days.

Charlie checked his watch Tuesday morning.
He had to pick up Denice at the Burbank Airport at
11:00, but Harold Tishman had agreed to email him
the outline of the murder movie as soon as he got into
his office at Pinnacle around 9:30.

"Why didn't you have him send it to our computer
at the office?" asked Maureen.

"The guy is scared to death even working there,
okay? But he needs the job and he trusts me—at least
up to a point—so let's roll with how things are, not
how we'd like them to be. I'll forward it as soon as it
comes in."

Blake and Maureen left for the office, and Charlie
waited for an email that never came.

At 9:45 Harold ducked his head into the office
of the second assistant director, the only other person
in the building who was already working.

"Hey, Roberto? I think I left my inhaler in my car,
so I'm going to zip out to the parking lot to get it. I
mean, in case anybody asks where I am."

After he left, Roberto shook his head. No one ever
gives a damn where the writer is.

In the parking lot Harold slipped into his car,
checking all around to make sure there was nobody in
any of the nearby vehicles before he took out his cell
phone. Even so, he kept his voice low when the call
connected. "Charlie? It's gone."

"What do you mean?"

"My hard drive's been wiped. The outline isn't
there anymore. What the heck's happening?"

"I don't know," Charlie answered honestly. "But
you're safe. Nothing's going to connect you to me or
anything I'm involved in. Did you ever make a paper
copy of the outline?"

"No. Oh, God! Something bad's going on, isn't it?

Am I going to lose my job?"

Desperate to keep his one inside link to Pinnacle, Charlie assured Harold that if by some fluke he lost his position at the studio, he would be offered the script for *The Brothers Gunn*. "Sammy's talking about a budget of around twenty-eight million, so you'd be making at least a couple hundred grand."

As Charlie had hoped, that calmed Harold a bit, enough for him to agree to meet with Charlie and "two associates" after work tonight to give them a verbal synopsis of the murder movie he had been working on prior to *The Devil's Platoon*.

After Charlie phoned Maureen to advise her of the change of plans, he called Max Keller. "Maxim, you got a tux?"

"Bill Blass. Why?"

"Flick off the mothballs. I'm sending Ethel and you to the Pantages to see *The Book of Mormon*. And you get a candlelight dinner at Spago beforehand."

"Do I have to blow you?"

After he hung up with Max, Charlie got in his Alfa to pick up Denice. On the drive to the airport, he realized his promise to Harold meant he would be committed to following through on what had been, up until then, only a means to an end; he was going to have to play along with Sammy Greenbaum—at least through the completion of a script for *The Brothers Gunn*.

Kill me now, Charlie thought. I'm back in show business.

Once Charlie called with news of the vanished murder movie outline, Blake and Maureen began going over all the crime scene photos, documents and interview transcripts pertaining to Cody Mason's death. He had been the co-founder of Pinnacle, along with Micah, and they believed his murder must tie in to something else the studio was involved in. That fake murder—the one in Harold Tishman's movie outline—would have to wait until tonight.

At 11:45, Keesha joined them in the fishbowl. "I'm walking over to Ziggy's. What do you two want?"

Before they could place their orders, however, Blake and Maureen saw a tall, dark figure striding down the short hall from the reception area to the door of the conference room. Libby Johnson.

Maureen smoothly pulled over the open map of the Pinnacle lot to hide the incriminating evidence, while Blake moved quickly to block the doorway.

"Libby!" he said jovially. "Nice to see you."

"Cut the crap, Ervansky. And tell me what you're up to." At six-foot-three, Liberty Johnson was one of the few people who could go eye-to-eye with Blake, and she did so now in the doorway of the conference room. He didn't budge, knowing his body was the only thing between his former colleague and everything on the table that may have been acquired in a less-than-one-hundred-percent-legal manner. Maureen leaned her slight form back against the conference table, casually attempting to block Libby's view of the documents poking out from under one side of the unfolded Pinnacle promo brochure. Keesha did the same for the other side, her more substantial body doing a slightly better job.

"I don't know what you mean," Blake said mildly.

"*Bull. Shit.* Who hired you to nose around in the Mason homicide? And how did you gain access to official police files?" She darted her eyes venomously at Keesha, who responded by folding her arms across her chest and glaring back.

"The only work we have is a couple security contracts. And I promise you, *no one* is paying us to mess with your case."

Libby didn't believe him, but stopped short of calling him a liar to his face. "Then how do you explain those documents your two pals are trying so hard to hide?"

Blake looked over his shoulder. "Oh, *that*? It's leftover paperwork from when Gail Hatcher hired us to help clear Micah's name. That job was over before it ever got started because, as you know, Micah was eliminated as a suspect almost immediately." He stood his ground as Libby fumed. "You're welcome to check that out with Mrs. Hatcher," he said innocently. "She'll back up what I'm saying."

Libby didn't buy it, not for a second, but she had no desire to interact with the odious Gail Hatcher, something she suspected Blake was counting on. She leaned in to him so she could lower her voice and not be heard by Keesha and Maureen. "I'm trying to cut you some slack here out of respect for your recent bereavement." His light flinch told her she had hit where she had aimed. "But let me warn you, you are lifting your leg on turf that has already been claimed. So back the fuck off. You clear on what I'm saying?"

"Crystal."

Libby now leaned to her right, so she could make eye contact with Keesha through the glass wall. "And, by the way," she said, louder now. "Lt. Rhee's access code has been invalidated. We don't want any nosy skells getting their hands on private police business." With a last warning glare at Blake, she pivoted and stormed off.

Once Libby cleared the hall, Keesha sputtered her indignation. "Didn't I tell you? The new title went straight to that woman's bald head!"

"No, she said it was a jurisdictional beef. Frank Goodwin is about to be indicted, and I think Libby doesn't want anything to rock the boat on her first high-profile case as a lieutenant."

Throughout the whole encounter, Maureen hadn't spoken a word, so Blake turned to her. "Anything you want to say?"

"Yes," she replied, turning to Keesha. "Roast beef on pumpernickel, extra mayo, and a side of slaw."

Three floors below in the underground parking lot, a furious Libby Johnson climbed into her car and slammed the door. She hoped Blake would back away from this thing. She wasn't lying about it being a turf squabble, but she had not even hinted at its true parameters.

Tall as she was, Lt. Johnson was neck-deep in something *very* big and *very* dangerous. She had given Blake all the warning she could risk giving; if he chose to ignore it, she couldn't protect him.

Charlie emerged from the building with Max and Ethel, the two octogenarians in evening wear. He ushered them into the idling limousine, waved as they pulled out, then turned and started walking back toward his car. Once the black Lincoln had turned the corner, though, Charlie reversed direction, going into the building. Blake and Maureen, watching from half a block away, got out of the silver Mercedes and joined him at the entrance.

The three rode up in the elevator to Maureen's old apartment, where Harold Tishman nervously paced. Charlie made intros, then asked Harold to tell them about the missing movie outline.

"It was right after I started there. Mr. Briggs told me he wanted the studio's first big release to be a stylishly noir murder mystery, and asked me to come up with some ideas. He very specifically wanted an air-tight, perfect murder and he wanted the killer to set up someone else to take the blame."

Harold had spent two weeks fleshing out an idea before pitching it to Briggs, who then had a couple suggestions. Make it two women instead of Harold's idea with two men; set it in Chicago instead of LA; change the murder weapon from a knife to a gun.

"It was all cosmetic; he didn't really tinker with my basic premise, that you could establish the perfect alibi with three phone calls between the killer and the victim, covering the time frame in which the murder occurred."

He described the "accidental" recording of the first call, giving the police two sides of a conversation that seemed normal enough. Then, after the recording stopped and the victim hung up, the killer kept talking, establishing the idea of an intruder.

Blake and Maureen listened, fascinated, when Harold claimed if two locations were close enough to share a cell tower, it would be impossible to determine where a call between them originated. In his plot, as soon as the first call was done, the killer drove to the victim's house, shot her rival, then stood over the body to place the second call, a pre-recorded message she played into the victim's phone, while simultaneously triggering a remote device to play back the identical call at her own home so it could be captured by a listening device. Taking the victim's phone with her, to use in a later frame-up, the killer rushes back to her own house, making the third call immediately.

Harold, not knowing anything about the phone calls the night of Cody Mason's murder, had no idea his plot had been used as a template for a homicide. Every day in Los Angeles, writers commit murders, rapes, embezzlement and home invasions on paper, while in real life they could never be held responsible for anything worse than slipping a couple Splenda packets into their pockets before leaving the table at Du-Par's. But Blake and Maureen realized Dominic Briggs had taken Harold's idea and run with it, adding the realistic touch of bugs from a paparazzo in Micah's house. And he must have been the one who tricked Rosa Padilla with the phony lottery ticket, choosing her for her closeness in age and size to Jane.

Charlie decided not to tell Harold what was going on. If charges wound up being filed against Briggs, Harold could always tell police later about his movie outline. He did, however, encourage the writer to recreate the synopsis as well as he could remember it—using his *home* computer, not the one in his office at Pinnacle. To seal the deal, Charlie said he would take the idea to Sammy Greenbaum for possible sale.

Charlie went home to spend the rest of the evening with his fiancée, but Blake and Maureen drove to their office to analyze this new wrinkle while it was fresh in their minds. Cards went up on the storyboard, all of them pointing to Briggs as planner and Micah as perpetrator of the crime. All that hair, button and broken twig "evidence" was obfuscation designed to lead law enforcement away from Micah, who, when he'd been in Mason's office a couple weeks before the crime, could easily have pulled a few hairs off Frank Goodwin's jacket with a piece of tape. The button he would have ripped off with his fingers.

There was still no clear motive. Neither Micah nor Briggs benefitted directly from the agent's death, although Cody's ex-wives were now much better off.

The two biggest question marks were how Micah got to and from a house nearly two miles away in the limited time frame bracketed by the first and third phone calls, and where did he dump his bloody clothes? In Harold's story, the killer was conveniently having landscape work done, so all the evidence was covered by a bed of day lilies and gladiolas, but the two detectives knew from reading the police reports that Micah's yard had been dug up and searched. Maybe the landscaping he was having done at the time was only another phony trail to waste police time. Maybe it wasn't.

They would split up tomorrow, Blake to question the owners of Guerrera Gardens and Landscaping, Maureen to see if Briggs had an alibi for the night of the crime and why he might want Cody Mason dead. And, although it wasn't on her "to do" list, Maureen would figure out how Micah could have gone back and forth between the two houses so fast.

Carlos Guerrera was supervising a koi pond installation at Tori Spelling's house, so it was his son who greeted Blake Wednesday morning. The young man wore the cheerful smile his father had taught him to give every potential customer, but when Blake flashed his ID and said he had questions about the job at Micah's, Ricky's expression turned fearful.

"Oh, God, I was afraid of this. But I swear, my men didn't do the damage. It was already there when we came back Monday morning. Will you tell Mr. Deifenschlictor I'll make it right and I'll pay for the fix, but can we *please* keep my father out of this?"

Blake realized the babbling kid thought Micah had sent him. "Well, if it wasn't your fault, I'm sure Mr. D. isn't going to ask you to pay. Why don't you explain it all to me so I can report back to him."

When Ricky returned to Micah's house with his crew of five a few minutes after 7:00 Monday morning, he sent the men to mulch and water the large flower beds they had dug in on Saturday. Finishing the fountain was a one-man job and Ricky would do that himself.

He picked up the box with the fleur-de-lis finial for the fountain's massive, urn-shaped center piece, and an eight-foot length of one-inch pipe threaded at both ends. The fountain's sprayer mechanism had already been fitted into the finial by Carlos Guerrera, right before a bout of sciatica knocked him off the job, so all Ricky had to do was lower the pipe through an opening at the top of the tall urn, hand screw it into the fitting below, then set the finial on the protruding pipe. Before tightening it, he would apply viscous bonding material to the top of the urn and the bottom of the finial, wiping away any excess with a damp cloth. After fifteen minutes he could turn on the fountain's motor and water connections.

He went over everything in his mind as he walked toward the fountain, knowing only perfection would satisfy his father. This was the first major job Carlos had ever sent him out to supervise, and Ricky knew the sudden passing of the torch had less to do with trust and more with the sciatica attack.

He set down the pipe and finial by the side of the wide bowl of the fountain, then took off his work boots and brushed the dirt off the bottoms of his socks to ensure he wouldn't scratch the Parian marble basin.

Everything went smoothly, and Ricky hummed to himself during the twenty minutes it took to install the pipe and bond the finial to the top of the urn. Stepping out of the fountain, Ricky checked his watch to start the count until he could turn on the water.

As he retrieved his shoes, then walked around the fountain to check on his crew, Ricky saw something that wasn't possible: scratches in the marble floor of the basin. Glancing around to make sure none of his men—or, even worse, Micah—were looking in his direction, Ricky rounded the scalloped periphery to examine the scratches.

Scratches?! They were gouges! Like someone had stepped into the fountain and ground in his heels. It has to be torn out and replaced, Ricky thought, then realized that's what would happen to his own ass if his father found out. He rubbed the area with a soft cloth, already knowing the pitting was much too deep to be burnished smooth.

He sweated out the minutes, turned on the water and started the motor. Once the basin had filled with a foot of water, and once the surface of that water was being dappled by drops flung from the liquid plume rising out of the finial high above, the damage wasn't visible and tears filled his eyes.

Ricky had hoped no on would notice until the fountain's first cleaning, because by then he could claim vandals must have done it after it was finished. "Please tell Mr. Deifenschlictor I'm sorry. I should have said something as soon as I found the damage."

And you should have told all this to the police, Blake thought. He didn't know yet how the fountain figured into the homicide, but the timing of the installation was unlikely to be coincidence. "I'll tell you what I'm going to do, Mr. Guerrera. I promise you Micah will not come here asking for reimbursement on the repairs, but I think you can understand why he'll want to use another company for the job."

"Of course, perfectly understandable," Ricky said, happy that he wouldn't have to dip into his meager savings to pay for the fix, thankful Micah wasn't going to beat him to a pulp, but mostly relieved his father wouldn't find out about the screw-up.

"One thing, though," Blake added. "I'm going to need all the plans, blueprints, whatever, so I can show them to the guys who do the repairs."

Blake had the fountain blueprint spread out on the conference table when Maureen came in. "Did you talk to Mason's assistant?" he asked.

"Waiting for a call-back. But I was looking over the photos Libby's team took at Micah's house, and I think I know how he got to and from the crime scene without a car."

"And *I* know where he stashed the bloody clothes."

"You first," Maureen said.

He showed her a drawing of the fountain's three components: wide, flat, scalloped-edged bowl ten feet across, massive urn-shaped center piece, and fleur-de-lis top decoration. "Micah sent the landscapers home on Saturday, *before* they could cement on this top bit."

Maureen leaned in to read the specs. "You think he shoved his clothes and shoes down through a three-inch hole?"

"No. Even if it had been possible to squeeze them through, they might have blocked the connector pipe below. If the gardener hadn't been able to screw in the vertical pipe Monday morning, he might have taken the fountain apart, or it might have sent up enough of a red flag for Libby to look into it."

"Literally," she said.

He told her his theory, that Briggs and Micah had added the fountain idea to Harold Tishman's murder plot on their own. "Remember, in his story the evidence was buried under a newly planted flower bed." The fountain was a last-minute addition to the project, he told her, and it had the landscaper scrambling to do it in time. Blake thought Micah had come back from the murder scene, stepped into the flat basin, then lifted off the urn and set it aside. After stripping down and tucking anything that might incriminate him *around* the open pipe, he lifted the massive urn and seated it back in its carved channel. By the time

Libby had her search warrant, the landscapers were finished, and it was a sealed, working fountain."

Maureen picked up the blueprint and looked at the image of the center piece. Her eyebrows went up when she read the notation alongside the illustration. "I hate to pee in your corn flakes, but this weighs 420 pounds." She turned, expecting a look of surprise or dismay, but Blake was grinning back at her.

"Yeah, that threw me for a few minutes; then I remembered reading when I was a kid about Micah having made the Olympics weight-lifting team, so I had Keesha Wiki the stats. He qualified in 1976 by hefting 475 pounds. Even adjusting for his age, isn't it possible he could still lift 420 if he had enough motivation?

Before Maureen could respond, Keesha entered. "I've spoken to almost everyone on that production list, and they all say they'd use Pinnacle again. The consensus is it's a good facility with reasonable prices. And everyone confirmed the dates of their shoots."

"So, it's a dead end," Blake said.

"Not necessarily. I noticed an unusual pattern as I went down the schedule; there were never more than two stages in production at a time. If One and Two were working, Three was vacant. If One and Three were working, Two was vacant. Not once in twelve months were all three stages in use at the same time."

It made no sense. If they were hiding something big enough to need a movie sound stage, how could it be mobile enough to move around like that? And if it was small enough to move, why waste valuable production space to hide it? Why not tuck it into a shed somewhere on the lot?

Keesha went back to her desk and two new cards went up on the story board. The first one said *empty studio*, and the second *fountain/bloody clothes*? A story was emerging, but there were too many loose ends to prove anything. And, of course, the unspoken question that always hung between Maureen and Blake was: where's Jane? She could easily be hidden in something smaller than a sound stage, but that rotating empty stage was tantalizing. Blake unconsciously touched his shirt front over the diamond heart, then turned to Maureen. "You said you figured out how Micah went between the two houses?"

"Maybe. But, we'll have to go to my dad's to run some tests."

"What kind of tests?"

"I saw how enviously you looked at my Vincent and dad's Low-Rider, so Charlie went out and bought you a bike."

On the drive to the house, Blake protested that he couldn't accept a motorcycle as a gift. Charlie would have to take it back and get a refund.

As they turned into the cul-de-sac, Blake saw Charlie straight ahead in the driveway of the big Spanish house, standing next to a shiny blue and silver bike, a two-wheeler about the right size for an eight year old.

Maureen eased the car onto the circular drive. "Libby only analyzed the tread contents of Micah's bike. The smaller one belonging to his kid never came off the wall pegs." She stopped near her father.

The first few tries were comical. A six-foot-four-inch man on a bike designed for a child is all knees and elbows aimed at four different compass points. As he got used to his mini-ride, however, Blake was able to tuck himself in fairly tightly. More importantly, he built up speed, tearing down the cul-de-sac to Nichols Canyon and back. As Charlie and Maureen watched, Blake jerked the handle bars and skidded to a stop right in front of them.

"I think you're right about this," he said to Maureen. "How did you figure it out?"

"He didn't seem like the suburban parkour type to me, and his kid's bike was the only vehicle no one ever looked at."

During the lunch Denice had prepared, Maureen got the call from Cody's assistant. She left the table to speak with her, and when she returned she told Blake, "We may finally have a motive."

Karen Chapel had not told Maureen anything she hadn't already said to the police, but once the BHPD had Frank Goodwin and all the evidence against him, they had stopped looking at Pinnacle Pictures. Karen didn't *really* think her boss would have sold the agency and moved over to help Micah run the studio, but he had been kicking the idea around for a few months before his death.

After lunch Blake and Maureen went back to the office and put another card on their story board. Someone had been willing to kill Cody Mason to prevent him from moving over to join Micah at the studio. They couldn't believe it was Micah himself, as all indications were they had been besties since the actor was a teenager. No, this more likely had to do with Dominic Briggs protecting his control over both the studio and the star. Charlie had told them Briggs acted the part of "lord of the manor" when he greeted Sammy Greenbaum and him, but Maureen had not been able to find much information on the guy. Maybe Briggs couldn't afford to have Mason snooping around the lot because of whatever it was being hidden and moved from stage to stage.

Maureen asked Keesha to swap cars with her overnight, as she and Blake wanted to test out their bike theory on the path between Cody Mason's house and Micah's, and neither of their 550SLs had the room to cart around a bicycle. Keesha was happy to hand over the keys to her utilitarian Toyota and drive home in Maureen's Mercedes.

After Keesha left for the day, the two detectives studied their storyboard—the picture of the case they were trying to build. So far, Jane's name did not appear on any of the posted cards, but they were both aware tomorrow was the day DNA results were due in from the lab in West Virginia.

They didn't have a solid case against Micah and Briggs, but if Blake biked the round-trip tomorrow morning within the time established by the phone calls and the M.E., Maureen knew they'd have enough to take their theory to the police.

"Knock, knock." Charlie entered the fishbowl.

"Hey, Dad. What's up?"

"Denice is working all evening to get things set for next week's grand opening, so I thought I'd see if you kids wanted to join me for dinner. Maybe Thai food?"

Maureen checked her watch. "At 5:15? Were you angling for an early-bird special?"

"Up thine. I'm not that old yet. I thought I could pitch on the case with you for a while first. Anything still dangling?"

Blake snorted. "How about everything?"

"What my eloquent partner is trying to say is that while we have ample information on many disparate fronts, we don't have the *complete* package on any of them, so we're still looking for the one string that ties it all together."

"Then throw me your best curve ball. Maybe fresh eyes can spot a forest there among all your trees."

Maureen looked at Blake, who shrugged and said, "The empty studio?" She then told Charlie about the strange production schedule with only two stages ever working at a time and their theory that something big was hidden on the lot, being moved from one stage to another to escape detection.

He heard her out and said, "I don't think *any*thing is moving from one stage to another. I believe the whole stage is moving."

They looked at him with incredulity. Had he forgotten how humongous a movie sound stage is? You can't hitch it to the back of a pickup truck and drag it around like a mobile home. Charlie saw their skepticism, but went on. "Okay, Maureen, let's say you're a day player going onto a lot for a week's work on a sitcom. You're supposed to report to Stage Ten, but you've never been on that lot before. How do you know where to go?"

"I'd ask the gate guard."

"Who has five cars stacked up behind yours and only enough time to check your name against the drive-on list. No, all he's going to do is wave you toward a parking lot and bark at you to pull up."

"All right then, after I parked I'd look around for a number on a sound stage." She stopped to explain to Blake that every stage displays its number high up near the top in huge painted numerals.

"*Painted*," Charlie echoed.

"Isn't that what I said? *Painted* onto the exterior wall, so you can see it from anywhere on the lot."

"When Briggs was driving us around, I noticed something odd about the stage numbering. At the time I thought they were only trying to be different, because the numbers on the Pinnacle stages are separate pieces *mounted* onto the exterior walls."

Blake and Maureen let this sink in, then Blake said, "Meaning they're moveable."

"Not easily, though," observed Maureen. "They're

forty or fifty feet up, depending on the stage."

Charlie grinned at his daughter. "And what piece of equipment could get you up there? Spoiler alert: you'll *always* find one on a movie lot."

Maureen smiled. "A crane! Jesus, Blake, that's it! They're moving the numbers around so nobody figures out there's one stage that's always out of production."

She immediately called Keesha and asked her to fax the aerial photo of the Pinnacle lot to all those businesses she had contacted. "Have them mark an X over the stage where they shot."

Micah's ex, Deidre, snuggled into her Italian silk sheets, a satisfied smile on her face. She hadn't screwed a man so thoroughly since her split from her husband. As for Dominic Briggs, screwing Micah's ex had been a genuine pleasure.

The mutual screw job had taken place earlier that day at a table in the Polo Lounge, where, over a prestige cuvée, Deidre signed away her son's share of Pinnacle Pictures for twice what it was worth. She had good reason to believe she had gotten the better deal. Of the two founder/owners, the one with the brains was dead, and the other one, judging from the last time she had seen him, was losing his mind. The guy running the studio, Dominic Briggs, was nice enough and he seemed pretty smart, but he had zero experience in the movie business. Deidre knows Hollywood is a town that spreads newcomers on toast points and has them for appetizers. How long would it be before the dinky production facility in the Tujunga boonies went belly up, leaving her poor son with no money to buy a Rolls Royce for his mother to drive him around in?

Deidre had left the meeting with a life-changing

check, a strong desire to hit Neiman's, and the belief that she had wrapped Dominic around her pinky.

Briggs himself had walked away from their get-together with two things on his face: a smug smile and a kiss-shaped blotch of Christian Dior's "Red Riot." After pouring an entire bottle of champagne into the trashiest of Micah's ex-wives, Briggs had persuaded her to sign over the share of Pinnacle she controlled.

That was a coup in itself, but Dom could now use the sale to leverage away the smaller pieces owned by the *other* two former Mrs. Deifenschlictors. He would make certain they heard whispered rumors about the sale by the final former wife, ensuring they would suspect Deidre of *knowing* something and bailing before a disaster. Then he would step in and allow them to unload their holdings on him.

Everything was going according to plan. Micah had unwittingly signed over power of attorney to Dom the previous weekend, so now it didn't really matter if *The Devil's Platoon* was completed or not. Briggs would play along, "directing" the film until it was either done or had crashed and burned because of Micah's instability. By taking the director's job, he guaranteed his continued control over the actor, even onto the set, and had headed off the possibility of a *real* director gaining the slightest influence over the star. The assistant director understood his job was to shoulder virtually all of the directing duties, and for this he was being paid much more than his usual fee. Plus, he had been guaranteed a *genuine* directing credit on Pinnacle's next film, a rom-com to be shot in...oh, how about Tahiti?

The next morning Blake made three round-trips between Micah's house and Cody's, as Maureen clocked each one. By the time they put the bike back into Keesha's car and headed to the office, they knew Micah would have had enough time to kill Mason and make it back home within the established window.

They walked in to the smell of coffee and, as they crossed reception toward the archway at the back, Keesha handed Blake a large envelope. After getting their coffee from the kitchenette they went into the fishbowl. While Blake opened the envelope, Maureen posted another card on the board—*getaway bike*.

"What's that?" she asked, turning from the story board.

"Your dad was right; they're moving the numbers around on the stages. Look at this." He showed her Keesha's chart. Of the two dozen clients she had been able to reach last night and this morning, all of them had shot on one of only two stages. Blake pulled out an aerial photo of Pinnacle to check the stage layout.

Because land is so expensive in Los Angeles County, and because each movie studio has only a finite amount of it, sound stages are normally jammed together tightly. Pinnacle Pictures, however, having a hundred acres to work with and plans for only three stages, had been able to do things differently.

Once Cody Mason heard Micah's idea for creating little "locations," planted and landscaped to look like something other than southern California, he had asked the contractor to spread out the sound stages and put the five-acre locations in pairs between them. When the work was completed two years later, the lot was laid out with a road in to a central hub containing a small executive office building, as well as three other structures housing support staff, cafeteria, screening room, gym, equipment storage and wardrobe department. An editing bay and recording studio rounded out the facilities at the heart of Pinnacle.

The stages were set back a half-mile from the hub and separated widely enough that anybody working on one stage wouldn't even be aware of the existence of the others. Cody thought it gave the lot a boutique feel, but Dominic Briggs had taken advantage of that separation for other uses.

Blake and Maureen looked down on the image of the fanned-out stages, noting the one farthest east was the one none of the clients had marked with an X. Between that stage and the perimeter fence lay two large plots of land labeled K-5 and K-6. And on the other side of the fence was the property belonging to Dallis and Ostin Bates.

"I thought you'd want to know as soon as the call came in," Keesha said from the doorway. "The DNA results prove the woman who died in the fire was *not* Jane."

The breath went out of Blake and he closed his eyes to keep it together. Keesha discreetly withdrew. Once the glass door had closed, Maureen quietly said, "We have enough. Let's take this to the police."

"Which police?"

"I don't understand the question."

"The sheriff up in Tujunga where Pinnacle is? That jerk from Hollywood with jurisdiction in the arson/homicide? Or maybe Beverly Hills because they covered the murder that got the whole ball rolling?"

Maureen hadn't thought that through. She only knew they now had enough circumstantial evidence to justify an official investigation.

"And don't forget," Blake continued, "everything we got that first day is covered by privilege."

"Even without it we can show motive, how Micah got there—"

"Which we cannot prove. We have a half-assed theory that Micah pre-recorded his second and third phone messages, then used some unknown remote device to play them back in his own house for the benefit of hidden microphones, while simultaneously playing them into Cody's cell phone and land line."

"Blake, they can check the treads of Micah's kid's bike, prove that was his modus transportatis."

"Nine weeks ago when they were fresh, maybe. But any grass or leaf parts dried up long ago. They won't prove anything."

She didn't understand why Blake was suddenly pissing all over the work they had done. He had been right there with her, ferreting out every scrap of information. Now he was giving up? She watched him staring down at the sound stage where no movie was ever made, finally understanding. Softly, she said, "We're not taking this to the police, are we?"

"*I'm* not." He tapped the photo. "Jane's there; she has to be there." The man who had been so hesitant to believe his wife was alive, now embraced not only her continued existence, but her precise location.

"Let's say you're right; she's there. The problem is we don't know what *else* is there."

He looked at her with an expression devoid of emotion. "I don't care. I'm going in after her."

Maureen knew that on some level he was right. If—*if*—Jane were being held in that isolated sound stage, and *if* the various law enforcement agencies involved waived the usual dick-measuring contest over who had first dibs, they would still have to apply for a search warrant. By the time they finally began questioning people and searching the place, there would have been ample time to move Jane. Or worse.

No, a small strike team was much more likely to elude discovery while locating and extracting her. After that, they could turn over everything they had to the police. "Okay, I'm in."

They decided to go Sunday morning. That would give them two full days to plan, and they assumed it would be a time when few people would be on the lot. They didn't know *The Devil's Platoon* was set to begin shooting on Monday or that Briggs and his comrades-in-arms planned to spend all Sunday at the mystery sound stage where production was up and running.

Maureen went to the office Friday morning, but only long enough to sign the stack of paychecks Keesha had waiting for her. After that, she went back to Charlie's house so she and Blake could go over their maps and information.

They would drive as far as The Blind Pig, then collect the Vincent Black Shadow for the ride toward the Bates trailer. Leaving the Shadow camouflaged and hidden, they'd circumvent the former meth lab on foot, then enter the Pinnacle lot at the southern edge of K-6. They would then make their way across the five-acre parcel to the stage.

Maureen gathered what she'd need to cut through the fence and break into the stage. She also gave Blake a shopping list for himself which included the brand of sturdy, but flexible, boots he would need. Also, leather or canvas jeans—no denim. First aid kit. Two extra-large sweatshirts. Blanket. Gatorade.

That's when Blake stopped jotting things down and looked at her. "Are we going on a rescue mission or a picnic?"

At first she couldn't believe he could be so naive. Did he think this would be like a scene in a movie, with the reunited lovers successfully dodging a hail of bullets while they made their daring escape? She needed to give him a wake-up call, but did *not* want to scare the hell out of him. "I hope we find Jane when we go in there," she said calmly. "I really do. But she's been missing more than six weeks, and we don't know what shape she's in. She could be injured, starving. She might not be able to walk."

Understanding transformed his face when her words registered, as the healthy, happy Jane of his fantasies, the girl waiting for him to rescue her, suddenly turned into a more realistic Jane: neglected, dehydrated, perhaps hurt. Had she been beaten? Raped? She was halfway through her second trimester and had probably not seen a doctor. What if she'd had complications with the pregnancy?

Once Maureen saw he had adjusted his thinking to the reality of the situation, she went on. "With two sweatshirts, a knife and a pair of tree branches, I can make a stretcher if that's the only way we get her out of there. The blanket and Gatorade will keep her comfortable and hydrated while you two wait in the forest and I ride into Tujunga for the sheriff and an ambulance." She could have said more, but it would have been overkill; Blake's grim expression told Maureen she had made all her points.

"What else do I need to get?"

"Boots, pants and a heavy jacket for Jane. If she can walk, we'll have to kit her out so she can make it back through the woods with us."

Denice noticed the solemn activity Saturday morning, but mentioned nothing to Charlie. She had been living here only a short time and for all she knew it was normal for Blake to be slipping in and out, always returning with a large package he took back to his room. And the fact that Maureen appeared to be both focused and distracted at the same time when she infrequently emerged from her room—for coffee, a sandwich, rags and oil—didn't surprise Charlie's fiancée. Maureen had been tolerant of Denice's presence in her father's life, but no one could accuse her of being welcoming.

Ignoring the intense bustle, Denice concentrated on Charlie, who was pulling together a wedding and a honeymoon in record time. The diner would open next Friday, with Denice working full time that first week to make sure Cindy knew how to run everything by herself. Then, one week later, she and Charlie would be married in a civil ceremony to be followed by a reception at the Bel-Air Hotel.

The names he had run by her—Villa d'Este, Le Crillon, Chateau Eza—were unfamiliar, but Charlie's enthusiasm was endearing, and all she wanted to do was make him happy. So, she relaxed and left the planning in his capable hands.

In Blake's room Maureen went over the checklist, making certain they had everything they'd need. Whatever Blake didn't have on his body would be stowed in the backpack he would carry.

Maureen set a 3:00 A.M. wake-up time, wanting to be inside the Pinnacle fence before full daylight, then went to her room for final preparations. She didn't know if Jane was inside that stage, but Blake believed it—*had* to believe it—with all his heart, and she was going to play along. She also wasn't sure it was smart, the two of them going in alone, but Blake would do it with or without her, and Maureen knew he had a much better chance of coming back alive if she went with him.

She laid out a selection of handguns on the bed, evaluating each one before making her decision about what to carry. Putting the also-rans back in her gun cabinet, she took up the soft rags and prepared to sink into the soothing, Zen-like state in which she always floated while breaking down and cleaning a firearm.

Charlie woke up to the smell of coffee at 3:30. Denice slept soundly next to him, and Maureen had never been much of a morning person, so his first thought was that the timer on the coffee maker had malfunctioned. Barefoot, he padded down the hall to the kitchen, flipping the light switch and confronting a nightmare.

As his eyes adjusted to the overhead light, the nightmare coalesced into his own daughter. Charlie had not seen Maureen in full motorcycle leathers for a long time, and he noted she had dulled the normally reflective studs and zipper-pulls.

"Sorry," she said, slightly louder than a whisper. "I tried to be quiet."

"I had to get up to take a whiz anyway," he lied. Charlie took in the gun at her waist. Presumably, it would become invisible once she zipped her jacket closed. A few inches to the left of her huge, pewter belt buckle hung a leather sheath which held a hunting knife. "Tell me you're not on assignment for *them*."

"Oh, God, no. They're out of my life forever."

"Then what?"

"We're doing some early morning reconnaissance."

His eyes dropped to the knife and gun. Even a former comedy writer and TV producer knew you didn't arm yourself like that for simple recon. For a moment Maureen thought about telling him the truth, that the knife was only there for show, a pawn to be sacrificed, but if she did, Charlie was smart enough to figure out the second part of that truth: if Maureen found herself in close enough combat to be able to use the knife, she was as good as dead. Not having either the time or inclination to share her survival tricks with her father, she fell back on her old stand-by. "Don't worry, I'll be fine."

Blake entered, carrying a medium-sized backpack. He was as ninja'd up as Maureen was, so Charlie shook his head, sighed and walked back toward his bedroom. Maureen turned to her partner as soon as Charlie was gone, "We have ten minutes if you'd like coffee."

She called Fluffy from the car, so he was at the door of The Pig at 4:30, groggy from sleep and wearing boxers and a tank top. He was unsurprised by their S&M-ish outfits, but then in his younger days, Fluffy had been a roadie for Kiss. "She's fueled and ready."

"Thanks, Fluff. I need to ask one more favor; if we aren't back here by 7:00 o'clock, call the sheriff and tell him we're being held on the Pinnacle lot. He should look for us at the stage that's farthest east."

"Got it."

Blake and Maureen would *not* be back by 7:00, and Fluffy *would* call the sheriff. But when Dale Trainor and three of his deputies arrived at the lot, they wouldn't be able to get within a quarter mile of the easternmost stage.

This time Blake knew to wrap his arms around Maureen and stay tight against her back when the Vincent Black Shadow took off. Through the double layers of leather between them Maureen couldn't feel the heat from his chest, only the pressure. She knew this was most likely the last time they would ever be so close physically and she savored the contact for the entire ride, tamping down a feeling of loss when she stopped and he withdrew his arms from her waist.

She walked the Shadow twenty feet into the trees before rocking it back onto its stand. After checking her compass with a tiny flashlight, Maureen signaled Blake to follow, then plunged into the dense forest.

Once they were past the Bates trailer and through another few hundred yards of vegetation, they came to a five-strand barbed-wire fence with signs posted every twenty feet. Even in the pre-dawn semi-dark, they could read the ominous words: TRESPASSERS WILL BE SHOT.

Maureen dropped to her knees and fished out the wire cutter from her jacket. "You might want to stand back while I do this," she said to Blake. "Barbwire has a nasty habit of slashing unpredictably when it's cut."

He realized now why she had carried her helmet on their trek through the trees, as she slipped it on and bent closer to the bottom wire.

In Dominic Briggs' office, five men sat around talking, smoking cigarettes and drinking coffee. He and his three partners were enjoying downtime and camaraderie before golf-carting over to the stage.

Micah wore his combat fatigues. He had an M-14 resting across his knees and a .45 holstered at his hip. His eyes were vague and his left hand twitched every now and then. He had swallowed a couple of oxy's on waking an hour before and they were beginning to smooth off the ragged edges of Mr. Toad's Wild Meth Ride—the last, he had promised himself, until the movie was wrapped. Prior to the arrival of the other three men, he had insisted Dominic inject him with AAS. That triple-indulgence in less than twelve hours eradicated what little remaining self-control he had, so while his brain succumbed to the invasion of the white plaque, and the soup surrounding that dying organ soured and spoiled, Micah faded away and was replaced by Capt. Luther Hardy, USMC. Luther was jumpy because he *really* wanted to kill someone, but he wasn't allowed to until cameras rolled tomorrow.

As the former Marine known as "Ace" joked with

the man he thought was still Micah—"Yo, gyrene. Movie star mañana, right?"—Dominic's attention was caught by something on his computer screen. A small warning flash made him knit his brow as he keyed in a code. He looked at the schematic that now appeared on the screen, a red light pulsing on a spot along one of the outside lines.

"Fuck! The perimeter's breached!"

"Where?" Ace barked, rushing with the other two former Marines to surround Dominic and view the screen. Fingers tapping frantically, Briggs isolated a line representing the entire eastern fence.

"Halfway down the outer edge of K-5. Get your weapons and meet me at the stage. It's going to take them some time to cross that swamp." As the others scrambled to leave, Briggs turned and said, "Micah, you stay here. I mean it, don't leave this room."

Briggs knows the last thing he needs is for Micah to shoot some trespassing tweak or hunter. Dom and his boys will scare the shit out of the intruders, maybe even kick their asses a bit, but they'll send them on their way alive, so as not to bring any unwanted attention to the studio.

Their running footsteps clatter down the hallway, the sound cross-fading with the steady hiss of the monsoon rain pelting the dense marshes of the Mekong Delta. As Luther rises from his chair, the crackle of a radio man's call for reinforcements echoes in his dying brain, and his move to the desk is accompanied by the staccato *ak-ak-ak* of a machine gunner holding position against attacking enemies.

As the imaginary battle rages in Luther's mind, his eyes are drawn to the pulsing dot on the screen. The war—*his war*—is right there, beckoning him.

Wait, wait! A second blip signals a frantic call for help in a another location. K-6. Fighter jets scream overhead, carpet bombing the jungle, laying ground fire for those Marines about to be overrun by a tide of Viet Cong. A grin distorts Luther's lower face, never reaching his vacant eyes. Exploding grenades drown out the *helpme!helpme!helpme!* screams of dying men and the red dot beats in syncopation with the rifle fire only he can hear.

There is his enemy, his heroic destiny. Another few seconds and he's gone...in every sense of the word.

At an isolated spot along the fence surrounding K-6, Maureen cuts through the fifth and last strand of barbed wire.

The transition was jarring when Blake and Maureen crossed the fence line, moving from under the shading boughs of Douglas firs, California walnuts and Jeffry pines and into a lush thicket of towering bamboo. Staying on a northwest compass heading, they could hear water rushing nearby, presumably the man-made river featured in the Pinnacle brochure.

They found a rough path and followed it for the short distance that it went in the same direction they wanted, but when it curved away from their heading, Blake and Maureen were forced to continue pushing through the dense, unfamiliar flora.

Capt. Luther Hardy crouched down, listening to movement in the surrounding jungle. Viet Cong. How many he couldn't tell. The war wasn't scheduled to start until tomorrow, but the enemy had apparently slipped through for an early advantage. He moved quietly through the foliage, avoiding the spots where he knew traps were already set.

Because of the twelve-inch difference in their heights, Blake could see over the spiny tops of the sedge and stunted trees springing up from the moist ground but Maureen couldn't, so he took the compass and the lead.

When Luther got closer to the sound of human movement he raised his head high enough to take a quick look, then dropped down into the protective cover of the undergrowth. He had seen only one man. Luther moved away in a wide arc, intending to get in front of the lone V.C. and ambush him in the clearing up ahead. He removed a handful of loose cartridges from the thigh pouch of his fatigues.

Maureen tugged on the back of Blake's jacket, and when he turned she signaled him to stop and drop. He squatted down so his head was well below the tips of the reedy growth. "Listen," she whispered, her lips close to his ear.

Holding very still, Blake focused. Soon he heard a soft *thump* from somewhere up ahead. After a half-minute, they heard it again. Five or six seconds passed before a repeat. "Animal?" Blake asked softly, his own lips grazing the strands of red-gold hair that had escaped her scrunchy and now floated around her ear.

He was so close she could smell his after shave, and it was killing her. "Maybe. Could be a branch blowing against a tree."

There was a long wait, then another light *thump*. Maureen tapped Blake's chest and pointed straight ahead. She then touched her own chest and signaled that she would circle around and come in from the side. She crept away and Blake gave her a lead since she had more ground to cover. During the wait, he heard the *thump* twice. When he moved forward, still crouched low, he slipped out his Glock and held it in front of him.

Maureen had also taken out her weapon, a 9mm Browning Hi-Power, as she moved through the sedge, always keeping the *thump* to her left. The HP was her favorite handgun, but she felt better knowing it wasn't the only firearm on board.

One last cartridge arced into the air and tagged a half-buried tree root in the clearing, before Luther heard the enemy approaching. He tucked himself down, allowing the V.C. to pass within yards of him. Leaving his M-14 on the ground—he preferred to kill at close range with his .45—Luther rose without a sound and fell in behind his prey.

At the edge of the clearing Blake stopped and looked around. No movement; no sign of life—animal *or* human. Then a glimpse of something half-hidden by a tree root, its polished surface glinting for a split second as the leafy canopy fluttered in the breeze, allowing a narrow shaft of sunlight to penetrate to the ground. He was about to step forward when he felt a gun barrel connect with the back of his head.

"Drop your weapon and get on your knees, you gook bastard!"

Deep in the trees Maureen heard the command and knew Blake was in trouble. Unable to see over the sedge tops, she moved through it in the direction of the voice, making as little noise as possible.

Blake allowed the Glock to fall from his hand, holding both arms out unthreateningly. "Hey, I think there's been a slight misunderstanding here."

"Oh, you speaky-de-inglish, huh? They teach you that in combat school, you FUCKING SLOPE?"

The shouting came from very close behind him, and Blake felt droplets of spittle fleck the back of his neck below the gun barrel. Ducking and spinning to tackle the guy was out of the question, as Blake recognized Micah's voice. *If* he could somehow avoid the gun and get him into a clinch, Blake was likely to have his spine snapped. He knew Maureen was probably already sighting her shot, so better to keep the separation between himself and Micah.

"I'm American, dude," he said in an upbeat tone of voice. "Seriously, if you'll let me turn around so you can see my face, I'll prove—"

"Shut up! Shut up! This is how you tricked Cody isn't it? Got him to drop his guard so you could jam that knife into his gut. Jesus! He was only nineteen years old, the best damn soldier I ever knew."

Okay, Blake concluded, he's barking mad with a dollop of bat-shit crazy. And where the hell is Annie Oakley?

"NINETEEN!!" Luther screamed into Blake's ear. "Any you *murdered* him!"

Maureen was now close enough to the edge of the clearing to have a partial view through the screen of green stalks, but Blake was in front of Micah across the open space, so she couldn't get a true shot. She could break cover with a lot of noise and draw his fire, but that was risky. She wouldn't be able to shoot until Blake was clear, giving Micah several seconds to aim at her and get off a round or two. That was a .45 he had pressed into the back of Blake's head and she did not want to be even *grazed* by something that gonzo, especially out here in the middle of nowhere. Also, if she made a sudden move, Micah might plug one into Blake out of reflex. As she debated retracing her steps to come up *behind* Micah, the scene changed in the clearing.

"Listen, I'm really sorry about what happened to your friend, but I swear I wasn't—"

The thundering report of the .45 cut off his words and a column of dirt exploded upwards, scary close to Blake's feet. As he froze, so did Maureen, hidden in the sedge and fearing she was already too late.

"I told you to SHUT THE FUCK UP! Now put your hands behind your head and get on your knees."

When Blake didn't respond fast enough, Micah swung the gun and slammed it into the side of his head hard enough to stagger him. "ON! YOUR! KNEES!"

Blake complied, feeling like the main event at an execution. At least with him on his knees Maureen would have a clear shot. Although his head still rang and he felt blood soaking the collar of his sweatshirt, he kept the Glock in his line of sight, hoping to lunge for it and roll to his feet after Micah took the first bullet from Maureen.

Distracted as he was by finding his best friend's killer, Luther didn't see the woman rise from the grass at the same time the V.C. sank to his knees.

Maureen raised the Browning, but knew she had to make Micah aim the .45 at her, so as not to get Blake accidentally killed. She liked her chances much better now, and in a straight-up shoot-out, she knew Micah would be the loser. Taking a deep breath and holding the Hi-Power out in front of her, Maureen plunged through the last few yards of reedy growth, her third step bringing her to the edge of the clearing and landing her right foot on a steel bar.

The noises came in rapid overlap, causing Blake and Micah to turn at the sound of the woman crashing through the surrounding jungle. Then they heard the metallic *sproing* and snap as a trap was triggered and its toothed arch leapt up to bite into Maureen's leg from both sides.

The trap's chain axed her forward momentum, but she had already launched herself, so her body was fully extended when she slammed into the ground face first. The impact shattered her nose and sent the Browning into a long, aerial arc.

Pulling his hands from behind his head, Blake dived for his Glock, but just as he heard Maureen's cry of pain, he felt Micah's steel-toed boot slam into his ribs with all the strength that overdeveloped leg could deliver. The blow sent Blake rolling, and by the time he curled himself into a ball to brace for the next kick, his Glock and Maureen's Browning had been scooped up and dropped into one of the cargo pockets of the fatigues Micah wore.

Maureen raised up on her hands. Blood streamed from her nose, tears filled her eyes, and she gasped as she fought to remain conscious. Noting she was still armed, Luther crossed to her, but he also kept an eye on the prostrate enemy puking in the center of the clearing.

"I'll take that pig-sticker on your hip, if you don't mind," the captain said, aiming the .45 at her. He sounded calmer now, in control. Trembling with the bone-deep pain in her leg, Maureen unsnapped the leather sheath and withdrew the hunting knife slowly, holding it by the blade and extending it in reverse. Luther took it and hurled it away into the trees.

"Please, my leg," she choked out, backing up to get into a sitting position, ostensibly to check the damage from the trap jaws.

"Fuck your leg. Lift up the cuff of those leather pants." Maureen glared at him and spat blood at his feet. With a flick of the .45 he communicated his lack of tolerance for petulant resistance.

Blake slowly got to his knees, but Maureen could see blood pouring from his head wound and strings of vomit trailing as he gagged. He was injured too badly to have any chance in mano-a-mano combat with the monster standing over her, so Maureen knew she'd be playing this little game of "death or dare" by herself. With an angry show of reluctance she raised the hem of her left pants leg, revealing the Walther TPH snug in its compact holster.

Luther laughed, waving his weapon to get her to

pull back her hands. He relieved her of the dainty handgun and stashed it with the others, *after* he had caressed her calf. "Now that you're declawed, little puss, you wait right here for daddy."

His meaty paw came down to roughly cup the back of her head, fingers digging into her hair for a better grip. As he jerked her head up and bent to kiss her, Maureen didn't dare try to push him away. Instead, she pulled back against his hand, saying, "I'm bleeding." She popped the "b" hard enough to spatter his approaching face with some of the blood dripping from her nose to her chin. He paused, grinning.

"A bloody battlefield never stopped a Marine," he teased, before mashing his lips onto hers. He ground them from side to side, raking her broken nose and bringing fresh tears to her eyes. Still, Maureen kept her hands down.

He released her and straightened up, his face now a macabre half-mask of gore. "Don't you worry, Red, there's plenty more where *that* came from. But first I have to go kill that sumbitch over there."

Maureen prayed he'd take his time doing it. She twisted around to examine the trap, whimpering as the movement wrenched another wave of pain from where the trap jaws held her. The jagged metal bit deeply into the leather encasing her right leg, but she could see the sharp tips had been filed slightly and painted with a thick rubberizer. Even so, the stunt man who was *supposed* to step on this for the camera would be protected by thick padding from his ankle to the top of his calf. The points might have been dulled, but the spring itself was full, bear-catching strength, as she found out when she tried to pull the jaws apart. Nerves and muscles were being crushed under the pressure, and Maureen's foot was already numb. She glanced over her shoulder to make sure Micah wasn't still near.

Blake staggered to his feet, leaning sideways to protect the two ribs whose splintered ends rasped against each other with every breath he took.

Maureen saw Micah circling him, and hoped she'd have enough time. She reached for the large pewter belt buckle riding below her waist, but blood dripped down on it as she leaned over, slicking the release catch.

"Where's Jane?" Blake demanded, straightening up through excruciating pain.

Continuing the circular stalking of his quarry, forcing Blake to turn in order to face him, Luther asked, "Who?" He was very obviously enjoying the game.

"You know who! My *wife*! Where is she?" After he shouted, Blake gagged in agony, and not only from the broken ribs.

Good, Maureen thought, keep him talking. She released the catch on the buckle, took hold of it and slid out a razor-sharp, five-inch blade that had been sheathed inside the belt—what old-time cops used to refer to as a grand jury knife, one you threw down next to the body after you realized you had shot an unarmed man. With another quick check to verify she was unobserved, Maureen began slicing her pants leg an inch above the jawline of the trap, every movement accompanied by a gasp of pain.

"Oh, you mean *Blondie*," Luther snarled. "I guess you figured out it wasn't her we torched."

"Where is she?"

Since Luther Hardy wasn't a real person, only a character in a script, he couldn't pull up any *actual* memories. All he could do was parrot and embellish the words he had heard Dominic Briggs drilling into Micah for weeks. "You have any idea how much a rich rag-head will pay for a blue-eyed, all-American girl? Those oil sheiks love them some sweet blonde nookie. Natural too; we checked."

Blake forced himself to stay silent, turning to face his circling tormentor, watching for a mistake.

"And here's another thing those turbans'll pay big bucks for: cute little American babies, as long as their hair is light and their eyes are blue. Maybe they raise'em for sex slaves. Start training them young so they have all the skills by the time they hit puberty."

Woozy from pain, Maureen worked steadily with the knife, trying to cut a big enough opening where she needed it. But the leather was sturdy, the knife handle was slick with blood, and it was taking more time than she had thought it would.

"You sick son of a bitch," Blake hissed, staggering forward, despite the grinding in his rib cage.

Luther dodged the drunken lunge, continuing his stalking-in-the-round. This time when he spoke, the matter-of-factness had gone out of his voice and he sounded angry. "You know what they won't pay one goddamn dime for, though? A fat, sloppy pregnant bitch."

Maureen wasn't quite ready, but Blake was about to talk himself into a bullet and she knew she couldn't hold off a second longer. "Hey, asshole!" she shouted. Goliath's expression turned to one of disbelief that David had challenged him. "Yeah, I'm talking to you, G.I. Joe!" Realizing the V.C. was trying to maneuver behind him, Luther spun quickly, swinging his gun to slam it into the side of the gook's face. Stumbling backwards, Blake went down again, but was still conscious, still looking for an opening.

Maureen struggled to her knees, fumbling behind herself with the knife as Micah advanced. "Yo, big man! Try to get me, you elf-dick shit-weasel!"

Luther's voice dropped to a threatening snarl. "You stupid cooze. I was going to give you the ride of your life, but now I'm going to blow your goddamn brains out."

"You couldn't give a ride to your own hand, you impotent freak," Maureen challenged, dropping the knife and pushing her hand through the cut in the leather.

His face was now half-blood, half-rage, but he hadn't yet raised the .45. He wanted her to know who he was, who she had crossed, before she died. "You think you can take me on, little girl?" The .45 began its upward arc. "I AM A UNITED STATES MARINE!"

"Yeah?" she shouted, freeing the Baby Browning from where the trap jaws had sealed it against her leg. "Well, *SEMPER FI*, motherfucker!" She whipped up her gun and fired at Micah/Luther/Goliath before he could blink. Dropping his .45 and grabbing his twice-hit right arm, the big man went down in a ball of searing pain, shocked that real bullets hurt so much more than movie bullets.

Blake snatched up the .45 while Micah writhed on the ground. He stepped over to the injured man and aimed at his head. "Where is she?"

"Dead! We killed her because she was no good to us! Now get a medic, I need help!"

Maureen looked on, and for a heartbeat she was willing to let Blake pull the trigger. If Jane really *was* dead, maybe someday he might....

But, oh, God, could she really watch him step over that moral line she had crossed so long ago and join her on the dark side? Was she going to stand by and let him kill something in himself by executing Micah? When his finger began to squeeze, Maureen had her answer. "Blake, no!" she screamed. "Help me!"

As if snapping awake from a nightmare, Blake

realized she was still caught in the trap. Leaving Micah bellowing for help, he limped over to her. Kneeling, he laid down the .45 and put his hands to the steel jaws. Straining, feeling his own rib ends grinding against each other, Blake pulled with everything he had. Maureen's hands, snugged next to his own, whitened with effort. Slowly, they pried the teeth apart enough for her to drag her leg out. "Move your hands," he shouted, and as she did he let go. The trap thunked violently, shark teeth chomping only air.

Before Maureen could say anything, Blake had grabbed the .45 and gone back to finish the job. Her first attempt to put weight on the injured leg dropped her to the ground, but when she saw Blake point the gun to fire, she found the strength to rise and launch herself toward him, howling, "No-o-o!"

Blake couldn't hear her. He was in another place now, a place where Jane was truly dead and the squirming piece of shit at his feet had hurt her. When he saw Maureen hurtling toward him, he instinctively lashed out with his left arm, deflecting her momentum and sending her wind-milling toward a massive tree at the edge of the clearing. She frantically tried to stop her stumbling trajectory, but when her hand rammed into the tree, both bones in her left forearm snapped. Blake turned toward the sound of the break and her scream, horrified by what he had done in his fury-fueled trance.

And then they were hit from all sides by armed men swarming out of the surrounding jungle. Blake crashed to the ground as two of them tackled him; Maureen, struggling to her knees, trying to protect her shattered arm, was body-slammed into the tree a second time. Luther, thinking the Viet Cong were overrunning his camp, made the fatal mistake of pulling out Blake's Glock and firing. He died almost instantly in a hail of bullets from the fully-armored DEA agents who screamed at Blake and Maureen, "DON'T MOVE! DON'T FUCKING MOVE!"

Only when the agents had secured the scene and stopped shouting did Blake and Maureen become aware of the sounds of a gun battle raging nearby.

"If anyone knows a reason why this man and this woman should *not* be joined in holy matrimony, keep your pie-hole shut."

Max Keller, newly ordained by an online divinity college, (*"Godliness is only three easy credit card payments away!"*) conducted the wedding ceremony for Charlie O'Brien and Denice Cantrell. Charlie had been all for postponing the nuptials after the shoot-out at Pinnacle had left his daughter facing two surgeries, one to reconstruct her radius and ulna with titanium rods, and the second, a cosmetic procedure to put her nose back where it belonged.

He nearly fainted when he saw her at the hospital before she had been cleaned up. The front of her shirt was drenched in blood, her left forearm made an unnatural thirty-degree angle, and her right leg was swollen to twice its normal size. And when he learned an overzealous DEA agent was the one who had slammed her into a tree and damn near crippled her, Charlie wanted to have the man sued, fired and killed.

It was Maureen herself who talked him down. She was foggy from the pre-op meds, and her smashed nose made her sound like a stoned Elmer Fudd, but before they wheeled her in to reassemble her arm, she told Charlie the DEA agent was only doing his job, that he had no way of knowing she wasn't part of the group running the most sophisticated meth superlab in California history. Even drugged up the wazoo, she had the presence of mind to shield her father from the knowledge that it was Blake who had broken her. Not that she forgave the bastard, no way, but she knew this was between him and her to work out. If they ever could.

When Maureen's eyes fluttered shut and the nurse told Charlie he'd have to leave, he bent down and kissed his daughter's forehead, then went to talk to Blake. He was still being questioned in his *own* hospital room by the Drug Enforcement guys and that tall black police lieutenant, so Charlie visited Jane.

She was being held overnight for observation, as the doctors weren't sure what effect six weeks of exposure to meth fumes might have had on the fetus, but she seemed in good spirits when Charlie sat with her for a half hour.

Jane hadn't seen Blake—he was already in federal custody by the time the agents stormed the sound stage, shot it out with Dominic's crew, and freed her from the nine-foot-square storage room where she had been held—so she was naturally worried about him. Charlie assured her Blake had nothing more than a couple knots on his head and two cracked ribs that would keep him out of any upcoming salsa dance contests she might have had her heart set on entering.

She laughed, placing a protective hand on the belly that pooched up the hospital gown. "I think we'll both be out of competition for a while."

Charlie told her he was flying her parents in that same evening. A car would pick them up at the airport and bring them straight here to the hospital. "And when the crepe-soled gestapo throws them out tonight, the car will bring them to my house. Mrs. Taylor has already made up a room for them and they can stay as long as they like."

"I think you're about the kindest, most generous man I ever met. Maureen is lucky to have you for a dad."

Tears stung Charlie's eyes, so he diverted her focus away from himself. "How are *you* feeling? I mean, really," he said, taking her hand.

"You know what they were going to do to me? Hold me in that little room until the baby was born, and then sell us both."

"Those jackwits."

"When I said Blake and Maureen would rescue me, they laughed and told me why no one would ever come looking."

"Then I assume you know about the house being gone," Charlie said tentatively.

"*And* about that poor girl they killed to make it look like I was dead. I'll be straight with you, Charlie, those guys shared the skit out of me."

She would have been even more shared skitless had she known that Micah, after learning a pregnant woman was being held captive on Stage Three, had wondered out loud what it would be like to "bang a babymama." Having seen Micah's violence against the good-time girl whose jaw had been broken, and not wanting to lower Jane's resale value to his Middle-East contact, Dominic Briggs had told the horny creep the little blonde had miscarried and bled to death.

Charlie's thumb absently stroked the back of her hand, causing Jane to look down at her naked ring finger. "Those ear-holes took my engagement ring when they kidnapped me," she said sadly.

Once he left Jane to rest, Charlie asked to have a note taken in to the room where Blake was still being interrogated. A few minutes later Libby Johnson came out.

"Hi, I'm Maureen's father—"

"I remember you, Mr. O'Brien. You helped us out last year on the Dev Roberts case."

He made his request and Libby went back in the room. She spoke briefly to Blake, who looked through the glass at Charlie, worried Maureen had already told him what he had done.

From the encouraging smile Charlie gave back to him, Blake assumed *that* confrontation would come later. All he could do now was not be any more of a shitheel than he already had. Bowing his head, he reached back and pulled the chain from around his neck, handing it to Libby.

After confirming Maureen had already gone into surgery and would not be out of recovery for many hours, Charlie drove to the Beverly Hills jewelry store of Gerard Duval. The pink diamond was reset in the fastest time money can buy, and when the DEA was finally through with Blake, Charlie was waiting with the ring.

Knowing how furious Blake had been when he learned of Charlie's financial participation in the original purchase, he was hesitant when he stopped Blake on his way to Jane's room and handed him the small velvet box. Charlie stood ready to justify his action in order to brighten things for Jane, but Blake was a different man from the one whose ego had been bruised by Charlie's earlier generosity. He had lost *everything*, and it was only through the efforts of this man's daughter that he had the most important part of it back. And his repayment of *her* generosity? He had nearly killed her in a fit of rage.

"Thank-you," he said in a whispery voice Charlie attributed to the four-hour debriefing and a cracked-up ribcage.

In the two weeks since the raid on Pinnacle, Frank Goodwin had been exonerated in the murder of Cody Mason, Maureen had undergone a second surgical procedure, Blake and Jane had moved into an apartment while they decided what to do with the burned-out lot on Lookout Mountain, and Libby Johnson herself had wielded the sledge hammer that broke open the fountain at Micah's house, uncovering a wetsuit, a child's baseball bat and the rest of the blood-caked evidence.

If Blake's ribs hadn't already been broken, she might have taken the sledgehammer to him, too. They met for lunch a few days after the raid, and Libby was finally free to tell him what had been at stake while he and Maureen were poking around in Cody Mason's murder.

The DEA had been watching Pinnacle for months, cautiously building their case before making a move. When one of the two principals was murdered, they assumed an internecine power struggle was going on, so they bided their time while they gathered more information. Libby had been brought into the loop because she headed up the homicide investigation and the Agency wanted her to report anything she found that might tie in to the suspected superlab. Maureen and Blake had inadvertently dropped a turd in the punch bowl by stumbling onto the crack lab belonging to the Bates brothers. The DEA was confident Dallis and Ostin had been set up to be thrown under the bus if one of Pinnacle's supply or delivery trucks was ever stopped and searched. Worried the Bates bust would alert whomever was calling the shots for the drug op on the lot, the Agency had asked Libby to get the two detectives to back off.

When the main strike force was approaching Stage Three and heard the shot south of them, the agent in charge dispatched a dozen men to check out the gunfire and arrest anyone else on the property, which is how Blake and Maureen were caught up in the admittedly vigorous sweep.

Today, as Max Keller conducted the unorthodox and often hilarious wedding service, Maureen and Blake were in the audience. They hadn't spoken since the day of the raid—Blake from shame, Maureen from anger—and Jane was uncomfortably aware of the altered dynamic between them as she sat holding her husband's hand.

Jane knew everyone had believed she was dead for a month and a half. Was it possible Blake and Maureen, thinking she was permanently out of the picture, had done something they now regretted? A sharp kick interrupted her speculation, and Jane brought Blake's hand over to rest on the spot where the future President of the United States landed another solid one from inside. Blake smiled, gingerly putting his arm around her before they both turned back to the ceremony.

But Jane noted that on their way back to the bride and groom, Blake's eyes swept over the guests on the other side of the aisle, his smile fading when he saw his business partner. With her splinted nose, and her left arm in a cast and sling, Maureen sat ramrod straight, her eyes never turning from the wedding couple.

Toward the end of the reception four hours later, Maureen stood alongside the getaway limo, assuring her father once again that she was healed enough to take care of herself while he and Denice toured Italy, France and Spain. She woodenly hugged her new step-mother, kissed Charlie's cheek, then waved her good arm until the rattling trail of cans disappeared down Stone Canyon Road.

The reception was winding down when she returned to the ballroom, the band having traded Michael Jackson for Michael Bublé. Max Keller maneuvered Ethel Rosen and her aluminum walker across the floor in a romantic—if shuffling—waltz. Keesha and Fran tenderly held each other as they swayed to the music without moving their feet.

Blake and Jane danced, too, her blonde hair spilling against his jacket as her cheek nestled his chest. He held her protectively, eyes closed and his head bowed over hers. Maureen watched them from the door of the ballroom, knowing they would leave soon to go to their new place in Santa Monica.

Perhaps sensing he was being observed, Blake opened his eyes and lifted his chin from Jane's hair. When he saw Maureen watching, the shame of what he had done to her flooded back. He knew he would have to talk to her soon to make things right between them, and to pay whatever penance she demanded.

Maureen took a hard look into Blake's pleading eyes, fixing the picture in her mind before turning away and heading out. Charlie and Denice weren't the only ones hitting the road, and it would be more than a year before Blake saw Maureen again.

ACKNOWLEDGMENTS

Our gratitude goes to Pat Bedford of Lynchburg Choppers for letting us tap into his knowledge of vintage motorcycles.

We send special thanks to Richard and Lori at Richard's Custom Jewelry for giving us a peek into the world of rare gems.

As always, former Marine Catherine Murray not only talked the talk, but walked the walk. Oo-rah!

Please turn the page if you would like to read the opening chapters of MURDER: TAKE FOUR.

MURDER: TAKE FOUR

Executing a long con requires specialized skills, from selecting the perfect mark, to bleeding your victim dry once the rip-off stars align in your money house. Along the way you must remain dependable and trustworthy, never dipping in for a snack, always keeping your eye on the full banquet down the line. Of the many skills needed to be successful, however, patience is paramount.

For two years, Margrit Taylor and her partner had patiently worked a long con on Charlie O'Brien, the amount at stake so large they had been prepared to run the grift for at least one more. But then the miracle happened, a turn of events they never saw coming: Charlie's daughter, Maureen, voluntarily handed over the keys to the castle, enabling the con artists to set everything in motion to relieve the former comedy writer and television producer of twenty-eight million dollars.

Drinking wine at sunset on a luxurious barge in Bordeaux, France, enjoying his extended honeymoon with Denice, Charlie O'Brien had no clue he was about to go from multi-millionaire to barely-hundredaire.

Blake Ervansky stared at his cell phone, as if seeing her name on the screen could bring her home. He had known things weren't perfect between them since their house burned down, but when Jane left a couple weeks ago, ostensibly so her parents could meet their first grandchild, Blake had assumed she and the baby would be back soon.

Only now did he understand the reason for her tears when she had embraced him so fiercely in the slow-moving airport security-check line, the reason she had insisted he carry little Z-Bean during the inching forward to the ticketed-passengers-only club that was the gate concourse of LAX's Terminal Two. Jane had been telling him good-bye, giving him one last opportunity to hold the two people he loved more than his own life.

On the call a few minutes ago, Jane had assured Blake she did not want a divorce—yet—but that she had already begun the process of getting re-certified as a teacher in West Virginia. It was too late in the year to get a full-time position for the upcoming school term, although she felt certain she would get enough substitute teaching work to avoid being a financial drain on him.

The realization that she was leaving him stabbed into Blake with a double-edged blade: one edge pain, the other humiliation. Hearing her promise she and his child wouldn't become a burden to him had been the coup de grâce, the stroke that broke him.

Jane hadn't said it cruelly. Not even harshly. She had laid it out with the same patience and gentleness she always used in her kindergarten classroom. Maybe that's what had made it so real for him. His sweet, beautiful wife believed he would quibble with her over money. Blake would live under a bridge, go without food—he would do anything for Jane.

Anything, that is, except tell her the truth about what had happened between Maureen and him.

Maureen O'Brien pulled the sweaty doo-rag from her head, exhausted after hours of loading the truck. As the smallest member of the crew, and as the only woman, she felt obligated to prove herself equal to the physical challenges of the job every day, not willing to give the other roadies a reason to complain about her. They already didn't like sharing their tight sleeping quarters with her, but she had turned down the offer to ride on the much cushier band bus because it came with the caveat that she would have to bed Def Perception's lead singer, Snowy Ellis.

Once the instruments, lights, scaffolding, sound equipment, pyrotechnics and stage set-pieces were inventoried and locked away for tomorrow's long drive to Cincinnati, the roadies headed for a nearby bar to pick up *trashe blanc* women and drink cheap beer. The members of the band were being sucked-off by a better class of ho and drinking twenty-year-old scotch, but the results would be the same in the morning: grim hangovers and a high probability of at least one new STD.

Maureen declined the half-hearted invitation to tag along with the rest of the crew to Three Dollar Bill's, and she didn't even think about accepting Snowy's standing offer to join him in the suite. Instead, she walked to the ATM of a Citibank branch around the corner. Inserting her card, she followed the simple prompts, then entered her withdrawal request. The screen blinked twice before telling her the amount entered would overdraw her account. Def Perception covered most of its roadies' expenses, but every two weeks or so Maureen took out a couple hundred from her own account for what Charlie used to call "walking around money." Of course, he had been the show-runner on his cop series, *The Brothers Gunn*, so there were multiple hundreds on him at all times, cash being the immediate solution to ninety-nine percent of any last-minute problems on a TV stage. Maureen liked to have a few twenties for the occasional meal away from the band, personal feminine products and a better brand of bottled water than the one provided to the support serfs on the tour.

She interacted again with the ATM, very carefully entering her PIN and the amount, but the double blink once again preceded an identical response: overdraw?

Shit. How can people who manage a 30-city show tour be unable to direct-deposit a paycheck?

Every other Friday, DP's manager showed up with paper checks for the crew. Since the concert venues were not often within walking distance of a branch of her bank, Maureen normally mailed her checks back to Charlie's house so Mrs. Taylor could deposit them for her.

Frustrated by the ATM's insistence that she had a balance of only $50, Maureen took out the card for Charlie's account. She would call the bank tomorrow to straighten out the screw-up on hers. But then the ATM screen claimed her father's account would also be overdrawn by her $200 request. A glance at the balance showed the same $50 as her own.

Cursing colorfully, and with references to both male *and* female genitalia, she stepped away from the ATM to call Charlie's housekeeper. Mrs. Taylor had been specifically instructed to transfer ten grand from his savings to his checking every time the balance fell below a thousand dollars. That was almost a year ago, right after Charlie and Denice Cantrell had begun their European honeymoon, leaving Maureen in charge of the house and paying the bills every month.

The ATM's rebuff had pissed her off, but the cell phone's snotty insistence that the number she had dialed was no longer in service chilled her. Peering through the window of the closed bank to see the time, she realized California banks would be open another few minutes. Accessing the automated information service on her phone, she dialed the number it gave her and asked to be connected with the manager.

When she hung up minutes later, Maureen O'Brien—who had been stabbed by the bodyguard of an enemy combatant she had killed in his sleep, who had faced down AK-47's, man-eating tigers and a nut-case former Marine torn between shooting her and raping her—trembled with fear.

This can't be, she told herself, scrambling to come up with a scenario where she had not lost all her father's money. *Lost, hell. I gave it away*. Maureen had put Mrs. Taylor's signature on the accounts, all so she could hit the road and do some world-class sulking over Blake's betrayal.

She knew she had to move fast, had to fix the problem before Charlie found out, before she had to tell him she had *not* been living at the house in Nichols Canyon the whole time he had been away. *Not* been the person dutifully paying all the credit card bills from this luxury trip with Denice.

After Maureen gave the airline ticket agent her American Express number, she held her breath, not sure if the card had been compromised, too. When it went through without a glitch, she closed her eyes with relief; she had a seat on a flight leaving for LA in three hours.

Three hours, plus the length of the flight, plus the time needed to rent a car and drive from LAX to Charlie's house was too long to wait for answers. She needed someone who could go to the house right now to find out what was happening, and it couldn't be anyone who might call her father. Someone she could trust. But who?

Months before, she had deleted Blake Ervansky from her speed-dial, except her brain did not have that convenient one-button memory wiper. With no place else to turn, Maureen entered his phone number.

About the Authors

Marsha Lyons and April Kelly were debate team partners at Colonial High School in Orlando and roomies at The University of South Florida, before Marsha went to law school on a mission and April went to Hollywood on a whim.

While Marsha's career includes teaching at the FBI Academy at Quantico, becoming the youngest Assistant U.S. Attorney in Miami, and going into private legal practice, April's began in stand-up comedy, moved into writing on shows such as Mork & Mindy and Webster, then to producing her own shows like Boy Meets World.

Throughout their wildly different professional lives Marsha and April have remained best friends, finally deciding to put their separate talents together to write a showbiz crime novel, MURDER IN ONE TAKE, their debut as a team. MURDER: TAKE THREE is the third book of the series.

Marsha is married with children, and April is single with dogs.

**If you liked Maureen O'Brien
and Blake Ervansky...**

...check out PI Rick Valentine
in April Kelly's new series,
previewed on the next page.

"Trust me, I'm almost a detective."

VALENTINE'S DAY
by
April Kelly

The ink is barely dry on Richard Valentine's private investigator's license before his very first client frames him for a homicide, forcing Rick to accept help from ex-boss and top LA sleuth Dako Farona to get himself out of trouble.

Rick has no love for Farona, who paid him only slave wages during three years of legwork, but he gets caught up in one of Dako's cases after learning it links back to his own father, a police officer killed in the line of duty while Rick was still in kindergarten.

When someone sabotages the case by shooting Farona, Rick steps in to take over and, with a little help from the women in his life—including his octogenarian landladies, the duplicitous receptionist at Rick's old job and Dako's beautiful daughter—the neophyte detective morphs into a semi-seasoned PI while unraveling the heartbreaking truth about his father's murder.

For author biographies, sample chapters and a
complete list of our books, please visit
www.flightriskbooks.com

Flight
Risk
Books

Cover design by April Kelly

2.1.6